It's a Kink Thing

FOR THE LOVE OF KINK

M.C. ROTH

For the Love of Kink
ISBN # 978-1-80250-760-7
©Copyright M.C. Roth 2024
Cover Art by Kelly Martin ©Copyright April 2024
Interior text design by Claire Siemaszkiewicz
Pride Publishing

This is a work of fiction. All characters, places and events are from the author's imagination and should not be confused with fact. Any resemblance to persons, living or dead, events or places is purely coincidental.

All rights reserved. No part of this publication may be reproduced in any material form, whether by printing, photocopying, scanning or otherwise without the written permission of the publisher, Pride Publishing.

Applications should be addressed in the first instance, in writing, to Pride Publishing. Unauthorised or restricted acts in relation to this publication may result in civil proceedings and/or criminal prosecution.

The author and illustrator have asserted their respective rights under the Copyright Designs and Patents Acts 1988 (as amended) to be identified as the author of this book and illustrator of the artwork.

Published in 2024 by Pride Publishing, United Kingdom.

No part of this book may be reproduced, scanned, or distributed in any printed or electronic form without permission. Please do not participate in or encourage piracy of copyrighted materials in violation of the authors' rights. Purchase only authorised copies.

Pride Publishing is an imprint of Totally Entwined Group Limited.

If you purchased this book without a cover you should be aware that this book is stolen property. It was reported as "unsold and destroyed" to the publisher and neither the author nor the publisher has received any payment for this "stripped book".

FOR THE LOVE OF KINK

Dedication

For Q

Chapter One

Clint

Clint let out a gasp, dragging his covers back and stumbling off the couch before his eyes were half open. The claws of his nightmare clung deep, every marred piece of flesh tingling in memory and agony. His brain was so fucked that he could *feel* the suffering of his dreams.

His body flashed hot as he clutched the arm of the couch, his legs trembling under his own weight. Fire was tricky. What used to give him the greatest pleasure had also ripped his nerves apart, leaving him numb along the ravaged parts of his flesh.

The accident. He shuddered, pulling his shirt over his head before tossing it onto the floor. The air conditioning was cranked despite the cool night, but it still wasn't enough to destroy the memory of smoke that clogged his nostrils. Sweat poured from his body, streaking down his back to the waistband of his track pants.

He ripped them off next, tossing them next to his shirt. *Too hot. Too hot.* They landed in a heap next to a similar pair that was riddled with just as many holes.

Squeezing his eyes shut, he pressed the heels of his hands to them, trying to squash the phantom flickering of lights and the pounding headache.

It didn't seem to matter how much time had passed or how many times the nightmares woke him. It never got any easier.

The same face still haunted him, so clear that he could feel himself touching Ross' lips, his mouth open and slack and his sightless eyes staring. *No more words. No more songs.*

"Fuck." Reaching for his blankets, he ripped them from the couch, tossing them among the rest of the clothes. They were damp to the touch, reeking of sweat and that sour tang of fear that coated his tongue and made his mouth run dry. No amount of alcohol or water would quench his thirst enough to remove that taste—not when most of it was in his mind.

It had been better when he'd been sleeping on the small waterproof cot in the old club with little for blankets and a sore back so he rarely slept deep enough to dream. But in the virtual lap of luxury and the comfortable couch, his mind had taken to wandering at night.

The king-sized bed was out of the question.

All it would take was one faulty wire in the walls, and it would all go up in flames. He knew the builders and trusted them enough to sink a few million dollars into the construction, but everyone made mistakes. A slip from an electrician or a bad day at work and *poof.*

"Fuck. Stop thinking about it." He bit his lip, growling under his breath as he stalked to the bathroom. The plush carpet was soft against his bare feet, but just as warm as the rest of him. He needed ice, or ceramic tile cold enough to suck the fire right out of him.

Flicking the bathroom light on, he started the shower, adjusting the water as cold as it could possibly go. There had been a time in his life when cold showers had had an actual purpose, but now they barely helped him cope.

But how could he avoid them when Ross' memory had been all but erased in the new build? Everything they had grown together from the ugly ass curtains he'd picked out, to the bar top that was hard to keep clean on the best of days. Even the fucking rat trap Clint had kept under the bar after Ross had seen one of the buggers scoping out the place — gone.

The only thing left were the dreams.

His skin prickled as he ducked under the water, a shiver running over him. In the dead of winter, it would be cold enough that it would feel like dunking under ice and trapping himself beneath a surface, where frost would be a blessing.

His jaw trembled and his teeth chattered of their own accord, his body fighting the brutal temperature. *I can last. I can do this.*

Finally, the fire started to simmer from its inferno, tapering to the numbness that was a part of his life now. The phantoms wisped away, his head clearing until he could see the beige tile of the bathroom and the black countertop through the sheer glass shower stall.

I'm awake. This isn't a dream.

The numbness was easy to deal with compared to the rest. If someone got frisky in the bar and tried to land a punch, he hardly felt the bruise if it landed anywhere on his chest or stomach. He was lucky that he still had most of the feeling in his hands and could still mix a drink. *Yeah...lucky.*

He'd had to take care of fights more often than not since he'd owned the kink club Unkinked. Even after he'd moved the club from a bar to a more private setting, there had still been a few incidents. There was always drama in his life and people coming and going. It was the ones who stayed that made the lifestyle worth living.

Maddy, Trick, Derreck, Malone, Keady... He couldn't list all the ones who had become the closest to his heart, even if they didn't quite fill the gaping hole.

The truth was, he loved people, but they were assholes. Even his best friends were assholes when the mood struck them.

Trick, whom he'd known for years and had mentored, had still violated the community's rules. And Derreck, his virtual fucking rock, had cracked before his eyes over a man who had weaseled his way into Clint's employment, not to mention the stunt Keady had pulled—and Nikita, the secretive bastard.

Grabbing his body wash, Clint squirted some onto a cloth, running it over his skin as he tilted his head into the spray. The scent of citrus cut the last of the lingering smoke, soothing the ache in his chest.

Without them, he was nothing but a nurse turned kinky bastard. At the same time, sometimes he wondered where they would be without him. It was the selfish thoughts that had kept him from locking the doors and wandering off.

Why couldn't I have been there for them sooner? Where did I go wrong? How the hell am I going to stop the next crash? He hadn't found a cure for the drama yet.

He stayed in the shower as long as he could take it, roughly scrubbing his hair just before he stepped out. There wasn't a spot of steam in the room, but his eyes were still cloudy, barely able to focus on the mirror that hung above the vanity. It wasn't doing him any justice this morning.

Layers of black and gray were smeared beneath his eyes in a shadow that was so permanent he wondered if he'd ever looked any different. His eyes were bloodshot from what he could tell, with a touch too much scruff on his chin, as usual. *Handsome devil.*

Ross had called him that every day, no matter what role they had been in. Two switches, living in a twenty-four-seven, should have been a fucking disaster, but for them, it had worked. There had never been another man like Ross. *There never will be.*

He'd had his show, his high, and he'd lived that part of his life. Sure, he dabbled with his Dominant side sometimes, especially when he was figuring other people's shit out, or looking after the godforsaken bills, but his submissive side was buried so deep that he was never letting it out again.

Cutler had tried…

Clint shivered, sliding his hand up his chest to the hardness of his sternum. His heart beat slow and steady, a simple thump beneath his hand that gave no indication as to how important it was. The last time it had raced had been with Cutler, but he hadn't let go. There was no way he could with Ross' memory just as fresh as it had been the day he'd passed.

He moved his hand lower, settling his fingers by his belly button. If he closed his eyes, he could almost imagine it was someone else wrapping their hand around his waist, ready to tug him back into their chest. The embrace would be warm and strong, their scent calming his racing nerves as his mouth went dry.

But no.

Those days were over.

Not bothering with a towel, he made his way to the closet, rifling through the drawers until he found something comfortable. Most of his things had holes in them now from too many washes in the crappy machine he'd had at the club. His new washer was a highly efficient beast that only used a tablespoon of soap.

Sticking his fingers through one of the holes in a shirt, he grumbled under his breath. His pointer finger went straight through without much fuss, and that was the smallest of the few spots. His pants were in a similar state, but he couldn't exactly go without those.

Before seven in the morning rolled around, he headed out of his part of the house into the area where his real home was. When he'd hired Shelvin to build him a kink haven, he hadn't really expected it to turn out so well. And Elliot, Shelvin's sub, had kept Shelvin's feet on the ground through the project so it hadn't gone too far out of scope.

They'd been so worried about the money.

Clint scoffed, running his hand along one of the gray walls as he headed to the open play area. He didn't give a shit about the money. When someone got enough zeros to their name, the value of those zeros truly stopped mattering.

He used to be the kind of person who would do anything for an extra shot of cash. Funnily enough, it had been the reason he'd approached Ross in the first place. The man had been a known playboy, with a bank account that was the talk of the town. *If only they had known.*

Clint had hoped that maybe he could be a sugar baby for Ross, back when he'd had a look that had been closer to that of a twink than the muscle mass he had now. That hope had lasted until the first time he'd dominated Ross, and the real rush had begun. He hadn't exactly known he was a switch—just that he wasn't exactly a sub. Ross hadn't known either, but fuck, it had been magical.

Until it hadn't been anymore.

Scrubbing at his face, Clint flicked the lights on for the open play area, pausing for a moment to take in the sight. It would never get old—the room, the implements or the memories of screams and moans. To some, it probably looked like a torture chamber, but it was a playground for kinksters of every kind.

Some preferred the cross as the perfect tool of restraint, while others steered closer to the impact tools on the wall. The couches had been an excellent idea that Maddy had thrown in during the build. *What better way is there to watch someone get their ass beaten than reclined on a La-Z-Boy?*

They'd settled on a waterproof material that didn't recline, but it was close enough. The lack of a bar was the only thing that unsettled him about the place. But the bar had been Ross'. It hadn't been right to just move on and replace it.

Ross had built the bar top at the old club, spending days sanding and staining it until it had been perfect.

Clint had never expected someone like him to be so good with a hammer, but maybe it had made sense. Those same fingers could wield a whip, knife or flame with equal determination.

Fuck. Staggering, he grasped the edge of the nearest couch as his eyes prickled. Strength drained from his limbs in an instant, and his knees hit the floor, bile burning in his throat as his chest went tight. *Fuck. Fuck.*

He couldn't do it. Not on his own. The walls were empty, the heat an echo of what he'd built with Ross.

"Clint!"

He turned to the sound, flinching when he saw Maddy standing at the entrance of the room. His eyes were wide as he rushed across the room, his feet pattering on the floor.

Double fuck. He had all of two seconds before Maddy knelt next to him, his eyes searching for some kind of wound. The way he settled on Clint's scars with longing, even if only for a moment, made it so much worse.

"S'okay, kid. I just tripped and banged my knee is all. I was just feeling sorry for myself," said Clint. His words were slow before he forced in a deep breath. The smile was harder, barely touching his lips before it slipped away again. It seemed to fool Maddy, though, who instantly relaxed.

He was a sweet kid, but naïve as all hell. As far as Clint knew, he'd been a forty-year-old virgin before he'd met Derreck and that ship had sailed in a burst of pure sadistic drama.

"Don't call me kid," said Maddy, a pout touching his lips before he stood, fiddling with his hands. "I'm probably older than you, you know."

Nope. "Only in your looks," said Clint. The grin came easier as Maddy sent him a glare. Tugging at the couch, he tested out his legs, only making it halfway before his knees started to tremble.

"Do you need help or something?" asked Maddy, taking a step back, despite his words. A snuggly guy, he was not. And although he did get close to Derreck, his touches were often more exploratory than affectionate. *Almost like a cat's.*

"I think I pinched a nerve," said Clint, screwing up his face as he managed to heave himself the rest of the way onto the couch. Every limb trembled, and he clenched his jaw as his teeth threatened to chatter. His side ached, his skin tingling as it flared pink under his gaze. Sometimes it felt like he was still in the past — still on fire.

"Uh-huh." Maddy crossed his arms as he took a seat of his own.

There were a few inches between them, and Clint had the strangest urge to close the gap. He shook his head, trying to rid himself of the fleeting thought. Maddy was not his type in the least, and Derreck would probably murder him if Clint made a move on his sub. *Just a hug?*

"What are you doing here so early?" asked Clint, once his voice was finally a bit steadier. "I'm not paying you overtime." That was a joke. Maddy wrote his own damn paychecks after Clint had maybe forgotten a few times. He paid himself what he wanted, and Clint signed on the dotted line. When it wasn't enough, Clint made sure to add an extra zero.

"Derreck was just getting back home, and he woke me up with cold hands," said Maddy, shrugging as he continued to flick his gaze up and down Clint's body.

"I blew him, but I couldn't get back to sleep, so I thought I would work on cleaning up the *Feel* room after that fiasco last night."

Oh man. Clint let out a groan, letting his head fall into his hands. "I forgot about that."

Maddy widened his eyes, raising one eyebrow. "How? I mean, that was a literal shit show."

Yep. That was one membership that Clint was terminating with extreme prejudice. There was a reason he had themed rooms for certain kinks. *Just another asshole stomping on the rules.*

"I'll take care of it. Let me set out the impact stuff first. Keady pulled a cleaning shift last night, and they are spotless, sanitized and ready for the next ass." *Whenever I can get my ass off the couch, that is.* If he stood now, he would just go down again, even if he was feeling a hell of a lot better.

Maddy's presence always did that somehow.

"Your mind has been wandering a lot lately," said Maddy, making no move to stand. "It was worse in the old bar when you were trying to do things on your own. I thought you were doing better here, but now you just seem…different."

Clint let out a whistle, trying to lighten the mood. "That's heavy coming from you."

He wasn't even trying to be insulting. Maddy was just one of those guys who failed to see optimism sometimes. *I'm fine…really.*

"Well, you don't listen to anyone else who says anything." Maddy scratched his chin where a small flake of dirt came away. He looked at it, a fond smile on his face. "And I used to get like that way before I found Derreck. Maybe you need a scene."

A choke caught in his throat that he tried to turn into a cough, covering his mouth with his hand. "A scene is the last thing I need. I get to be a part of a dozen of those every day."

"No, you don't," said Maddy, sending him a fierce look that was probably the sole reason people didn't mess with him, even when Derreck wasn't around. "You watch...that's it. I spent my whole life watching people and wondering why nothing made sense. I didn't actually become a *person* until I met Derreck."

Heavy. Clint grimaced, shaking out his hand when his fingers started to tingle again. His hands hadn't even been burned that badly, and they didn't have scars, but the nerves were still fucked. "That's different."

Maddy let out a humorless laugh before he stood from the couch. "You keep telling yourself that, boss, and someday you might start to believe it." As he walked away, he paused at the entryway, shooting a look over his shoulder. "Go back to sleep. I've got this."

Chapter Two

Scotland

Tattooing himself was one hell of a bad idea. It wasn't the pain, which was barely more than a sharp tickle, or the buzz that put some people on edge, either. The big problem was that he'd gotten to a spot that he couldn't fucking reach.

"Well, that went to hamburger in a handbasket." He let out a sigh, wiping at the last trail of ink before grabbing for the spray bottle. The hit of cooling liquid was instant, quenching the burn that had risen to the surface of his skin.

It was only supposed to have been a small piece on a stretch of blank skin near his kneecap. He hadn't planned on giving the rose quite so many petals, and his original placement he'd had in mind for the stem had changed when he'd thought of turning it into a chain.

He'd just been so wrapped up in not messing up the freehand design that he'd forgotten exactly how far his reach was. He hadn't figured it out until his back and neck had started to protest and the tip of his machine had disappeared out of view.

Now he had a half-piece that was probably never getting finished, and an obsession that belonged to his new machine that he'd found online. His old one had been clunky and noisy, but this tattoo machine fit easily in his hand, the buzzing muted and not quite enough to make his fingers tingle.

I had to try it out first.

He cracked a grin, trying to catch sight of where he'd trailed off. His skin tingled, flushing warm, like he'd spent too much time in the sun.

Of course, even as beautiful and quiet as it was, it was really nothing next to his main obsession. Blue eyes, blond hair and a five o'clock shadow occupied his thoughts ninety percent of the time when he wasn't focused on his art. The other ten percent was pure private time. No one but a trusted partner was seeing that part of him.

Wiping the area one last time, he reached for his roll of dermal cover sheets, cutting one to size and pulling the paper off. It was pure adrenaline to press it to his open skin, gently smoothing it in place before peeling off the plastic backing. All that was left was a sticky film no thicker than cellophane that would speed his tattoo along to healing.

His skin was hot as he touched it through the film, tracing the fresh lines that were darker than the gloves he wore. It was already weeping in some spots, and soon the ink would spread, turning into a smudged mess that would only be removed when he took the plastic off a day from now.

It would be fine, until the itch set in. To him, the itch was the worst part.

Stripping the gloves from his hands, he tossed them to the nearest garbage can, easing the paper towels and wells of ink inside before tossing the half-dozen needle tips he'd used into the sharps bin.

When he'd ventured out on his own in the tattoo world, he'd been nearly certain that he would never make it. His personality rarely matched that of other artists, and his style was different, to say the least. His old place with the neon sign and the constant drama had been easy to leave.

A few clients had turned into dozens, and it had spiraled as word spread of his work. His clients were like walking billboards, and everyone who asked them who their artist was inevitably ended up on his website or his doorstep.

He still couldn't believe it, really. He didn't think he was *that* good, no matter what his clients said about it. He just loved art, and the people were pretty damn awesome, too...for the most part.

Now he was booked up for two years, and only working three days a week in a shop of his own where the overhead was the only thing that kept him from knocking it back to two. And when he wasn't working, he had his side business that was more for fun than anything else.

His phone hummed against his desk along the far wall, the buzz shattering the endorphins that had started to build. Usually, he turned the thing off when he was working, but today was technically his day off. He hadn't been able to resist trying out his new favorite baby when it had shown up in his email as delivered. He'd rushed into town, kicking off his shoes as he'd torn the package open.

Giving his hands a wash, and failing to get most of the splatter off, he grabbed his phone by the time it started its second round of ringing, putting it to his ear.

"We have a problem."

Scotland chuckled, shaking his head as he wiped his arm over his forehead. "Hey, Maddy."

The sadist had wormed his way into Scotland's heart as soon as he'd started going to Unkinked. He was the strangest mix of shy and social butterfly, dipping into gossip only to tilt his head in confusion a moment later. He also seemed to have the strangest mission lately, not that Scotland minded at all.

Not when his crush was the prize.

"I'm serious," said Maddy, no hint of humor in his voice. "Clint fell this morning."

"Shit." Scotland dropped his hand towel, the fabric falling from his fingertips unchecked. "Is he okay? Did you need a doctor or something?" He knew a few. Hell, he'd tattooed one's sub, and they were part of the community.

"Uh—no, he's not that old. He didn't break a hip or anything," said Maddy, completely deadpan. Confusion was laced in his voice, so pure that it broke Scotland's heart. "I think he was dropping."

Scotland blinked in surprise. "But Clint hasn't scened with anyone in forever." Watching didn't count—not when you were doing it without a real partner or aftercare.

"Well, he did once, but that was a while ago," said Maddy. "And no one is supposed to know that..."

Well, it was news to him. Terrible fucking news. Or maybe it wasn't so bad. If Clint hadn't gone back for seconds, then he couldn't have gotten too attached.

"Why do you think he's dropping, then?" He reached for the hand towel, scooping it off the ground and tossing it toward the laundry basket under the sink. He hated the crunchy feeling towels got after he used them more than once, so he always kept an ample supply.

"He looks exactly like I do when I drop," said Maddy, letting out a little huff. "He can barely sleep and wanders around like he doesn't even know where he is sometimes. He smiles, but it's not real—not if you truly know him. And he didn't just fall... He just collapsed like all his strings had been cut. If I hadn't been there, I doubt he would have bothered to get up."

Okay, that's worse than I thought. "What did he say?"

If anyone would know about a drop, Clint would. He was the local king of kink, for Christ's sake.

"That he tripped," said Maddy, scoffing. "But I saw it. He did *not* trip. He's dropping."

He scratched his scalp before dragging his fingers along his chin. He'd shaved that morning and he'd be good for another two days before he got any hint of scruff. He'd tried to grow a beard once, but after two weeks of a five o'clock shadow, he'd given up.

"I know you're worried, Maddy, but I think you're reading into this too much. Clint is tired. He has been since I've met him." He couldn't recall seeing him in any other state, even though he was always sexy as hell. "Maybe he just needs a vacation."

He wished he could do more, but Clint had made himself abundantly clear on multiple occasions. He wanted nothing to do with Scotland, and there was no power on earth that was going to change that. That didn't mean Scotland couldn't obsess over him a bit—or a lot.

"Tired people don't scream in their sleep and cry when they think no one else is there," said Maddy, his voice rising. "They don't hug and rock themselves when they think the door is locked. There's something wrong — really wrong."

Scotland bit his tongue, clenching his hand into a fist. If he had his way, he'd be at Unkinked right now with Clint in his arms. He had a feeling that ship had sailed, though.

"Maybe he *really* needs a vacation?" That excuse sounded weak, even to his own ears. "What do you want me to do?" *Everything — anything, and I'm there.*

Maddy let out a long sigh, his breath muffling against the phone. "I don't know. Derreck didn't have any input, either. He respects Clint too much to force him into anything, but I can't see how there is any other way."

Respects him too much? "I guess that implies that you respect him too little?" Scotland tilted his head in confusion, battling with his humor. *Now is not the time. This is serious, dammit.*

"He's my boss, so…"

And didn't that speak a thousand words. Whoever Maddy had worked for before must've been one sorry sonuvabitch.

But what the hell were they going to do? If Maddy was right, it was only a matter of time before Clint had a complete meltdown. Someone couldn't carry that kind of weight and end up as a healthy person on the other side. Stress warred with your soul and usually won in the end.

"Let me come by the club," said Scotland, reaching for his wallet and tucking it into his pants. They were black, too, not just because they made his ass look fantastic, but because it hid the little splatters of ink that were sure to be everywhere by the end of each working day.

"Okay, but wear something that will catch his eye," said Maddy, his voice suddenly rushed. "Shit, I gotta go. With any luck, you'll get laid."

Scotland snorted, shaking his head. "Who taught you that? I never thought I'd hear you say the word 'laid'."

"Nav."

"Of course." There were so many people in the community, but it was hard not to get to know the regulars. Trick and Nav had had their membership fully reinstated while Scotland had been there—after an apparent incident, that was.

Not my pig, not my farm. There was a reason he tried to stay out of gossip, even as much as Maddy tried to drag him back. Everyone sounded terrible in the middle of a hearsay battle, but he always tried to see the best in people. It usually worked out okay.

"Shit, he tracked me down. I'm supposed to be stocking the supply room right now. Bye." Maddy ended the call with a click, and Scotland couldn't help but chuckle.

Their friendship had happened by pure chance, like so many other things in his life. One minute, Scotland had been admiring Derreck's ass, and in the next, Maddy had had a baseball bat over his shoulder and death threats on his lips.

"You look at my Dom like that and no one will ever see you again. I know exactly where to hide the body, too."

Scotland had laughed so hard that he'd fallen off his barstool and straight onto his ass, holding his sides as his chuckles refused to abate. *"I was actually wondering if he'd bury me alive if I slipped you my number."*

He could have loved a sadistic sub like Maddy in his bed, but he was even better as a friend. That, and Derreck was a pretty intimidating guy. He didn't have to lift a finger for people to get out of his way, and he'd probably never had to raise his voice in his life.

Even with the offer to Maddy, Scotland already had his crush by then. There was only so much longing he could do without breaking down a little.

Clint had been behind the bar that day, moving his hands quickly to keep up with drink orders, and striking up a conversation with anything that moved. He was rugged, in an 'I slept on the floor' kind of way, with arms that displayed exactly how many cases of beer he could carry in a single trip.

One look and Scotland had been lost. He hadn't seemed to be able to find his way since.

Chapter Three

Clint

Reaching into his pocket, Clint felt for the remote to the sound system. Shelvin had insisted that he could adjust it from his phone until Clint had pulled out his archaic flip phone. Shelvin had almost fainted. The architect was against texting, but a flip phone had been almost beyond his comprehension.

He flicked the volume down, letting out a sigh as the rock music lowered to something a little more tolerable. He loved music in any form, but with a headache, the grinding guitar was killer. And no amount of rubbing his temples seemed to help over the last few hours as the temperature in the building rose and the occupants amped up the volume.

The soundtrack of his life was like a twenty-four-seven adult video, only way, *way* better. His life had every sense, not just sight and sound, and he could watch a couple go from budding amateurs to pros at anything from Shibari to flogging.

Sighing, he leaned against the wall, giving in to the urge to rub at his head. He did feel a tad warm, with sweat beaded along his hairline that clung to his fingertips.

Maybe I'm coming down with something? He'd hardly ever gotten sick at the bar, but that may have been because of the slightly excessive use of vodka. *Definitely the vodka.*

"You okay, Clint?"

Fuck.

Maddy was driving him up the wall, and every time he asked, Clint just gritted his teeth, counting down the hours until he could do another round and park himself in the recovery room for thirty minutes or so. With the Dungeon Masters on site and domestic servant subs volunteering their time, the club almost ran itself. But Clint didn't want to leave too much up to fate.

He'd been in the right place at the right time on too many occasions to sit back and relax. And even though kinksters were usually a friendly bunch, he'd still broken up more fights than he could count.

"I'm fine, Maddy," said Clint, failing to keep some of the edge out of his voice. "Don't you have someone else to worry about? It's a headache, nothing more."

The air shifted as Maddy leaned against the wall next to him, his shoulder only a few inches away. He'd pulled on long sleeves, which was strange for him, since he'd finally become comfortable in his own skin.

When Clint had first met Maddy, he'd done his best to ignore the marks that covered most of Maddy's body. He had his own, and he knew what it was like being unable to control his own skin, and if anything, he'd learned Maddy was stronger because of them. Still, he had his days where he covered himself in long sleeves and pants, shielding himself from prying eyes.

He knew Maddy was in his element on the days he strolled around topless.

"Just a headache," Maddy mused, biting his lower lip. "And *just* a fall earlier."

Brat. The last thing he needed was one more person on his case. He had enough friends to last several lifetimes, and they all seemed to want to check in with him lately. *I'm fucking fine.*

"Don't you have a Dom to go bother?" asked Clint, scanning the crowd for Derreck's form. He winced as his temples throbbed, the low lights in the club still a bit too bright. "Or is he working again tonight?"

Derreck's work schedule was more haphazard than Clint's, but that came with the territory. When you dug graves for a living, you never knew when peak season would be. Frost was a bitch, too. Luckily, they were at the end of summer at the moment.

"He's in the basement tonight as Dungeon Master, remember?" Maddy turned to him, raising one brow with a look that was a tad judgmental.

He didn't, in fact, remember that. He hadn't thought the event was until tomorrow, actually. *Did Maddy plan something without me?* He was looking after the club more and more as he became comfortable.

The new system was completely computerized, but sometimes Clint found himself out of the loop. He used to know who was where, and exactly what they were doing.

"Shibari?" asked Clint, racking his brain for what event it could be. The mirrors in the basement, along with the enforced rebar framing were perfect to tie someone up and give them a little spin.

In the initial sketches for the new build, the basement had been unfinished. But that had changed right quick. There was nothing scarier to subbies than a dark basement with the slight scent of dampness, despite the dehumidifying system and sump pumps. Some of the best gang bangs had taken place down there.

"No. Wax play. We thought the basement would be best because of the flooring. It's easy to scrape any spills off concrete, compared to some of the other materials." Maddy looked toward the crowd that had gathered by the cross, smiling at the display.

Clint's heart dropped like a stone, settling into his gut and sending bile creeping up his throat. "Wax?"

"Yes," said Maddy, letting out a yawn that was wide enough to crack his jaw. "I told Derreck you okayed it. I figured you wouldn't mind because it's just a few candles."

His palms went simultaneously cold and sweaty, his body flushing so fiercely that he wondered if he would hit the ground after all. *Just a few candles.*

"What the fuck is wrong with you, Maddy?" Clint pushed away from the wall, rage simmering beneath his skin as he narrowed his eyes. "I hired you to help me out with this place, not burn it to the ground." A few gazes turned their way, but Clint ignored them, storming to the doorway as his heart pounded.

Just a few candles. It's okay. It was absolutely *not* okay, no matter how many times he told himself that. The skin along his belly tingled, flaming hotter as he pictured the flickering blaze. He knew how quickly a single spark could turn into an inferno. The wood in the house was still fresh, and it could go up in flames in an instant.

"Shit. *Shit.*" His shoulder thudded off the doorway as he broke into a run, darting down the hall and nearly crashing into Betty and her new sub, Gus. His shoulder ached, but he shook it off, picking up his pace with adrenaline alone pushing him onward.

"You okay, Clint?" Betty called after him.

He shook his head, dragging in a deep breath as his vision started to swim. There were too many fucking square feet between him and the basement.

Nightmare was the room that led to the basement, and it was aptly named. Maddy had actually come up with the idea for it, and the builders Shelvin and Elliott had been too happy to go along with it—Shelvin more so.

Maddy. He shook his head, tossing his guilt to the side as he flicked on every switch just inside the door. Light flooded the room, along with screeching music and a thumping beat loud enough that his headache burst into a full-on migraine. The door to the basement was shut, so he grabbed for the handle, tugging hard even as his sweaty palm slipped.

The smell hit him first.

At one time it would have reminded him of birthday candles or campfires—and burnt marshmallows with the crispy caramelized surface. The heat had always been so soothing, banishing every cold thought and aching bone.

Now it was dread and thick agony that almost sent him to his knees.

Clutching at the railing, he stumbled down the stairs, his head buzzing as he hit the landing. His heart nearly stopped at the sight, every hair on his flesh standing at full attention.

There could have been a thousand candles, but it was impossible to tell with the mirrors that lined every wall except a quiet space at the far end. Light flickered on each surface—an orange and yellow flame taunting him with hints of brutal red.

There were two couples involved in the madness, one's back nearly painted blue with flaking wax that shone against their skin in a crusty shell. The candle was burning low in a measured grip. All it would take was one wrong move and it would be on the floor, ready to catch at the nearest piece of cloth. Derreck was on the other side of the room, probably too far to do anything about it in time.

Where the hell are the fire extinguishers? If he had his way, they would be stacked in every room.

"Fuck! Put it out!" Clint yelled as loud as he could, his voice echoing in the space. Derreck looked his way, but he didn't move. He didn't *do* anything.

One of the Doms hesitated, wax still dripping and the flame sharpening as more wick was exposed. It grew before his eyes as a bit of black soot licked the edges of the brightness.

"Clint?" Maddy's voice echoed from the top of the stairs, but Clint was already moving, running to the nearest flame and pulling the squat column of wax from the Dom's hand. Molten wax dripped over the edge, coating his fingers in a film that was ecstasy and agony as the flame seared him.

His mind blanked. He didn't know the Dom — not in that moment. He'd probably spoken to him dozens of times, but he was a stranger, smashing on territory that didn't belong to him.

"What the hell?" The Dom took a step back, nearly stumbling as Clint cupped his other hand over the top of the candle, smothering the flame with sheer force. His hands flared from the heat, the little smoke that escaped sinking straight into his lungs. It cut off his air, his nightmare thrumming into existence with the force of a slap.

"Water. I need water." Clint looked around, but the nearest sink was too far. And where the hell was the fire extinguisher? A bit of wax stuck to his palm as he pulled one hand away, the familiar sensation wisping over his nerves.

Only one reflected candle remained. It was in his hands in seconds, the sting joining that of the first as the flame touched that same spot that blushed red in the center of cooling wax. It was blue, swirling with purple as one drop ran free, spattering onto the ground.

"Um—red?"

That single word had Clint shuddering to a halt, his breath catching in his throat. The sub looked back at him, his skin shiny as he raised himself off the table and turned toward Clint. It was his eyes that really struck Clint—full of such sad confusion that it nearly felt like he'd been slapped.

The sub, he knew. Heath had come to the community nearly broken from a previous relationship where his partner had tried to pass off abuse as kink. He'd just started opening up over the last few months, trying out a few scenes and finding himself a devoted Dom.

Heath had mentioned something about wax play before. Clint couldn't remember the details, but he recalled revealing a bit of himself—admitting to his past love of fire.

"What's going on?" Heath looked to his Dom, who was already approaching, wrapping his arms around Heath, despite the wax that was still tacky. The Dom's gaze wasn't confused at all. He was *pissed*.

"It's okay, darling." He held Heath to him as the second couple moved away, the suspense broken as everything came hammering down.

Shit. What the fuck am I doing? Clint took a step back, thudding into someone behind him. He whirled on Derreck, whose eyes were unreadably dark.

"You burned your hands," said Derreck as he reached for the candles, slowly pulling one from Clint's grasp, then the other. He passed them to Maddy, who had somehow made it down the stairs, even with tears on his cheeks.

There had been very few select times where he'd seen Maddy cry, and each of them had destroyed a small piece of his soul.

"I'm sorry," said Clint, staring at his palms as his stomach dropped. He'd interrupted a demonstration, but more importantly, a *scene.* He'd always promised his kinksters a safe place to fulfill their desires, but he'd just freaked out and smashed that all to bits for two couples who were looking less impressed by the minute.

"Shit, I'm so sorry." He closed his hands, bringing them close to his chest as his own eyes stung and the mirrors began to blur. His hands trembled, his grip weak as he tried to stay on his feet, flinching away from Derreck's outstretched hand.

"I gotta go." Turning, he did something he'd promised himself that he would never do again.

He ran.

Chapter Four

Scotland

Leather pants were something that he'd never been able to squeeze his thighs into, but jeans were fucking money. It didn't seem to matter which brand he tried, his thighs always maxed them out, the muscle straining against the fabric. It made up for his slight lack of ass, at least.

He ran his hands over his thighs one last time, digging his fingertips into the thick material that didn't have an ounce of wear on them. Most of his things got stained so quickly with ink that they didn't last long in the closet. It was too bad he looked like shit in black — like an emotional black hole.

It was the same reason he kept his hair colorful. The tips of his black hair were neon blue at the moment, and he liked it better than the previous purple. He tried going blond once, but he was not going down that road again. It wasn't a good look for him.

None of the colors seemed to catch Clint's eye, though. He'd tried rainbow shirts, high boots and aviators, and Clint had only asked him what he wanted to drink at the old bar. A getup made of entirely leather straps that showed off his assets a little more than he was comfortable with had had a similar response at the kink house.

So tonight, he'd gone with a salmon shirt and light blue jeans to prowl the halls. He'd already had two conversations and gotten someone's phone number, but he hadn't spotted Clint anywhere. *Not that I'm looking for him.* It was easier to tell himself that than face the inevitable heartbreak.

"Scotland!"

He turned to the voice, grinning at Keady, who was dragging Cutler along with an excessive amount of enthusiasm. Keady had been a completely different person when Scotland had first met him in his tattoo chair, tasked with making swirling designs around a few fresh scars. Cutler had been there, too, and it had been hot as fuck to watch him take control of the scene.

If only. That heady experience was nothing compared to what it would have been like for him to be in the chair with the needle buzzing against his flesh. It was one thing to tattoo someone's sub, but it would be completely different to be the Dom ordering it done — or the sub whimpering under the needle with a sharp gaze on him.

Puffing out a breath of air, he held his arms wide, pulling Keady into a brief hug when he closed the distance. Cutler grinned at him, all teeth and predatory glee. Scotland had almost fallen for that gaze when he'd been balls-deep in Keady's ass, but a pair of blue eyes was where his heart really was.

"You look like you're trying to impress someone," said Keady, throwing his arms around Cutler's neck as soon as he stepped back. He raked his gaze over Scotland's form and lifted one brow. *You used to be shy.*

"I knew you'd be here," said Scotland, grinning wider as Cutler smirked. "I dreamed of your ass this morning, so I wondered if Cutler was willing to share again."

Keady flushed, ducking his head before he cast his gaze around. "Do you have to say it so loud?"

Scotland snorted, hiding his chuckle behind his hand. It was amazing how Keady could be a mix of an exhibitionist and shy at the same time. The first time they'd met, Keady had hardly been able to speak to him at all.

"I'm always willing," said Cutler, the grip on Keady tightening, despite his words. "I don't think a hundred cocks would keep my slut satisfied, so I'm open to helpers."

Oh, you poor, sweet boy. Keady couldn't possibly get any redder.

"SB, what the hell?" asked Keady, letting out a little groan as his eyes sparkled.

These two were so cute together. And somehow, Cutler let Keady get away with the nickname SB, which stood for '*sadistic bastard*'. It was a great name, though. Sadists were the best.

"You going to get another piece?" asked Scotland, glancing to Keady's arm where his first tattoo was. He'd been great for a virgin, not even asking for any breaks for the entire thing. Arms were a good place to start—not like the crazy bastards who got the top of their feet done...or their neck.

"I think so," said Keady, shuffling his feet as he clung tighter to his Dom. "Just waiting on orders." He gave Cutler a pointed look, who responded with one raised brow.

Maybe cute hadn't been a good way to describe them. *Intense* was much more accurate. *Oh, to be a fly on the wall for those scenes.* He'd heard some rumors.

"Have you seen Clint around?" asked Scotland, letting out a sigh as he scanned over the room again. He was still fairly new to the community, having become a member just before the big move. He'd stumbled upon the place during an open house and had instantly fallen in love. His last community hadn't been nearly as welcoming to people like him, and by the end, he'd had enough.

He shook his head. Kink to him had always been second nature, but he didn't exactly devote every moment of his life to it, nor did he care if he fit into certain boxes or not. And the gossipers could go fuck themselves.

Cutler had breezed through the same community as him, not staying long before the whispers started, and he'd moved on. They'd been wrong about Cutler, anyway, and that was reason enough for Scotland not to believe a single other word they said.

"So you *are* on the prowl." Keady grinned, his previous nervousness apparently forgotten. "I thought Maddy was pulling my leg when he said he'd called you here to the rescue. But if anyone can rescue Clint, it's you."

Where was this vote of confidence coming from? Clint had hardly spoken to him, and he doubted that was going to change any time soon. He wasn't much for the matchmaking scheme.

"I'm not going to be any help at all if I can't find him," said Scotland, craning his head back to look at the door. He'd thought he'd heard some commotion earlier, but the Dungeon Master must've taken care of it.

"Did you check the recovery room?" asked Keady, his gaze straying away as something presumably caught his eye. "He hangs out there and chats with people sometimes like he used to do at the bar."

Scotland followed Keady's gaze, widening his eyes at the extreme display of restraint that Keady was looking at. It was too close to mummification to tick his boxes, but the sex that had just begun was nice.

Maybe the recovery room would do him good. It had been so long since he'd scened that he was probably feeling lower than normal. The gangbang with Keady and Cutler had been awesome, but it hadn't been nearly enough to get Scotland to fly.

"Thanks," said Scotland, already starting to turn away. *On second thought.* "I was serious, though. If you need an extra hand tonight—or cock—I'm game." It was always a good idea to have a backup plan.

The place was fairly busy, but it was so much bigger than the old club that it almost had an empty feel to it. He wasn't sure if he'd preferred the loud music and press of bodies or this calmer version.

It was a good thing that the people hadn't changed. They were still kinky as fuck and most were out for a good time. It was easy enough to avoid the few assholes. He'd be able to hold his own in a fight, but Scotland detested getting his hands dirty like that. If he broke his hands, his business would go bust.

Most of the doors to the specialized kink rooms were closed when he ducked around the corner. His membership included access, but they had to be booked ahead of time. Some of them were booked for weeks ahead on the weekends but open Tuesday afternoons for people who apparently had no day jobs. He still hadn't managed to see the inside of most of them.

He had, however, had the privilege of *Nightmare.* His skin prickled just thinking about it, the memories making his cock twitch.

He shook his head, smiling as he walked past the notorious room. Keady probably had an even fonder memory of it. The only thing that had dampened Scotland's time that night had been when Clint hadn't made his promised appearance.

Something that was getting a little too frequent.

The door to the recovery room was open, but he tapped on it gently anyway before he stepped inside. Soothing peppermint and lavender scents struck him first, then the murmur of conversation.

It was the perfect spot for couples to regroup after a scene in relative peace and privacy.

He paused in the doorway. Derreck was on one couch, a bawling Maddy in his lap, with Clint across from them, his face ashen. He was cradling his hands to his chest, the skin on his knuckles hidden behind bits of colored wax.

Derreck flashed his gaze to the door, and Scotland struggled not to take a step back. If there was one man in the world he'd never be able to top, it was Derreck. Maddy seemed to have him wrapped around his little finger, though.

Why is Maddy crying? There didn't seem to be any fresh marks on him that he could see, even if he was mostly clothed, but pain rarely made Maddy cry. In fact, Scotland couldn't think of a single moment that he'd ever seen Maddy more than a little upset. He was shy, more than anything, and innocent in a way that was rare when it came to kink.

"Am I interrupting something?" asked Scotland softly, preparing to retreat until Clint turned his face toward him. *Oh, baby.*

Clint's eyes were bloodshot and dark, the tip of his nose red to match his splotchy cheeks. Scotland caught a look at his hands as he moved, gasping at what he saw.

He was across the room in moments, kneeling on the floor in front of Clint. He grasped one of Clint's hands, pulling it to him. His skin was hot to the touch with a few blisters surrounded by wax in the center of his palms that looked like he should be in agony. It was the type of burn someone could get when they were fucking around with fire.

His thoughts turned to the scars he knew were hidden beneath Clint's clothes.

"Jesus, what happened?" Scotland grasped Clint's other hand, hissing at what he found. The blisters were raw and fresh, the skin shiny and stretched thin over his frame.

"Nothing," said Clint, drawing his hands back before tucking them under his thighs. He didn't flinch, even though it must have been agony. That type of wound would have stung and throbbed in the worst way.

Scotland rocked back on his heels before standing to cross the room. Every nook and cranny in the place was well stocked, and he wasn't disappointed when he found some aftercare cream in one of the drawers. It was a small tube, probably meant for a couple to take along with them after an impact scene, but it was full and sealed, so it would have to work.

"Give me your hand." He lowered himself next to Clint, twisting off the cap with his teeth and dragging off the thin aluminum film. Bitter and spicy peppermint struck him, a tiny bit getting on his teeth and filling his senses with a medicinal taint. He rarely used cream unless his partner asked for it, preferring the stretch of sensation that lasted long after a scene.

Clint shook his head, forcing his hands farther under his legs, his shoulders straining from the angle. "I'm fine. Don't worry about it."

"You are *not* fine," said Scotland, tugging at Clint's elbow. If the fucker wanted to play hard to get, now was not the time. With the tears on Clint's cheeks and the faraway look in his eyes, Scotland doubted that Clint had any idea about his current state. "Give me your hand, Clint. I'm not fucking around."

Clint narrowed his eyes, his jaw ticking as he clenched it tight. *I would kill to have that look in any other situation.* "Just leave it. I told you I'm fine."

His voice rose to one that Scotland recognized. Clint could break up a bar fight and bring a wayward scene to a halt with that voice, but it rolled off Scotland without striking true.

He couldn't just throw Clint over his shoulder and bind him to the closest cross, could he? Some of the paste seeped from the tube as he squeezed it, the greasy liquid dripping down his fingers. It tingled everywhere it touched, a strange numbness settling in.

Derreck cleared his throat and Scotland jumped, almost falling on his ass as he whipped around. He'd been so focused on Clint that he'd forgotten there was a much more intimidating man at his back.

"The way I see it, Clint, you've got two choices," said Derreck, running his hand down Maddy's arm. Maddy leaned into Derreck's chest before he wiped his eyes with the back of his hand. There were splotches on his shirt as if he'd been crying for quite some time, a tiredness to his expression that Scotland had never seen. The innocence was shattered.

"Here it comes," mumbled Clint, jerking himself off the couch. Scotland did fall back at that, landing on his ass with an *oomph*. For a shorter guy, Clint was still pushy as hell when he wanted to be. Usually, he didn't have to be because people moved for him.

"I'm guessing Maddy gets an apology or you make sure I end up six feet under," said Clint, ticking off his finger despite how sore they must've been. Did he not even notice the burns? "You don't intimidate me, Derreck, and I have every intention of apologizing to Maddy. I was tired, I lashed out and said things I didn't mean. Maddy didn't deserve that."

"Sit down." Derreck's voice was like a dark pit, ready to suck his soul dry. Scotland swallowed as Clint slowly lowered himself back into his seat, his face pale. There were so many holes in his shirt that Scotland couldn't count them. Every part of the house was perfect, with high-end finishings that spared no expense. It didn't fit.

Is he going to pass out?

"You were close with option one," said Derreck, his hands tracing patterns over Maddy's skin. "No one would find the body, Clint. They wouldn't even know where to look." Scotland believed him. "But as for the apology — that one's not voluntary."

"I'm sorry —"

"Option two," said Derreck, cutting off Clint's hushed words. "You take some time. I don't care if it's a week or a month, but I don't want to see your face in the building until you figure your shit out."

Whoa. He wasn't sure exactly what he'd walked in on, but death threats seemed a little extreme, even for Derreck. Maddy huffed out a small sob, and Derreck tightened his grip, his eyes unfathomably dark. *Or maybe not.*

"You can't force me out of my home," said Clint as he jerked back to his feet. Scotland failed to scramble to his feet, squashing the tube of cream as he tried. It spurted over his hand, the cooling gel instantly numbing him.

"I'm not forcing you to do anything," said Derreck calmly. "You have a choice, like I said."

He *had* to be joking. *Will I die too if I laugh?* Clint owned the building. Derreck couldn't trump that.

"You need time to process, Clint, and to grieve. Ross is gone—"

"Don't say his fucking name right now," Clint snarled, whirling on Derreck. His lips were drawn over his teeth in a vicious grimace, his eyes wild. "Don't blame him for this, too."

Blame?

Derreck blinked, seemingly as shocked as Scotland. Scotland had heard the rumors of what had happened. People always talked, no matter the community. It had been *years*.

"I'm *fine*." Clint crossed his arms. He clenched his fists, a few flakes of wax breaking off and dropping to the floor, immediately lost in the plush carpet.

"It wasn't that long ago that you were walking through the rain with a polka dot umbrella to find me when Maddy was dropping. You weren't happy that day, but you were calm. You knew who you were and what you wanted. Where is that man today?" asked Derreck, his voice breathtakingly cool.

What? Picturing Clint in polka dots was hilarious and ridiculous. Scotland had only ever seen him in tattered shirts and ragged jeans.

"And before that — before everything," said Maddy, sniffing, "Nikita told me you used to patch him up at the hospital. He had a nickname for you there — Jester. You never let anyone leave before they laughed, even if you were sewing stitches into their skin. He'd pick fights, just to go see you."

Scotland quirked his lips. Clint was funny, but in that subtle way of someone who didn't know it. He never seemed to *try* to make people laugh. He just seemed too tired to accomplish that all the time.

Clint took a step back, his eyes wide. More wax dropped from him as his hands went slack. They were almost clean now, except for the burns that appeared even brighter. "I didn't know — I mean — that can't be right."

Scotland didn't blame his disbelief. The Nikita he knew was a badass mob enforcer with a twin brother who didn't give two fucks.

"Everyone in this building is here because of you, one way or another," said Maddy, taking the tissue that Derreck passed him. "But I feel like you haven't been here for a long time. I can still see you, but it's not really you. I didn't know you when Ross was alive, but every story I hear, it's like you were a different person back then."

Can you blame him? Scotland could only imagine the sorrow of losing a close partner. Sometimes there was no moving on from that.

"You haven't grieved," said Derreck with utter finality. "And you are about to snap and lose everyone you love. I know because I've been there."

Maddy sent Derreck a soft look, snuggling in closer. Scotland had heard all about them too and how they had come so close to breaking each other.

"I'm not," Clint mumbled, his eyes shiny. "Maddy, I'm sorry I yelled at you. You're the best thing that's ever happened to this place." He looked away, dropping his gaze.

"No, I'm not," said Maddy, laying his head against Derreck's chest. "You are, Clint."

Silence hung in the air, only broken by Maddy's sniffles as he wiped his nose. Clint bit his lip as he clenched and unclenched his hands. The wax was nearly gone, his skin flared red and painful-looking. "You're wrong."

"No, he's not," said Scotland, pushing himself off the ground. His ass twinged as he moved, a reminder that he wasn't in his twenties anymore.

Clint narrowed his eyes. "Stay out of this, punk. I'm not sceneing with you and I'm certainly not going to fuck you. Get that through your head."

Ouch. Is that all Clint thinks I want? He was so, *so* wrong. "If you won't take care of yourself, someone has to."

It was a low blow, even for him. Clint was a grown-ass, independent man, and Scotland knew well enough that he wasn't needed.

Clint brought up one hand, pushing a single finger into Scotland's chest. He wanted to grab that hand and kiss the soft, delicate spot on his wrist, but he was frozen, too caught to hope to move.

Clint was the only one who had ever made him feel that way.

"You know what? Fuck you, punk. Get out of my fucking club. I don't want to see your face here ever again." Clint's eyes were blazing, rage carved into his features as Scotland's heart sank. His friends and people he considered family were all here and Clint had the power to take that all away in a heartbeat. He just never thought he *would*.

Well, shit.

Chapter Five

Clint

Vacation. The word was practically poisonous — and even worse than a nightmare wrapped in broken limits. He hadn't taken a vacation as a nurse, and he certainly didn't need one from the club. But Maddy's suggestion of therapy had been even worse. *If I let a therapist in, I'll be committed for sure.*

"I'm so excited for you," said Maddy, grasping Clint's smaller bag from the trunk and tossing it over his shoulder. Clint grabbed the second one, pushing out a sigh as he let it thud to the gravel road. There were weeds growing through the road in large patches, some stretching higher than his waist where they'd burst through the crushed rock.

And the potholes had made Maddy crawl along in the car, barely getting over walking speed as they'd rocked back and forth. It was made for a truck with big axles and more testosterone than dick.

Clint let out a sigh, running a hand through his hair. *Where the hell am I?* There was no way that a vacation was what he needed, but it was only slightly better than the alternative of Derreck's first choice.

Maddy had insisted on driving, too, leaving Clint no way to escape the trip to their destination. There was a butterfly that was nestling on a nearby flower and a high-pitched sandpiper sounding the alarm as it zoomed down a dusty section of the path. *He knows me too well.*

If it had been Clint's choice, he would have turned for the city as soon as the lane had come into view. Of course, he loved the new home in the middle of the woods, but it still wasn't the same as the thrum of the city and the lights that could guide him, no matter what the time of night.

It wasn't that far from the club — maybe fifteen minutes tops. But it was off the beaten path, for sure.

"I've heard so much about this place," said Maddy, shielding his eyes before looking at the cabin. "It has five stars on all its ratings, and a few members have been out here, too. Apparently, the owner is a great guy, but I doubt you'll see him much."

Clint was doing his best not to look toward his future stay, his gaze firmly affixed on the suitcase that was now coated with dust. He hadn't even owned the bags before the move.

"Uh-huh." Clint crossed his arms and leaned against Maddy's car. Derreck must've buffed the exterior, because it was slippery to the touch and shiny except for the few bugs they'd hit along the way.

He'd never thought he'd be caught dead in a bed and breakfast, especially not a privately owned cabin that was somehow up for rent on a few popular websites. The concept was ridiculous.

The main house they'd passed hadn't looked half bad—for a hundred-year-old farmhouse—and the fenced paddock he caught sight of had almost caught his interest. The cabin, though? *Um, does it even have heat?*

He took a quick glance and wasn't impressed.

It wasn't that cold yet, but the nights were starting to get chilly. He hadn't thought to pack any extra blankets or mouse traps, for that matter.

"Do you like it?" asked Maddy, a smile touching his lips as he looked around. "I can't believe it's so quiet. I can hardly even hear the road."

"What road?" Clint chuckled at Maddy's glare. "That *path* was not a road, kid. But, yeah, I like it." Even after everything Clint had said, Maddy had still tried his best to find something when Clint had agreed to a vacation. The kid was gold, and he wasn't going to hurt him again. *That's a promise.*

Biting his lip, he looked back to the cabin. The exterior was made of wood logs that were slightly pleasing to the eye with a burnished stain that was nearly red. The deep green door with white trim seemed to suit, as well, and a few windows were spotted along the small exterior.

It was the inside he was worried about. "Don't places like this usually have mice?"

He'd had rat problems a few times in the old club, which seemed to come with the territory. The last one had taken him three sleepless nights to catch, and the thing had almost been as big as a house cat. He hadn't meant to kill it, either, but when it had run right by him while he'd been carrying the baseball bat while on the prowl, he'd struck out automatically.

"I think so?" said Maddy, scrunching up his nose. "If you have any problems, just contact the owner. I printed everything off for you." Maddy rushed over to the car, grabbing a piece of paper from the front seat before folding it and zipping it into Clint's bag.

"And what am I supposed to do out here?" Listen to crickets, that was for sure. There must've been a thousand of the things. The new Unkinked had its fair share, but not nearly so bad. There was always music there, though, and people. Even when the club was closed, the regulars were sometimes in the few rooms meant for overnight stays. He was never *alone*.

Maddy scratched the back of his head, squinting at the sun. "Relax, put your feet up, read a book. Those kinds of things."

He snorted, shaking his head. "Kid, I haven't read a book in twenty years. I live in a kink palace. No book could be better than that."

"Then the other stuff." Maddy pulled at the collar of his T-shirt before hiking the bag up again and heading to the door of the cabin. "I honestly didn't check to see if there was a television."

Wait…no kink and no television? Clint glanced at the car. The keys were still in the ignition.

"And how long do I have to stay in this place?" Clint rubbed the back of his neck as he looked away from the car. "I'm not trying to sound like an ass. I appreciate you planning this trip and all, but the whole cabin in the woods thing is pretty boring when you aren't starring in a horror movie."

"You'll be fine," said Maddy, pointing to the keypad at the door. "The code is 3-4-5-6 to get inside. The door locks automatically, so make sure you remember the code." He typed the code on the small keypad, twisting the door handle as soon as there was a click. "Wow, this is really nice."

Kill me now. Clint looked back at the car. If he made a run for it, he could probably make it before Maddy. But then Derreck would kill him for real for leaving Maddy here and for possibly breaking the car during his rush out of the lane.

Letting out a sigh of resignation, he stepped inside, squinting in the lower light.

"Wow," said Clint, letting his heavy bag slide to the floor as he blinked and looked around.

"I know," said Maddy, making a slow turn before grinning. "And it's all yours. You are going to have so much fun!"

It didn't look like fun, exactly, but modern appliances and one hell of a stylish interior certainly helped. The floors were spotless hardwood, and the kitchen countertops looked like granite, from what he could tell. The couch was a plush, leather-looking thing that appeared to recline, but it was only a two-seater.

That's going to be a trick to sleep on.

"It's nice," said Clint, slipping off his shoes and taking another step inside. He spied something along the far wall. "Oh, and thank God there is a television." It wasn't huge, but it was there, nestled between two bookshelves that were surprisingly full.

"You like it? Really?"

He didn't deserve someone like Maddy in his life, plain and simple.

"I love it." The smile was real this time. When he touched the back of the couch, he let out a groan. At least it would be comfortable. It smelled clean, too, with that fresh smell that came from something new.

"Perfect, because I've got you booked for the month," said Maddy, letting out a sheepish grin as he dropped the bag and took a step toward the exit. "I should go check on the club now, Clint. Bye."

"Now wait just a second." Clint was only a step behind and closing the distance fast. "There is no way I'm letting you run Unkinked for a whole month by yourself, Maddy. A week tops." He was already going through withdrawal. He hadn't seen a single nipple yet today. Shit like that took its toll.

"Derreck wanted three months, but I got him down to one," said Maddy, his smile looking a tad more forced as he took another backward step. The edge of the small porch was right behind him, and Maddy took a glance before making his way down the stairs.

"You can't just leave me out here," said Clint, motioning to the fridge which was probably empty. "I'll starve to death." He couldn't walk to town from this far, and it would take him a good day to hike back to the club unless he managed to hitch a ride with someone. *That's a good plan.*

But even if he got back, Derreck would no doubt be waiting with a shovel and a pre-dug hole somewhere.

Maddy shook his head. "You don't have to worry about a thing. The owner of this place had the option to have all your meals provided to you, and I've already let him know about your allergies. You'll be fine."

I am so not going to be fine.

"Bye, Clint." With one last step, Maddy turned, hightailing it to the car.

"What the hell just happened?" He had to laugh as Maddy stumbled just before he reached the car, catching himself on the trunk and probably scratching up the wax job as he caught it with his nails. "Karma's a bitch, kid."

As the car pulled out of the drive, swaying and thumping along the pitted road, a finality crept in that tugged something in his chest. For the first time in years, he was away from the club and well and truly *completely* alone.

But what the fuck was he supposed to do in a cabin for a month? Kink was his thing, and without it he was…

He shook his head, cutting that thought off before it could sink too deep. He'd been without kink for a long time, even if he immersed himself in it every day.

He strained his hearing, but the sound of Maddy's car had disappeared, replaced with crickets, wind and a few birds that were probably hopping around in the trees that surrounded the property.

His stomach grumbled, pulling him away from the door. He padded across the space, jerking the fridge open. It was only eleven in the morning, and he would be out of luck if meal time wasn't until after lunch. His breakfast had consisted of a cold coffee and glares from Derreck.

"What the hell?" his mouth flopped open against his will as he pushed the door wider, scanning the interior.

It was packed with everything from carrots to bacon and a few other things he didn't recognize. There was no way he could eat everything before it went bad, especially not on his own. *Is it the fucking apocalypse?* He kept his fridge fairly stocked at home, but often went for precooked meals for simple ease and time. There was no joy in cooking. *Not anymore.*

He stumbled to the cupboard, pulling the door wide. It was in a similar state, with boxes of crackers, chips and even the soup packets that he secretly got cravings for every few months. He wasn't sure if he'd ever seen so many varieties of canned beans before, and someone had obviously found out about his secret love of black licorice.

A white scrap of paper on the counter caught his eye, and he reached for it, flipping it over to read the scratched lettering.

~To get you started.
S.

"What in the ever-loving fuck?" This couldn't be just the start. He was going to gain fifty pounds in a week if someone expected him to eat this much. And who the fuck was S?

Something shifted in his gut as realization struck him like a force. Maddy had been so eager to pick the spot and had booked it without even letting Clint vet the place. He'd mentioned that he knew the owner, only to backtrack a moment later and claim that a friend of a friend did.

And leaving him without a car? It was like a final nail in his modern wooden prison.

He scrambled for his bag, reefing the zipper open and grabbing the folded paper that Maddy had tucked inside so casually. Clint hadn't even thought to ask for it or read it, so in denial of his fate.

"Maddy, you little brat." Clint fell back on his heels as a laugh pushed through his lips. It wasn't even funny, but he couldn't stop. *Oh, this is going to be hell.*

On the paper was information about the place like the Wi-Fi password and the door code, along with the owner's name and number. There was even a little quote from the bastard, which had presumably been done up by the host site.

If you need anything at all during your stay, just let me know. I always have a steak on the grill.
~Scotland

Chapter Six

Scotland

He wasn't sure if it would be better to rip the Band-Aid off and knock on the door to the cabin or act casually surprised when Clint stepped foot outside for the first time. He'd never been one to avoid a situation, normally, but Clint had kicked him out the last time they'd been in a room together.

He'd probably gone overboard. *Definitely.* He hadn't spent so much on groceries since he'd hosted the Super Bowl party with twenty guys. That had been enough potato skins and jalapeno poppers to last him a lifetime.

Would Clint notice the little basket of cherry tomatoes from his garden? Or the zucchinis that Scotland loved growing but never knew what to do with? He could only make so many muffins before he got sick of the green demons.

Turning onto the pitted road, he slowed as he started down the lane to his house. It was overdue for fresh gravel, but he kind of liked it the way it was. Visitors always drove slower when it was like this, and it gave the place a more authentic feel.

When he'd first bought the land, he'd found tracks of unknown people going onto the property. That didn't happen anymore when some of the potholes were bigger than castle motes and lined with enough muddy water that some of his guests hesitated at first.

He turned into his parking spot along the side of the house, rolling the windows up and shutting the car off. The engine ticked a few times as it cooled before falling silent. Closing his eyes, he took a deep breath.

If Clint reacted the way he expected him to, then he wasn't in for the quiet evening he needed. Maybe a medium-rare steak would change Clint's mind, along with sausages and a potato mix of his own creation. There was still some corn kicking around in the bottom of his own fridge, and there was bound to be a plateful of beans in the garden yet.

I'm doing it again. The last thing he wanted to do was push Clint away by getting over-eager. Steaks would do…and the corn.

He crept out of the car, gently shutting the door and glancing toward the cabin as he made his way to the house. Only the corner of the building and the yard at the guest house were visible because of the curve of the land and the trees that guarded that part of the property. It was enough to give everyone privacy, but he could still keep an eye on the place to make sure nothing was on fire.

Some of his guests had been a bit…special. One particular city kid had moved the fire ring onto the porch and had started to pile massive logs into the thing in an attempt at a campfire. Scotland had been lucky that the guy had only had matches, otherwise the whole cabin would have been at risk.

He'd spent three months building it and another furnishing it, doing most of the work himself and even using a few trees from the forest on his land to make some accent pieces inside. He was damn proud of it, too.

Ducking into his house, he flicked off his shoes before strolling to the back patio. He had a better view from there, with the empty fire pit out in front of the cabin and the few Adirondack chairs set up around it. There was a charcoal barbecue there, too, that didn't get too much use, despite most people cooking for themselves.

When he had the place rented out, he usually avoided the back porch to give them more privacy, but today he couldn't help himself. He'd been raw since his last time at Unkinked. *How badly did I fuck up?*

Providing meals didn't usually come with the stay, but as soon as Maddy had mentioned looking for a place for Clint's vacation, he had jumped on the opportunity. Hopefully, it would make up for most of his recent blunder.

"I'll take care of everything," he'd said, a grin stretching over his face. "*Everything.*"

Maddy's grin had been confused at first, before realization had begun to dawn. He was cute but a little oblivious.

It wouldn't be the first time he'd had kinksters out to his place. In his old community, he'd had a few friends out, and even at Unkinked, word seemed to spread. It was relaxing to come home to his little slice of heaven with Dumb and Dumber grazing in the small paddock and a rope bunny strung up on the sturdy branch of a large oak tree.

Maybe Clint will let me string him up. Letting out a snort, he shook his head. There was no way in hell Clint would let him do that. He was the Dommiest Dom who ever Dommed. And he seemed to have a watchful eye for everyone except Scotland, no matter how hard he tried.

Maybe he had something against switches? It wouldn't be far-fetched, but Clint was just so damned nice that it was hard to think poorly of him. He helped people, even if he denied it.

Scotland's phone buzzed in his pocket, vibrating against the change in there. He grabbed it, bringing it to his ear without looking at the name.

"Hello?"

"It's Clint."

Scotland sucked in a breath, leaning against the wall as Clint's voice rolled over him. It was the first thing to draw him to Clint, the very sound of it sending a shiver over his body. His memory never did it any justice.

"Hey, what's up?" His voice was shaky, his grip on the phone fierce. *Fuck, I'm not in high school anymore.* He hadn't had this type of reaction to any man, but Clint always managed to do it to him. Maybe it was because he so often ignored Scotland, so when he finally looked his way, the full attention struck him so much harder.

"I saw you drive in. How the hell does this stove work? I'm starving."

He blinked. The stove? He hadn't bought anything complicated — just a nice model that had been on sale at the local depot.

"Just hit the power button — I'll be there in a second." He hung up, scrambling inside and throwing his shoes on. He took off at a jog to the cabin, panting as he reached the door before knocking. His heart was pounding, even though it had just been a short run, his gut jittery as adrenaline sparked through him.

When Clint answered, Scotland had to swallow to keep from drooling. The man was shirtless, his track pants hanging low and loose and showing off a dusting of hair above his groin. The lump just below that hair looked impressive, even if it was hidden away. The extent of the scars was a surprise, though.

Of course, he'd heard the stories about the burns, but he hadn't expected so many, the skin shiny and pink in a swirling pattern. *He's so strong*. To have survived something like that was a miracle.

"Hey," said Clint, scratching his belly as he took a step back to let Scotland inside. He turned, showing off the perfect dip of his back where a few prickles of sweat had gathered. Below that was the soft roundness of his perfect ass that flexed as he moved.

Scotland simultaneously lost the fight not to drool or get hard. His plan fizzled away to nothing as his mind went blissfully blank. Clint's nipples were that brown shade of rose that made his lips ache to suck and nibble at them. They would fit in his mouth perfectly one at a time, and they would glisten as he worshipped them. He could imagine the salty taste of Clint's skin, and the smell of his sweat as he dragged his nose over the plane of his chest.

"H-hey." Scotland shook his head slowly, trying to break the spell, but it clung tight. He'd never seen anyone so perfect or masculine, the hard lines of muscle just as prominent as the softer bits.

Clint chuckled, trailing his hand over his belly as if he didn't know how much he was torturing Scotland. *I'd pay to be that hand. My entire bank account for a night.*

"The stove?"

"Y-yeah. I got it." Biting his lip, Scotland toed off his shoes and strolled to the stove, the back of his neck prickling as Clint's gaze followed him. "You should just have to hit the power button, then mode and it will turn on at maximum. The plus or minus adjust it up and down."

He glanced at the pot of water next to the stove and the clumped and uncooked macaroni noodles within. There was no way he was letting Clint get away with eating cheap pasta on his watch.

"I did all that, but it just kept beeping at me," said Clint, rubbing the back of his neck as he approached. "I found the book of manuals on the counter, so I followed the directions there. I'm not sure what I missed. I've never used an induction stove before."

Clint was so close that Scotland swore he could feel the heat of him and the whisper of his breath against his neck. Clint was shorter than him, but he was a powerful man with a gaze that was knowing and intimidating at the same time. It was a struggle to keep from kneeling then and there.

"Did you put the pot on the stove first?" asked Scotland, reaching for the pot before setting it on the circular burner. "It won't start unless the pot is already there."

The beat of silence and Clint's 'oh' was answer enough.

"Don't worry about it. I've had a lot of people ask me about it. It was just safer to have one like this instead of a gas or electric stove out here." Not to mention that a tabletop stove weighed about twenty pounds. He'd done most of the work himself, and it had been the easiest thing to carry on his own and get hooked up.

"I was going to throw some steaks on the grill in a second. That's probably better than mac n' cheese." He swirled the pot once, but the pasta remained clumped in one bulky mass. How long had Clint been trying? The pasta looked like it had been soaking in cold water for a while.

"You know you don't have to do all this, right?" Clint stepped closer, his shoulder brushing his. The touch was nearly electric. There was only one thin layer of fabric between them — a layer that could be tugged off at a moment's notice.

"I want to," said Scotland, the truth of his words startling him. "I mean, it's really no problem." God, he sounded desperate. One phone call and he could get laid. Another phone call and he could have a fun scene that would take his mind off things. *So what the hell is wrong with me?*

"I don't know what Maddy and Derreck said to you, but I can take care of myself. I've been cooking my own meals since I was fifteen. I don't need someone else to do that for me."

Need has nothing to do with it. "Says the man who can't start a stove," Scotland muttered, biting his lip. "Just because you can cook for yourself doesn't mean you have to. Sometimes it's nice to have someone take care of you for a bit."

Sometimes it's the best ever.

Clint took a step back, a frown twisting his lips. "I don't need you to take care of me."

"Uh-huh." Clint was a cry for help if he'd ever seen one. He wasn't sure if he'd ever seen anyone so sleep-deprived with such a false smile on their face. And Scotland always had that itch to look after someone and he hadn't gotten to scratch it so long.

"I'm serious," said Clint, a wary look on his face as he crossed his arms. He flexed his biceps, the rigid muscle jumping.

"So am I," said Scotland, throwing caution to the wind. "You take care of everyone around you, Clint. You are super sweet to Maddy, Nav and every other sub, and you are like a rock to every Dom. You can only be a rock so long before you start to erode."

He closed the distance between them, reaching for anything to keep Clint from escaping. He settled his fingers on the drawstring of Clint's pants, holding the string tight. It was a struggle not to look down when Clint pulled his hips away, the fabric tenting as the string snapped taut.

"Let me treat you to a nice vacation. Let me help you relax while you're here and cook you a meal or two. Nobody will hold it against you, and I won't even tell anyone. I just want you to enjoy yourself."

I can keep my hands to myself. It would kill him a bit, but he could keep things platonic. Clint's health came first, and if Clint wasn't going to look after himself, then Scotland was going to do it for him.

"You're not my Dom, Scotland. This whole ruse isn't going to bring us together."

Scotland nodded sharply. *I knew that.* Even if he wanted that to change. He'd been waiting a long time. He could keep waiting as long as it took.

"I'm not treating you like a sub, Clint. I'm just trying to be nice. When was the last time you took a kind gesture at face value?" He struggled to keep his voice calm. Clint was not going to get a rise out of him. He took a breath, letting it out slowly. "This isn't about sex or kink."

"Says the man with his hand down my pants," said Clint, narrowing his eyes.

Shit. He must've adjusted his hand subconsciously, because he now had a handful of Clint's pants in his grip and a very decent view of a drool-worthy package. If he wasn't mistaken, the back of his hand was a little warmer where he'd just brushed the wondrous thing on accident.

"I'm making you dinner. It's up to you if you want to eat it or not." Scotland slowly pulled his hand away, giving Clint one last look before he padded to the front door. "And for future reference, if you don't want me to eye fuck you, try wearing a bit more the next time you invite me over."

He wasn't the type to blame the victim, but Clint was being way too shameless not to be up to something.

"There won't be a next time, boy. I can look after myself."

He shut the door quietly, letting out a sigh as his phone buzzed in his pocket. No one had called him 'boy' in a long time, and fuck, he missed it. He missed being attracted to someone so much that it almost hurt not to have them that instant, knowing that they felt the same way. It wasn't nearly as fun when it was one-sided.

When he glanced at his phone, he let out a wry chuckle. Maddy had sent him a simple text.

How is it going?

How in the hell was he supposed to reply to that? He'd tried to build a bridge, but he'd flooded the place instead. This was probably only the beginning. *It will get better.* Or maybe it was all downhill from here.

Swimmingly.

He sent back the text before heading to the other side of the house where the paddock lay. The grass was almost tall enough to cover the two occupants within the place, but he'd never been worried that a coyote would get them. Donkeys were kick ass like that, even when they were miniature.

Usually, he went straight to them after work, but he'd gotten a bit distracted along the way this time. Ducking through the fence, he glanced around, trying to spot their tanned coats against green. They were quiet when they wanted to be, always picking the most startling times to let out their ear-shattering bray.

"Dumb and Dumber? Where are you guys?" Two nearly identical heads popped up a second later, their long ears pricked toward him. It was no wonder that he hadn't been able to find them. They'd been at the far end of the nearly two-acre paddock in a lower spot where rain gathered to make a giant mud puddle every spring and fall.

A grin stretched over his lips, and he patted his thigh at the sight of them. They were both due for a brushing, with twigs and a few plants sticking to them. And it looked like Dumb had enjoyed his roll in the remaining mud, with brown streaked along his rump in large clumps.

Dumber extended his neck, letting out a loud bray as Dumb immediately trotted his way, the grass parting around him and a few grasshoppers taking off in the stampede. His ears wobbled as he ran, his tiny hooves clearing the rocks and downed branches that always managed to trip Scotland.

"Hey, sweetheart." he lowered himself to one knee as Dumber reached him, bracing himself as the donkey thumped its head into his chest. For small creatures, they had a lot of weight behind them and one hell of a center of balance. "You guys been good today? You didn't scare momma fox, did you?"

He scuffed Dumb's ears, chuckling as Dumber approached and started to nibble on his shirt. It really was no wonder he went through so many clothes.

The other morning, he'd looked out of the window, only to see a whirlwind of dirt as they chased a fox out of their field, braying and kicking as they went. Thankfully, the fox had made it back to her kits, who had been sitting by a fencepost playing.

Dumber glanced toward the cabin, letting out another long bray that made his ears ring. They were better than any guard dog known to man, and he'd never met a more loyal companion. They were smart as hell, too, despite their names.

"I know, I know." He glanced back at the cabin, catching a flash of light as the door swung open and Clint popped his head out. The only noise complaint he'd ever had at his place had been from the donkeys when a couple had brought their dog along, despite his no-pets rule in the house. Not that he didn't love dogs, but a lot of people had allergies, and it was difficult to get the hair out of the sofa.

"You can't run *him* down, guys. I'm trying to get him to relax." He let out a huff as Dumber nudged him, sending him to his ass. He got his feet under him as calmly as he could before standing. He had no doubt that he'd get a bit trampled if they got too excited when he was down.

Clint still wasn't wearing a shirt, but he had donned some shoes as he walked over to the fence, a grin on his face as he rubbed the back of his head. He propped one foot up on the lower board of the fence, crossing his arms over the top rail as he looked their way.

"I saw the fence, but I thought it was empty. Every time I looked out, I didn't see anything." Every bit of his anger seemed to have disappeared, his face smooth and relaxed as he slumped his shoulders.

"Yeah, they are good at keeping out of sight," Scotland patted Dumber before scratching his neck. He wasn't a big fan of ear scratches like Dumb was. "But don't let that fool you. They are little hellions most days, and they are very good at making sure you don't forget they are here.

"Yeah, that noise scared the hell out of me."

Scotland grinned. The first time he'd heard a donkey, he'd been expecting the typical hee-haw noise. He'd had no idea that they could sound like a cow had gone head-to-head with an ice scraper.

"Do you want to pet them? They don't bite or anything. Come on, guys." He patted his leg, heading back to the fence where Clint was waiting. They trotted behind him like they always did, probably expecting carrots from the way Dumber was nibbling at his back pocket. He slipped his wallet out of his pocket, shoving it into the front one, just in case. They would probably have a great time munching on his credit cards.

"They're like dogs," said Clint. His grin was one of the cutest and sexiest things Scotland had ever seen, with his eyes lit up. *I should have just put the donkeys in the cabin.*

He turned away, looking back to the pair. Clint had made it pretty clear that this was going to be a hands-off arrangement, so it was probably best to avoid looking at that attractive chest that was so hot it could melt butter.

"They're a hell of a lot smarter than dogs," said Scotland, ducking through the fence before turning back and kneeling down. Clint crouched beside him, bringing his hand up as the two popped their heads through the fence. "Dogs will fetch the stick for you. Donkeys are smart enough to trick you into fetching the stick for them."

Clint let out a hum, which turned into a gasp as he touched Dumber's neck. "They're so coarse. They looked so soft."

Dumb bobbed his head, searching for scratches of his own.

"Don't take any offense, buddy," said Scotland, letting out a grin. "You're still my little floof ball." He ran his hand over Dumb's face before rubbing the soft fuzz of his muzzle. "You should have seen these two when they were born. They were both so fluffy that they looked like they'd been struck by lightning."

Clint chuckled, reaching a second hand out to pet both donkeys at the same time. A few flies had caught up to them, buzzing around them, but Clint didn't seem to mind. "Were they born here?"

"Yeah." Those had been the days. "I got their mama off a farmer who didn't want her anymore. She was so depressed and had barely been outside the barn in years. The first three days she was here she wouldn't even step outside of the trailer, so I just left it in the paddock until she did." It had been so heartbreaking to see an animal afraid of the big outdoors, simply because she'd never been exposed.

"Next thing I knew, she was the light of my life. She loved everyone, except Samuel, funnily enough." He snorted, shaking his head. "She tried to run him down in the paddock. She was so huge at that point that it was like watching a bouncy ball chase a football player."

"Who was Samuel?" asked Clint, his expression soft as he gazed at the creatures.

"One of my old Doms," said Scotland, leaning away to crack his back. He'd been stooped over for far too long. "We were together for about a year until we both realized it wasn't going to work out."

"Ah." Clint nodded. "It happens."

"Yep." It had been a mutual parting that didn't give him much grief. He still saw Samuel sometimes, and he really hadn't missed him. "But anyway, here's this donkey running around all this space with a new diet and everything good, and she just kept getting fatter. I took her for walks every day because she'd follow me around everywhere, but nothing seemed to get the weight off."

One of his fondest memories had been walking through the bush with Penny at his side and stumbling on a herd of white-tailed deer. They'd taken off once they'd spotted him, and Penny had just flicked her ears and kept on walking.

"Then one morning I woke up and I didn't have one donkey anymore— I had three. Twins are really rare for these guys, and there was no way I was ever selling them. They stayed here, even after their momma passed a few years later." He swallowed as he remembered that day. He'd never been so fucking broken in his life. Luckily, he'd had a sub at the time who had been one of the sweetest guys Scotland had ever met. Riley had held him as he'd cried for hours.

He'd almost always had someone there for him, and someone who could hug him or hold him and cherish him after a long day. But when was the last time Clint had had that?

"Let me make you dinner, Clint," he said softly, giving Dumber one last pat.

Clint swallowed, tugging some grass and passing it through the fence to Dumber, who gobbled it as if it were candy. "Okay."

Chapter Seven

Clint

His plan to get Scotland to back off had pretty much crashed and burned. Truth be told, it was barely a wisp of an idea with a tad of cruelty thrown in. He'd waited for the disgust to bloom when he'd blatantly paraded about with no shirt on, but obviously Scotland wouldn't be deterred so quickly.

People usually stared at the scars, even when they tried not to. Then, the awkward questions would come. But if anything, Scotland was staring at his chest, his gaze zeroed in on one nipple at a time.

The fucking donkeys, though. He wasn't sure if he'd ever seen ones that were quite so small before...or adorable. That hellish noise they'd made had pulled him straight out of his hangry stupor.

And now, somehow, he was eating some of the best steak he'd ever had, on a plate piled with so many different vegetables that he wasn't sure if they'd ever fit in his stomach. The shit-eating grin on Scotland's face was even tolerable as the tender meat practically melted in his mouth.

"S'good," said Clint, stabbing another bean, mushroom and piece of steak before shoveling it in his mouth like a miniature kabob. When he moaned at the taste, a pink flush bloomed over Scotland's face.

The guy was cute — that he could come to terms with — but he was also dangerous.

"I can't promise every meal will be steak, but I'll try to keep you from getting hungry while you're here. And if you need a snack, just shoot me a text, and I can grab something on my way home from work." Scotland licked his lips, the blue tips of his hair falling forward as he ducked his head.

"Let me know the time, and I'll make sure I put on a shirt," Clint mumbled, looking off to the side. The house was tastefully decorated and bright, with a modern look, despite the century-old exterior.

"I don't have any rules out here," said Scotland. "If you want to walk around nude in the bush, I couldn't care less. You'll probably get a bunch of mosquito bites on your balls, though."

"No thanks." Clint grinned, closing his legs at the mere threat of bug bites. "I went on a camping trip with Ross when we first started going out. The temperature dropped to just above freezing every night. It was the only trip that I never had a bug bite. Usually, they love me."

Scotland took a slow bite, blatantly staring. "You must be sweet or something."

Clint straightened his spine before clearing his throat. The meat had made him sleepy, but a little light flirting and he was wide awake. "Or something."

"Did you guys do a lot of camping?" asked Scotland, snapping a bean between his teeth. "I rarely do, myself.

This place is already so close to camping that there really isn't a need. I don't need an uncomfortable mattress or to wake up covered in dew just to hear the crickets singing at night."

Maybe Scotland wasn't trying to flirt, but it still felt like it. Clint forced himself to relax. "Not really. Some glamping trips in cottages and the like, but rarely out in the tent. I'm not very good at the whole 'no electricity' thing. Not much of a boy scout, either."

Clint set his fork on the table, leaning back in his chair. "There's no way I can fit another bite." He rubbed his belly, which was full and stretched. He could go for a nap and Scotland would clean up, but that wouldn't be fair. "I'll do up the dishes."

"Don't worry about it," said Scotland, copying Clint's movements. "You're a guest. And besides, there is a dishwasher."

Asshole. The type that wanted to cater to his every need had never been *his* type. It always felt a touch unbalanced to him.

"I wasn't actually asking a question," said Clint, raising one brow as he grabbed his plate and utensils before heading to the kitchen sink, which was only a few steps away. Depositing his stuff on the counter, he returned for Scotland's dishes.

Scotland reached for him, grasping Clint's wrist as he went to retrieve the plate. Biting back his gasp at the contact, Clint tugged his arm, nearly whimpering when he wasn't able to break free. *What's he playing at? I...can't.*

It felt good to be powerless again. He didn't let his eyes flutter shut, no matter how tempted he was.

"I can't quite figure you out, Clint," said Scotland, turning Clint's wrist over in his grasp. His hold was tight, his finger digging deep into Clint's bones. The whimper was real as Scotland shifted his hold, forcing Clint a step closer.

"Do you want me to cherish you or did you want me to push you against the wall and fuck you, no matter what you have to say about it?"

Where the hell did that come from? He was pretty sure Scotland had been just another sweet guy a moment before, but now he was pushing buttons that hadn't been pushed in a long time.

"Traffic light system?" asked Scotland, standing from his chair without letting Clint go. *This is going so fast.* He wasn't at the club. He hadn't even had anything to drink, but his head was already swimming.

Clint swallowed dryly, not sure where to look. His skin prickled, a fire building in his gut that wouldn't be hidden for long with the way his pants were hanging so loosely.

"Yeah." *Shit. Am I doing this?* "J-just let me do the dishes first."

There was no way. Absolutely no fucking way he was getting laid tonight. His cock twitched as Scotland gave his wrist one last squeeze before letting go.

"Of course."

I could resist, but... It had been a while—too long. And it would only be once. Next time he'd have his guard up. *Fuck it.* Yeah, it was going down.

He grasped the plate, ignoring Scotland's smirk as he turned back to the sink and started up the hot water. A few drops of soap later and he plunged the dishes into the little clouds of bubbles.

When he felt the tell-tale tickle of Scotland's breath on the back of his neck, he let out a shuddering gasp, slipping his hands beneath the surface of the water as the cool fabric of Scotland's T-shirt touched his back.

"L-let me do the dishes," said Clint. A plate nearly slipped from his grasp. His voice sounded so meek that he wanted to pause and slap himself across the face. But he was already getting lost, the submission sliding over him like it had never left. *I can't let myself get too deep.*

"I won't stop you," said Scotland, setting his hands on Clint's hips. He curled his fingers, running them over the little dip on the inside of Clint's hips.

His skin prickled, his spine going rigid at the sensation that was so strange yet familiar. Scotland moved his fingers, teasing the edge of his pants until they slipped lower. The drawstring had already accidentally untied itself at some point, and they were barely hanging on.

"Keep washing," said Scotland. A moment later he pressed his lips to Clint's neck.

It was too good. The heated touch of soft lips against one of his most sensitive spots made him lose his breath and his mind, all in one instant. He tilted his head, giving Scotland access as he deepened the touch into something with just a hint of teeth and pain.

"I don't ask a second time, Clint." Scotland dragged his teeth over the sensitive tendon before biting down into Clint's shoulder.

Clint hissed, grabbing the dishcloth and scrubbing it against one of the plates a few times. Water splashed on his front and over the edge of the sink at his enthusiasm. He jerked as Scotland bit him a second time, harder and close to breaking skin.

"Do you know how much bacteria is in the human mouth?" asked Clint, twisting as Scotland nipped the back of his neck before gentling his kiss. "You can bruise me but don't draw blood."

Scotland chuckled, rubbing the tip of his nose along the top of Clint's spine. "You'll survive."

With that, he sank his teeth into the meat of Clint's shoulder, the sharpness digging deep. Scotland had always seemed so sweet and nice, if not a little desperate. *I didn't know he had this in him.* If Clint had known, maybe he would have given in sooner. *No. It's just this once.*

"Fuck." Clint dropped the plate into the suds, clutching at the counter as his knees went weak. It had been too long since he'd ached like that. His gut throbbed, his track pants giving everything away beneath the lip of the counter.

Keep washing. Scrambling for the plate, he gave it a few more rubs before tossing it into the drying rack. Suds flicked over the counter, a bit splashing onto the ground. *So much for cleaning up.* The sting faded to a throb, splitting into two as Scotland bit him again.

"Never took you for a fucking vampire," said Clint, his hands trembling as he searched for the utensils beneath the bubbles. Something sharp pricked his finger but he barely felt it.

"What can I say? I like to bite," said Scotland, a grin in his voice. "It makes me feel primal, like a beast that's getting ready to fuck you dry."

Clint's mouth was parched, a steak knife zipping against his finger as he met it under the murky water. He pulled his hand back with a gasp that turned into a moan as Scotland tugged his pants the rest of the way down and went to his knees. Blood dripped down his finger, immediately mixing with the water on his hand and turning pink.

"Lean forward," said Scotland, leaving no room for argument. *That voice.* It was the voice of his dreams and nightmares.

Clint swallowed harshly, bracing his slippery hands on the back of the sink as he leaned forward. He spread his legs as his pants were removed the rest of the way, tilting his ass out as his cheeks were spread.

He'd forgotten how good it was to have someone's mouth on him. The touch of a tongue against his rim and strong hands digging into the globes of his ass were like paradise. His body couldn't seem to remember what to do as he went to his tiptoes, shuddering and whimpering as suds dripped from his hands. It was stranger that he remembered...and *loud.*

"How long has it been?" asked Scotland, sounding so calm as he stroked Clint with one finger, teasing his rim and dipping only the tip inside.

Years. "A while." Clint let his head fall onto his forearms, warm water brushing his cheeks as the smell of dish detergent overwhelmed him. He'd scened with Cutler, but sex had been strictly off limits for that, along with any and all forms of penetration.

"Those dishes aren't going to wash themselves," said Scotland as he slid one finger past the tight ring of Clint's entrance. *Fuck.* He was full already, clenching down as his body protested.

"Jesus." Clint whimpered as he forced himself upright, nearly losing his balance as he plunged his hands back into the sink. "You are such an asshole." The water was getting cooler, or maybe it was him getting hotter as Scotland slid a second finger deep. It stung, stealing his breath as he tried to accept the intrusion.

"There's only one asshole I see right now, and it's not mine," said Scotland as he withdrew his fingers all at once.

Clint rocked back, chasing the feeling as emptiness washed over him. Truthfully, he'd never thought that he would be fucked again in this lifetime. Ross had been his one and only love. Nothing and no one had ever managed to be a blip on his radar compared to that.

"Hilarious." Clint hissed as he found the knife with his finger. Before he could get sliced again, he grasped the handle, tugging it out of the suds and tossing it into the drain tray. Everything would probably have to be washed a second time with how crappy of a job he was doing.

But he couldn't focus as Scotland stood, bringing his naked cock against Clint's ass and slipping the shaft between his cheeks.

"Condom." Clint turned his head as Scotland rutted a little deeper, the head of his cock pushing against his entrance.

"Who says I'm going to fuck you?" asked Scotland, quirking one brow. "You're a needy boy, but you can't even wash the dishes properly."

His knees went weak as Clint let out a keen, closing his eyes as the words rolled over him. He *was* needy, and he wanted it now. *Fuck, fuck, fuck.* He could barely breathe with how much he craved it.

"I'm trying, but you keep pushing me around." Even as Clint said it, Scotland nudged his hips forward, so Clint's hard cock was pinched between himself and the sodden countertop.

"You aren't trying hard enough."

Well, fuck this. There was no way he was going back to his cabin tonight without getting fucked, condom be damned. He'd never admit it, but he trusted the blue-haired bastard to keep him safe.

Shoving himself back with all his might, he whirled as Scotland stumbled, grabbing Scotland by the shirt to keep him from falling. The bite marks stung as he prowled ahead, pushing Scotland back until his ass caught the lip of the table.

One moment they were standing, and the next Scotland's leg caught on the table leg, sending them both to the floor. Clint landed on top, his breath squishing out of his lungs as his full weight landed on Scotland.

But he didn't need to breathe when that perfect cock was pressing against his ass, only an inch away from his hole. Reaching behind himself, he grabbed the shaft, tilting his hips as he aimed it at his hole.

"Clint, wait—"

The head of Scotland's cock popped through his entrance with a zing of pain that went straight through him. His chest went tight, warmth flooding his core as tears prickled at the corners of his eyes. He gasped as he sank down, taking him deep, despite the dry drag and overwhelming ache.

"Fucking brat." Scotland cursed, grabbing his hips hard enough to bruise. He didn't stop him, only squeezed hard as Clint pushed himself inevitably closer.

"What can I say?" Clint panted, his mouth hanging wide as the ache washed over him like sweet candy. "I'm greedy." He shrugged, despite the zing that traveled up his spine from even the slightest movement. His cock was throbbing, the scarred skin at his hip tingling. There was only one thing that could make it better.

He rocked back, cutting off his thoughts as Scotland sank a tad deeper, splitting him apart in a way that he used to crave. Bracing his hands on Scotland's chest, he eased forward, letting him slip almost all the way out before he drove back again in one sharp thrust.

"Fuck. At least let me get some lube," said Scotland, forcibly trying to cut off Clint's movements. His grip was sturdy, but Clint was stronger in this position.

All Clint had to do was jerk his hips, grinding down onto the blissful pain. *I missed this. Fuck, I missed this so much.*

"Don't need lube. I'm close." He was probably only a few stuttered jolts away from coming, the discomfort sending him there faster than he could have imagined. *Fuck stamina.*

Clint's back hit the floor, his breath whooshing from his lungs as Scotland flipped their positions. Emptiness shattered his haze as Scotland's cock slipped free from the movement, a heavy ache breaking through the fog.

"You don't get to come—not tonight." Scotland's eyes were pitch dark, his hair surrounding him like a demonic halo. Shoulders straining, he half-dragged Clint across the floor, hefting him straight into his naked lap.

"Fuck that—" Clint's words turned into a long groan as Scotland simultaneously slammed back inside and wrapped his hand around the base of Clint's cock in a punishing grip.

"Try not to scream."

Clint wouldn't have been able to scream if he'd tried. Scotland jackhammered his cock inside, hitting his prostate with every thrust. The onslaught of Clint's orgasm came and went, trapped beneath Scotland's hand as his grip went tighter and tighter.

Tears rolled down his face as Clint dug his nails into Scotland's ass, urging him faster and harder. His skin buzzed, his gasping breaths drowning out the blood rushing through his temples.

"That's a good boy," said Scotland as his hips stuttered and he buried himself all the way one last time. His cock pulsed, warmth flooding Clint's ass as his own orgasm flitted away to nothing, his cock throbbing and so painful that it only made the tears come faster.

Good boy. The retort fizzled on his tongue as Scotland slipped out with a sigh, warmth following the move in that embarrassing way that only ever happened after the best fucks. It may have been a long time for him, but he certainly wasn't tight after that pounding.

Scotland leaned on his hands, caging Clint's body in as he throbbed. The smirk on his lips had turned into something soft and knowing. "I think I got my answer."

Ah hell.

Chapter Eight

Scotland

With sex out of the way, and his balls aching with how recently they'd been emptied, things should have been easier. He'd pictured a snuggle session paired with an epic makeout before fucking Clint a second time, sweet and soft in his king-sized bed.

Instead, he was on his back on the cold floor, his pants around his knees and his ass sticking to the hardwood. The bruise on his head from when Clint had first knocked him down throbbed into a headache that promised to haunt him for the rest of the day.

"I am too old to fuck on the floor," said Clint, grumbling as he slapped the hardwood. "Seriously, my knees are screwed." He was too far away. When Scotland reached out, he couldn't touch him, skimming his hand over the blank space between them.

Scotland let out a grunt, trying and failing to turn onto his side. "Any other limits I should know about for next time?"

They hadn't exactly talked about it when Scotland had had the sudden revelation during dinner. One minute Clint had told him that they were never fucking, and the next he was pinned on his back with Clint riding him like some kind of horny cowboy.

"*Pfft*," said Clint, shaking his head as he made an attempt at reaching his pants which were pooled on the floor next to the sink. "Next time? That's a good joke. I'm never getting off this floor."

Scotland quirked his lips, even as his heart sank. He wasn't sure if Clint was serious or not. Hell, he was never sure of anything when it came to Clint.

"I didn't realize you were a sub," he said, grunting as he finally made it over onto his side, his back cracking as he adjusted himself. Scooting across the floor, he reached for Clint, dragging him closer despite the way his sweaty skin was sticky. "I pegged you for a Dom for sure."

"You did peg me, for sure," said Clint, a grin on his lips. "I'm a switch and proud of it."

"Huh." He leaned his head into Clint's shoulder, breathing deep. Sweat, sex and Clint coated his lungs, giving him something to drown in. "I didn't think there were any other switches in the community. Some people aren't exactly fond of men like us."

He dragged his lips over Clint's shoulder, kissing the edge of one of the bite marks left behind. It didn't make his sore back feel any better, but it sure was nice to see his marks on Clint's skin. "I wouldn't mind pegging you again. Just give me five."

"You going to let me come this time?" asked Clint, brushing a hand over his belly. His cock was still hard, but not nearly as red as it had been. He hadn't reached for it once, either. *Good boy.*

"Nah." Scotland smirked, hefting himself onto his hands and knees before capturing Clint's nipple between his lips. The small bud hardened at the touch, and he lapped his tongue over it. It was perfect.

"Seriously," said Clint, tapping at his shoulder. "No more. My ass hurts."

"I think you like that." Clint had responded beautifully, even though it must have hurt something fierce. Scotland knew how much it ached to be penetrated so quickly without a warmup, especially when it had been a while.

"Let me see," said Scotland. He also knew how rough Clint had been and how sensitive of an area it was. He'd had people legitimately hurt themselves by overenthusiastic sex before. He shuffled between Clint's legs, pushing them wide.

"Ow. I don't flex that way." Clint tucked his legs together, rolling away from Scotland's grip and getting to his knees. "I hate your floor. *Fuck.*" He grunted as he got to his feet, immediately moving to the counter and leaning heavily against it.

"Water's cold, too," he said, unplugging the drain before starting up the tap again and filling the sink with fresh bubbles and steam. Grabbing the washcloth, he wrung it out before cleaning the few dishes he'd put in the drain tray and starting on the ones he hadn't gotten to.

Is he fucking serious? There was literally cum dripping down Clint's leg, but he was doing the dishes. And was he humming? Scotland tilted his head to the side as he lifted himself off the ground, tugging his pants all the way off before planting his ass in the nearest chair.

"Did you want something for dessert?" asked Clint, throwing a smile over his shoulder. "If your freezer is stocked anything like mine, you've got a few options."

A smirk spread over his lips as Scotland leaned back in his chair. "I think I already had dessert. Your ass was the sweetest thing I've ever tasted."

Clint let out a little snort. "You just keep getting smoother." He shook his head, wringing out the cloth before heading to the table. He leaned over as he wiped the surface, catching the little crumbs that had strayed from their plates.

Scotland slipped his hand between Clint's thighs as soon as he came close enough, dragging his fingers through the sticky trail there. He bumped against Clint's entrance with one knuckle, reveling in the gasp. He was still so wet.

"I was thinking more along the lines of another round," said Scotland, cupping Clint's sac and kneading it until the cloth slipped from Clint's hand and fell to the floor.

If he had his way, he'd turn one more round into a dozen. Then maybe Clint would get hooked in the same way he was.

I should have taken my time. Clint seemed hesitant, and that put a shot of dread straight through Scotland's chest. If he would have known, he would have gotten the cock ring and fucked Clint for a solid hour. *It still wouldn't have been enough.*

Clint gave him a half-smile before leaning to retrieve the cloth and turning to the sink. He pulled the plug on the water, hanging the cloth as he reached for a dish towel.

You've got to be kidding me. "You don't have to dry them, Clint. It's called a drying rack for a reason." Air drying was the only way in his book. He only had the dishcloth to wipe his hands on after he washed them.

"It will only take me a minute," said Clint, letting out a small chuckle as he turned with a plate in his hand. "Just like you." His chuckle turned into a laugh as Scotland scowled and pursed his lips.

"How am I supposed to last when you're fucking yourself on my cock like a wild bronco? It doesn't help that you're cute as hell and your ass is tighter than a vise." He ran a hand through his hair, wincing when he realized that he'd just smeared cum through it.

Clint slid the last plate into its spot in the cupboard before he turned back, giving Scotland a long look. He felt his face flush as he looked down at himself, wondering what Clint was seeing. He was in good shape, but he wasn't a supermodel by any means.

And he did have a lot of tattoos, which were a turn off for some. The idea of that was ridiculous to him. Tattoos only made a person hotter.

The shiny film on the fresh tattoo on his leg didn't exactly look appealing. He'd almost forgotten about it, but it burned like fresh sunburn, the wrap already itchy as hell.

"You good?" asked Clint, scratching at the speckling of hair on his chest. "I don't know what you usually need for aftercare. I'm good and steady now. How are you feeling?"

When the hell had their places switched? And why the hell did he suddenly feel like he wanted to submit? Usually, he only had one role with the same person, either submissive or Dominant, but never both.

"I'm good. That wasn't my most intense scene — not by a long shot. And I don't usually drop too hard. I guess that's pretty common for switches." He shrugged, suddenly feeling exceedingly naked sitting in his dining room. His skin prickled in the cool air, but he was still wearing his shirt. Clint seemed to see right through it.

"Good." Clint nodded, reaching for his own pants and crumpling the fabric in his hand. "I'm only a few steps away or a phone call if you need me. I guess you have my phone number now, after all."

Scotland nodded, frozen as Clint padded over to the door still completely naked. He slipped on his sandals, heading out of the door before closing it shut softly behind him. The silence was near deafening in his wake, the kitchen hazy with the smell of sex and sweat.

"What the hell just happened?" He looked around the kitchen, the delicious meal like a distant memory. One thing was for sure. He still hadn't made any progress.

Chapter Nine

Scotland

What is the best channel for news?

Scotland glanced at the text again before rubbing his hand through his hair. His client looked to be getting a bit frustrated, and truth be told, so was he. His phone had been buzzing every time he got truly focused on the piece, so he'd had to take more breaks than usual.

Clint *had* to be fucking with him.

"Sorry about that," said Scotland, quickly washing his hands before tugging on a fresh pair of gloves. "We only have a bit of shading left by your wrist, then we'll call it a day."

His client gave him a weak smile. They'd been at it for almost three hours, and they were definitely approaching limits for the both of them. His back was still aching from his romp on the floor, and his client had been squirming for the past ten minutes.

"The wrist is the worst," she said, scrunching one eye as he flicked the machine back on and started in on the final section of the day. He was doubting the dark shadows that he'd planned for the spot, going for broader strokes instead. The darker it was, the more it was going to hurt.

"A recommendation from one tattoo junkie to another," he said, giving her a smile as he wiped the area. "Never get the top of your feet done. You think the wrist is bad? Sheesh." He shook his head. "I almost passed out on foot number one, and it took me six months to convince myself to finish foot number two."

He winced at the memory. That had been the bad kind of pain. He rarely reached that level, especially with tattoos. The stinging buzz had always been alluring for him, but the designs on his feet and wrists had been like tiny jackhammers digging into his bones. *Not cool.*

"Can't be as bad as childbirth," she said, shaking her head and grimacing as he made another pass.

"Not from what I've heard. I don't have first-hand experience with that one." He winked, holding back an eye twitch as his phone buzzed against the tabletop with another incoming text.

"They are pretty persistent," she said, glancing toward his phone. "New partner or jilted ex?"

He chuckled. "Always looking for the latest gossip."

Chewing his lip, he filled in another spot, digging deep to darken the blending. She didn't seem to notice this time, apparently too busy waiting for an answer.

"Neither, I guess. Hopefully the former, but he made it pretty clear it was a one-time thing." Epically clear — if walking out of his house naked and only checking in to make sure that they were both feeling level counted.

When Scotland had stopped by later, he'd made sure to go without a shirt while munching on a popsicle. Clint hadn't even looked interested when Scotland had licked his lips and sucked the thing straight into his mouth. Supremely unimpressed was more accurate for the look he'd gotten.

"But he keeps texting you? Sounds like you've already hooked him." She shifted in the chair, a bit of her blonde hair coming loose from its tie. She had four other tattoos by him, but most of them were covered. It seemed to mean that she was familiar enough with him that she wasn't worried about *digging*.

Yeah, but – "He's staying at my cabin right now and he's been texting questions about the place all day. First, he couldn't get the stove started again, then the dishwasher and the washing machine. He actually asked about a sewing kit first thing this morning, and now he's wondering about news channels. He sounds more bored than interested."

"Or he's just lonely." She hissed, her biceps flexing as he made the final pass. "You told me before that it's pretty quiet at your place. Maybe it's just too quiet for him."

"Huh." He leaned back, grabbing the cooling spray and a fresh paper towel before spraying and wiping her new tattoo. "I never thought of that." He'd never minded the silence or the chance to be away from people and live in his own head.

"What does he do? Maybe he's used to the hustle and bustle, and he can't figure out how to turn that off."

"He works at a – uh – bar. He's the owner, actually." He was not outing his kinky self to a client. Nuh-uh. He'd made that mistake before. "You're all set. Take a look in the mirror before I wrap it."

He put on another fresh pair of gloves, wrapping the tattoo and sending his client on her way after she handed him a hefty tip. When he grabbed his phone again and looked at the screen, he winced at the newest message.

Can I feed the donkeys? They look hungry. I forgot to ask their names.

Hitting the call button before he could back out, he brought the phone to his ear.

"And here I thought you were going to ignore me all day," said Clint. He didn't sound pissed off. He was maybe a little miffed, if anything.

"Sorry. I was at work." He brushed one hand against his leg where a bit of ink had pooled. It smeared against the fabric, all but disappearing if not for the sheen. "I just wrapped things up so I'll be headed your way in five. And I thought I told you their names—Dumb and Dumber."

Clint chuckled against his ear, a sound that went straight to his gut. If only he could get that noise to come out of Clint's mouth when they were in the same room. It would be so much better in person.

"I thought you were joking."

Most people did when he first told them the names. "Nah. They are smart now, but they were two of the silliest colts when they were growing up. Back then, I couldn't tell them apart very well either, so the names just kinda stuck."

He shrugged despite being alone, his face flushing as Clint laughed. If he put the pedal to the metal, it was still a good twenty minutes home. Usually, he took his time after a client to clean up and work on a few sketches. Now he just wanted to be back.

Maybe he'd be able to catch a glimpse of naked skin if Clint went without a top again—or that epic ass, which he'd dreamed about. He hadn't gotten nearly enough time to admire him properly, and the more he thought about it, the more he realized that he'd rushed things when he should have taken them slower.

Even just Clint himself would be the highlight of his day, which was just strange. Art was his life.

Then again, Clint *was* art.

"It's cute. Very mature." He could almost hear the eye roll. "I won't bug you if you're at work. I'll see you when you get home."

The line went dead with a click, and Scotland swallowed, even though every bit of saliva had gone dry. *Home.* He wasn't sure if he'd ever see a day when Clint would say that word and think about the same place as Scotland did.

Fuck, I'm getting soft. It was a crush and just a crush. He'd had dozens in his life. Some, he'd thought were more serious than they were, and others he'd been surprised to see tears when he'd broken up with them. Not a single one of them had ever lived with him, though.

"Crap." He brushed his hair back from his face, probably getting ink everywhere. It was just about time to change the color. With just dark hair, people often found him intimidating, but when he splashed a bit of color on his scalp, people suddenly opened up to him. And if he hated it, he could just cut the tips off and start over.

Time for something different. He had to get Clint off his mind somehow.

* * * *

Scotland tossed his keys onto the small antique table left behind by the last owner. The attic had been a treasure trove of multi-generational stuff. He'd given most of it away but hadn't been able to part with the table.

Taking a breath, he headed right back outside. The air was hot for so late in August, but the humidity had dwindled, so it was tolerable.

His shirt still stuck to his skin as he hurried around the back of the house, the rush from his drive home still clinging to him. The cabin looked empty, with the interior lights off from what he could see through the two square windows at the front. The porch light was on, though, casting a bit of light as the sky went from bright to gray.

The only thing he hated about the fall was how quickly his day ended when he was working. He would barely get home most days before the darkness started to creep in, the threat of frost looming just around the corner.

Before he knew it, he'd wake up to a dusting of snow clinging to everything green and turning it brown.

Two sets of long ears poked out of the grass in the paddock, but they weren't pointed at him for once. Clint must've gone through the fence, because he was standing a couple of feet from them, nothing but a few grasshoppers between them. He held his hand out, clicking to them as he gently called their names.

Scotland paused at the fence, slinging his arm over the top rail as he leaned against it. Most people were afraid of the two donkeys, probably too worried that their toes would be stomped or the donkeys would bite them.

They were the sane ones.

From what he could tell, Clint was in sandals and shorts, his toes an open target for hooves or carrot-seeking teeth alike. He seemed to have forgotten a shirt again, sweat shining on his skin as he took a slow step forward.

"You guys are the cutest fucking things I've ever seen," said Clint, his voice low. He brushed a fly away from his face, his gaze focused and determined as the donkeys continued to graze, popping their heads up to watch him every few bites.

Scotland kept quiet, hiding a smile behind his hand. His truck wasn't quiet, but Clint must've missed the sound of him pulling in the drive.

"Come here," said Clint as he made the clicking noise again. "I brought an apple I found in the fridge. I don't really like it, but I'm sure you guys will. And here," he reached into his pocket, pulling a second apple out, "I brought two. See?"

How am I not supposed to fall in love? Scotland grinned, chuckling as the donkeys rushed ahead at the sight of the apples, nearly bowling Clint over in the process.

"You guys are cute together," said Scotland, raising his hand in greeting as Clint looked his way in surprise. "Just don't let them put their heads between your legs."

Even as he said it, Dumber scooted a little closer to Clint as he chomped on his apple, dipping his nose down so it was at the level of the ground. Between one moment in the next, he closed the distance, tossing his head up between Clint's legs.

Clint let out a little cry as he was simultaneously sacked and thrown onto the back of Dumber, who immediately whirled and took off at a donkey lope, Clint clinging to his back as his cry became a scream.

Scotland ducked through the fence with a curse. "Dumber, you little ass, put him down!"

A puff of dirt rose into the air as Clint disappeared into the grass, Dumber bolting and galloping to the far edge of the field. Dumb trotted across the space to where Clint had disappeared as he presumably searched for another apple, his long ears pricked with interest.

"You okay?" Scotland called out as he jogged over to Clint, spotting his sprawled form in the trampled grass.

Clint threw his head back, letting out a laugh as he got to his knees. Dumb nudged at his arm, searching for another treat as Clint dusted some of the dirt off himself. Scotland held out his hand, helping Clint to his feet.

He didn't let Clint's hand go, tugging as Dumb put his head down and started to nudge ahead again.

"Not you, too, you ass," said Scotland, pulling Clint close and shielding him from his little prankster donkeys. Clint's breath puffed against his ear as he kept laughing, his grip weak on Scotland's hand.

Why did I think donkeys are a good idea?

"You okay?" asked Scotland, his breath catching when he realized just how close they were. With a field at the backs, there was only an inch between them, Clint's naked chest smudged with grass and dirt. All he had to do was lean down and turn his head slightly and Clint's lips would meet his. They tingled at the thought, his mouth dry as he took a deep breath through his nose.

Clint smelled of the afternoon sun with a touch of sweat and donkey. It was so familiar that Scotland went weak, his breath shuddering. Clint's laugh stuttered to a halt, his half-lidded eyes going wide as their gazes caught.

"I'm fine," said Clint, his voice raspy and low. "Just caught me off guard." He moved closer, until the distance was nothing, and Scotland could barely breathe. He was like fire against Scotland's body, his skin breaking out in goosebumps and tingles as every hard inch pressed against his own.

"They like to do that," said Scotland, licking his lips. He couldn't look away, finding a cute mole on Clint's shoulder and staring at it. There was a stretch of freckles he hadn't noticed the night before, and Clint's skin was tinged pink from the sun. "Take you off guard, I mean."

His heart pounded, and he pulled Clint tight, closing the final distance between them and bringing their lips together.

Clint gasped as they touched, and Scotland let out a groan as he leaned in, Clint so soft and warm that he was lost in seconds. Tracing the seam of Clint's mouth with his tongue, he dipped inside, touching and tasting as the sweetness turned addictive.

I could live off this. The moment, the touch and the taste of Clint would be enough to sustain him for a lifetime.

Clint's tongue met his own with a tentative touch that had Scotland's grip going tight, heat pooling in his belly. He slid his hand into Clint's hair, tilting his head and deepening the touch as a low groan answered his own. He tasted so fucking good, like licorice with a touch of whiskey and smoke.

There was innocence, too, of someone who had kissed and forgotten what it really felt like. Clint seemed hesitant, only following Scotland's movements, barely there in his touches that burned with concealed hunger.

He felt Clint tugging away, and his body acted of its own accord. His grip on Clint's hair turned punishing, their teeth clacking as he refused to give in. Twisting his tongue with Clint's, he took one final taste before nipping at his lower lip and digging his teeth in enough that he would leave a bruise behind.

They were panting as he drew back, Clint's lips glistening against the setting sun behind them. His cheeks were flushed, his mouth open and his lips bruised from more than just the single bite.

Christ, how can one person be so perfect? Scotland stared for a moment, trying to let everything sink in so he would remember forever. At any time, it could shatter before his eyes, just like last night. He needed Clint to be more than a wisp and a breath.

"Don't pull away from me," said Scotland, lowering his voice into a growl before he brought their lips back together, immediately taking possession of Clint's mouth. Clint only fought him for an instant before he gave in, melting against him and parting his lips.

Scotland lost himself, cupping Clint's hip with his free hand as he brought their groins together. He wasn't hard — not yet — but his gut was aching for more as Clint responded to him. If the kiss lasted forever, it wouldn't be long enough.

I'm in too deep. I'm drowning.

He drew back, sucking air through his mouth as his head started to swim. Clint's eyes were still closed, his head tilted back and his lips looking so soft that Scotland couldn't help himself.

With both hands, he grasped Clint's ass, sliding down to his legs and hefting him off the ground with a grunt. Clint seemed to catch on, wrapping his legs around Scotland's waist as Scotland went to his knees, tilting Clint back onto the ground. To hell with the bugs — and the donkeys, who were watching them with an attention that was just a tad creepy.

"I'm going to fuck you in this — "

"Ouch!" Clint yelped as soon as his back hit the ground, scrambling to the side and out of Scotland's arms. "Ow, Ow, fuck."

"Shit, are you okay?" asked Scotland, leaning back on his toes as he tried to get to his feet. His legs were like jelly and his knees hit the dirt again a moment later. "Did I drop you? Was it a rock?"

"No." Clint winced as he looked over his shoulder. "It was a thistle I think."

Oh shit. Scotland glanced to the spot he'd tried to lay Clint out in the grass. An absolutely massive thistle glared back at him, its sharp spines practically glinting, and the purple flower on top looking much too innocent. *So much for hot sex in a field.*

"Oh, I think they're stuck," said Clint, struggling to his feet as he kept trying to look at his back. "Ow, that is *so* not the kind of pain I need right now."

"Here." Scotland stumbled to get up, grasping Clint's hips to try to still him as he looked at his back. There was a trail of spines in his skin, the larger ones easy to spot against the pink scars, but others probably disappearing into his freckles. He knew how tricky the buggers could be, which was why he usually went around and pulled all the thistles a few times a year.

He'd been putting the task off for a rainy day that lacked inspiration, but obviously, it was overdue.

"Come inside, and I'll get the tweezers." Scotland glanced to the house. It was getting darker as the sun fell fast, the porch light flicking on automatically.

"Not if you're going to push me into another thistle the next time you get horny," said Clint, spinning so his back was out of view. "I can get them."

"Uh-huh." Scotland pinched Clint's side. It was the same thing he'd do to a bratty sub. "Get in the house *now*."

Clint sent him a glare, grumbling as he shrugged Scotland's hands off him. "Fine." He stomped toward the house, kicking up dust along his way. "But you're not fucking me. That was a one-time thing."

Scotland let out a sigh, running a hand through his hair as Clint disappeared into his house. Things were going swimmingly. At this rate, Clint was going to hate him for the rest of his life.

Chapter Ten

Clint

Clint pulled the blanket around his shoulders, tucking his feet into the edges. A few mosquitoes had already wormed their way inside to bite him, but he hadn't been able to muster the courage to go inside yet. His back was still stinging from every spot that Scotland had tugged a barb out, and Clint was determined there were a few he'd missed.

That wasn't the reason his skin was buzzing or why he'd retreated back to the solace of the cabin as quickly as possible.

His lips were still tingling, his fingertips and his chest practically vibrating. Even his hair was stinging like it had been tugged just right.

He dragged his hand over his mouth, the bruised ache flaring. The feeling didn't fade even as he bit his lip, chewing at the edge until he could taste copper.

"Stop it," he whispered, glaring at the light from the battery lantern he'd set inside the firepit. He hadn't known what the ring was until he'd spotted the charred logs within.

There was much more to the property than he'd expected, including a bug-ridden bush and the firepit surrounded by worn wooden lounge chairs. There had been a trail through the bush that he'd only explored a bit before he'd turned back, the bugs threatening to ruin his shirtless holiday.

The fireplace unfortunately wasn't tucked away out of view, so he had to see the shape of Scotland wandering behind a pane of glass. That man moved about his house as if he were on a mission, never seeming to rest, even when he was home.

Not that I've been watching.

Clint's stomach grumbled and he pulled the blanket tighter. He wasn't hiding—not exactly. He'd been hungry for a few hours, but there was nothing in the cupboards or fridge that was tasty enough to get him out of the chair.

"Here you are."

He looked up at Scotland's voice, squinting through the darkness and the overbright LEDs in the fire pit. Night had closed in around him while he'd been staring off into space, the crickets chirping even louder than before.

"Here I am," said Clint, pulling his legs up and resting his chin on his knees beneath the blanket. *Well, there goes my peace.* Who was he kidding? His entire day had been spent alone, and it had been the furthest thing from peace.

"Is there anything else I need to watch for in this place?" asked Clint, flicking his gaze over Scotland as he emerged into the light. "I've found the guard donkeys and the killer plants. Do you have a house cat that doubles as a secret agent?"

Scotland chuckled, lifting his hands until Clint caught sight of two plates balanced on his palms. "I brought dinner. Did you want to eat inside?"

His stomach grumbled again as he hugged his legs tighter. "No thanks. I'm good."

He struggled not to drool as the scent of roasted peppers and something sweet reached him. It smelled so fucking good, like something his mom would have made him when he was a little kid. *If she had been a Michelin chef.*

"Come on, Clint," said Scotland, letting out a sigh before he set the plates on the edge of the brick fire ring. "I know you aren't exactly here by choice, but that's no reason to be miserable. The company is good, at least."

Clint shot him a glare. He had to be joking.

So far he'd been fucked, carried off by a donkey and stabbed by the biggest thistle he'd ever seen.

"Okay," said Scotland, holding up his hands before he grabbed a chair and tugged it close to Clint's. "Maybe not the company, but the food?"

"Just the food," said Clint, reaching for the plate when his stomach gave another loud growl. Pausing, he touched the battery lantern, turning the brightness up. He'd had to turn it down when a plethora of massive moths had started to swoop toward the light. It had almost given him a heart attack when he'd seen the first one, which had seemed to be bigger than a dinner plate.

Setting the lantern back onto its spot, he grabbed for the plate. The center of it was hot while the edges were still cool as he balanced it in his lap. He pointedly stared at his food as he shoveled the first bite into his mouth, refusing to look at Scotland.

"Did you want me to start a real fire? We can roast marshmallows." Scotland grabbed his own plate, balancing it on one knee as he looked Clint's way.

Clint's heart stopped at the same time his gut went tight. "No."

The smell of ash and smoke didn't get to him as much when he was outdoors. It was unavoidable when he drove around in the summer. People were always lighting campfires.

But flames were another thing altogether. His skin prickled at the thought, his appetite slipping away to nothing as his mouth went dry. *No.*

"Sorry. I wasn't thinking," said Scotland, placing a hand on Clint's knee. He struggled not to pull away as the warmth sank straight through his blanket. It was nice and warm in the chill of the night. His lips tingled.

No. "It's okay," said Clint, clearing his throat. "Let's just eat."

"Were you 'little' with your husband?"

Clint choked on the piece of chicken in his mouth, accidentally spitting it out so it landed between their chairs. He hacked out a few breaths, setting his plate down on the edge of the bricks so he didn't lose the rest of his dinner.

"What?" His face flushed as he turned a wide-eyed look on Scotland.

"Were you little?" asked Scotland, his gaze steady and piercing. "Sometimes you go quiet, and you act little. I like it a lot. Have you ever explored that part of yourself?"

When did this turn into an interrogation?

"I've explored every part, punk," said Clint, untucking the edges of his blanket so he could put his feet back on the ground, bugs be damned. "I'm not a newbie— I'm the king."

Scotland set his plate down next to Clint's, holding his gaze steady. Clint itched to look away, those eyes burning into him and probably seeing too much in the darkness.

"Then you say something like that," said Scotland, "and it makes me wonder if you are okay." Scotland blinked, slow, steady, *soft*. He was that supportive best friend that had already been in his pants.

Clint swallowed, looking away. The chirping of the crickets was almost overwhelming without the sound of wind through the trees. His own heart was quiet and beating in metronomic thumps. "Like what?"

"You go from a kid all wrapped up in a blanket after rolling around in a field to defensive," said Scotland, squeezing Clint's knee. Clint hadn't realized they were touching, and he fought not to jerk away. "You say you're the king, but I'm not sure if you know how to play anymore."

Clint bit his tongue, the tang of blood filling his mouth. "You don't know me."

"I do," said Scotland, standing from his chair to move before Clint. His ass touched the edge of the plates, almost sending them into the ash as he dropped to one knee. "Let me show you that I do. I can prove it."

Clint pulled his legs up, trying to escape Scotland's grasp. The 'no shirt during vacation' suddenly seemed like a very bad idea. *The damn guy is persistent enough.*

"What do you have to lose?" asked Scotland.

Clint looked away, his face burning where Scotland's gaze touched him. *Why the hell did I turn the light up?* He should have just gone inside or watched for Scotland's approach so he could have disappeared when Scotland had started toward the house. "Nothing. You don't— Trust me. No one does."

The words stung at the same time his eyes did. *Do I really mean that?* He hadn't meant to say it. His friends had to know him…and maybe Cutler.

No. Not a single one of them knew the real him. Not even those who had known him when Ross had still been alive.

"Give me the chance to prove it. You still have your safewords if you need them. I won't hurt you."

Scotland's voice was like the sound of nails on a chalkboard during a migraine. "I'm not afraid to get hurt. I like it, actually." Clint waggled his eyebrows, slumping his shoulders when Scotland didn't respond with his usual quip and smirk.

"Not this type of pain," said Scotland, touching Clint's cheek.

Clint inhaled a sharp breath, his cheek burning. He hadn't felt the good kind of pain in a long time. So long, that he wondered if he would even like it anymore.

"You hate how you're feeling right now," said Scotland, trailing his fingers to Clint's lips. "You're so afraid to hurt that you refuse to feel anything at all. You throw yourself into kink and lust because you think that's the only thing left for you, but you can't do more than watch."

"What's your point?" Clint bit the inside of his cheek as his eyes burned for no reason at all.

Scotland was starting to sound like his fucking therapist. He'd only seen her a few times after the fire, and it had never helped. He hadn't wanted to talk about it then, and he sure as hell didn't want to now.

"Give me a chance."

A little gust of wind picked up, swirling around the fire pit and throwing up specks of white and gray. A few wisps of dust floated onto the food, coating the roasted pepper in a touch more charcoal. The ash stuck in moments, already starting to dissolve.

There was nothing to fear of the ash. He *knew* that, but he still dreaded the feeling on his tongue when he slipped the food into his mouth. He used to love that smell, the taste, and with his fucked-up brain, sometimes it still made him *want*.

"Fine." He spat the word, elbowing Scotland to the side so he could reach for his plate. His chicken was far too good for him to let it go to waste, even if he did have nightmares. If he didn't look at it too hard, he wouldn't see the dissolved ash, anyway. "Do your worst, but don't come crying to me when your Dom ass can't handle me."

"Okay," said Scotland, pulling away before grabbing his plate and returning to his own chair. "Finish your dinner."

Clint rolled his eyes, letting his inner brat out tenfold. The dynamic between a Dom and sub was sacred to him, but Scotland was pushing every single button the wrong way. "I was going to anyway."

Scotland paused with his fork hovering in front of his mouth. "I was going to anyway…" He lifted one brow, giving Clint a pointed look.

Oh, you've got to be fucking kidding me. "I was going to anyway, *Sir*."

Scotland's lips split in a grin. "Good boy. I never knew you'd be quite so easy."

Clint grumbled, scraping his teeth over his fork when he bit down a little too hard. "I'm not easy. I'm polite."

He was not tackling how nice it was to be called a good boy. He'd think about that when he had no choice, just before he fell asleep and into another nightmare. He heard the phrase all the time. Now was no different.

Scotland snorted. "Polite?" He stabbed a piece of pepper, holding it out for Clint. It didn't have a single speck of ash on it but was charred a bit from however Scotland had cooked it, the caramelized sugars sweet and aromatic.

Clint sent him a glare, even as he grasped the pepper between his lips. *Two can play at this game.* He was going to have Scotland so wrapped up in himself that he forgot Clint even existed. "Thank you, Sir. Dinner is delicious. I can clean up when you're done."

Scotland's grin was so pure that it made something in his chest pang.

"You're going to be too busy to clean up. But don't worry, I'll take care of you."

Idiot.

Clint reached for another piece with his fork, blinking as Scotland suddenly yanked his plate away. "Hey—"

Scotland tilted the plate, scraping the rest of Clint's food next to his own. Tucking the now-empty saucer under his full one, he stabbed another pepper with his fork, holding it out for Clint.

He should have just turned his face away or his nose up, but his stomach gave another grumble, reminding him that he was far from full. And the peppers were the best he'd had in a long time. He opened his mouth, reaching for the piece and gently grasping it.

"Thank you, Sir." He blinked, trying to shake off the fog that was nipping at the corners of his thoughts. It was *just* food. Sure, he was being somewhat hand-fed, but that was no excuse to let himself slip.

"You're welcome, love."

He swallowed the lump in his throat, dreading and yearning for the next bite. Hopefully, the term was a slip of the tongue.

* * * *

He wasn't sure where the plates had gone, but it didn't matter when he was perfectly full, his belly warm and stretched with how sated he was. The blanket had fallen from around his shoulders, leaving his arms exposed to the dark breeze and the occasional bug that didn't get drawn straight to the light.

It didn't feel quite so cold anymore, even though the leaves were rustling more now than they had all night. His skin was cool to the touch when he ran his fingertips over his arm, but the chill didn't sink any farther.

What time is it?

"You still with me?" asked Scotland as he returned. He touched the edge of the blanket, tugging it higher on Clint's arms until a warmth soaked into him that he hadn't been aware he was missing. "Are you warm enough, love?"

He nodded, words drifting away as he half-closed his eyes. Scotland hadn't stopped calling him that since he'd agreed, but he couldn't find it in himself to be upset about it.

I'm here. He shouldn't have eaten so much—or maybe it was because he hadn't slept well in so long. That was the reason he was half asleep and not the sweet hand-feeding and touches that had devolved into a kiss that had made his lips ache.

He was sure they were bruised, just like the spot on his back that had hit the ground and not the thistle. A few of the small spines were still tucked into his skin, stinging every time he moved. He leaned into them, imagining them pressing deeper.

"Good." Scotland leaned in, dragging his lips against Clint's in a chaste kiss. His eyes were bright in the flashlight—blue and endless. "I'm going to take your hands. You don't have to move at all. Keep your eyes open, though."

Clint let out a slow breath as Scotland reached under his protective blanket one hand at a time, grasping Clint's hands before kissing each wrist. Gently, he set them on top of the blanket, leaving them to rest in Clint's lap.

"I'm going to tie your hands now, love. You'll be nice and safe. No need to move at all. I'll do everything for you."

Clint hummed in acknowledgment. He wasn't going anywhere, and he was more than happy to let Scotland tie him up. Shibari was the best, even if his hands were a bit chilly now that they were out of the blanket. "Green."

Scotland must've grabbed the rope when he'd gone back to the house for a few minutes, because it wasn't something rough and prickly that could be found outside. It was smooth, but not slippery, and slightly cool as it was wrapped around one wrist, then the next. Scotland tightened it, making a simple slip knot that could be released with one tug of his hand or Clint's teeth.

Are we going to discuss limits? He wasn't sure if they were really doing this or if he'd fallen into a fucked-up fantasy. That would have been strange. He'd never dreamed about Scotland like that. The closest he'd come was reliving the memories of when he'd kicked Scotland out of the club that night and the way Scotland's expression had fallen in a way that managed to haunt him.

A click had his attention snapping to full alertness. The sound was something he'd recognize anywhere, imprinted on every synapse of his brain. Ross had smoked when they'd first met until Clint had finally managed to convince him to quit after years of putting up with the stale smell.

That click was ingrained in his memory just like the scars on his skin.

A single flame touched the air, hovering above the lighter in Scotland's hand so close that the bright light almost hurt his eyes. His heart pounded, sweat slicking his skin as he stared at it.

There was kindling next to the fire and a few shabby pieces of newspaper that would burst into flames at the first opportunity. It would only take a touch of the breeze for the dry fall grass to catch and spread.

His chest pulled tight, his heart pounding.

"I've got you," said Scotland, keeping his finger depressed on the fuel as he reached for Clint with his free hand. He tucked one finger into the rope at Clint's wrists, the tug focusing his gaze away from the tinder. "You couldn't even move if you wanted to, could you? No need to think of running away when I'll keep you safe." His voice was dark and soft, lulling Clint like a metronome.

He was right. Clint could barely twitch, let alone contemplate putting his feet in a way that he could stand without keeling over.

"No, Sir." His voice was just a bit slurred like he'd drank four glasses of wine at dinner instead of Scotland's lips. The fear trickled away as he focused on the ropes and the burn on the back of his wrist as he tugged at them. They were strong, resisting any thoughts of struggle.

"Good boy."

A shiver ran over his skin, the flame flickering a tad closer as Scotland shifted to tug the blanket from Clint's body. He tossed it to the darkness of the lawn, the smooth warmth of it disappearing. *Now* he was cold, the sharpness of the breeze raking over his skin.

He didn't move.

The flame went out as Scotland set the lighter on the brick fireplace. With that same hand, he slid between Clint's thighs a moment later, finding Clint's cock unerringly. He could imagine a warmth to his fingertips from the fire that burned against him, but it was all in his head.

Hell. He was hard, and he gasped as Scotland traced him through the fabric of his pants. Scotland's hand was heavy, resting against him as he throbbed.

"I want to see you." He grasped Clint's bound wrists, pushing them so they were over Clint's head and resting against the chair. He didn't need to be told what to do next, gripping the chair and holding on tight. It left his chest on display, his nipples hard and his skin tingling.

A few tugs and Scotland managed to get Clint's track pants down to the tops of his thighs. It took everything Clint had to help him, planting his weight on his feet so he could lift his ass from the chair.

The wood of the chair was smooth against his ass as he settled back down, nothing between him and the night as Scotland slid his pants the rest of the way free. A mosquito landed on his thigh, but Scotland quickly brushed it away before it could bite him. His skin prickled from the light touch, and he fought the urge to squirm.

"Such a pretty cock." Scotland grabbed for the lighter, pressing the igniter.

Clint's breath hitched as the flame appeared a second time, so much closer than the last. He was almost a part of the small circle of light and heat surrounding it, the little trail of smoke on top like a beacon.

"Your heart is racing," said Scotland, roaming with his free hand everywhere he could reach. He trailed over Clint's belly, teasing the underside of one bound arm before pausing to squeeze his pec and play with his nipple. The insides of his thighs were next, but Scotland never got close enough to Clint's cock to take the edge off.

"Beautiful," said Scotland, letting the flame flicker out as he touched the edge of one of Clint's scars. The skin was usually number than the rest, but it burned as Scotland stroked him, so sensitive that it was nearly painful.

Maybe it was all in his head. He hadn't *felt* like this since the accident. There had only been numbness or pain then, but this was something else.

The flame was back, inches from Clint's skin and flickering in the breeze that rustled the treetops. *I can feel it.* Fuck, he wanted it. He remembered what it felt like to have something so powerful at his beck and call—or wrapped around his skin for a split second before it was smothered.

The touch at his cock nearly had him coming as the lighter went out, only for the flame to spring to life a second later. The cool metal of the base of the lighter touched his chest as Scotland wrapped his lips around the head of Clint's cock.

The wires in his brain crossed. He could swear it was the heat from the flame wrapping around his cock as he closed his eyes, the cold metal disappearing as he was overwhelmed by warmth and suction. He could only breathe with the rhythm of sucks and the click of the lighter each time Scotland ignited it. His balls went tight, his groin pulsing as his orgasm rushed toward him at full speed.

"You are so very good for me," said Scotland as he pulled back, setting the lighter back on the edge of the fire pit. Clint's body buzzed, his fingers twitching as he stared at it. Even as the flame went out, he could swear that the tip of the metal glowed. If it were to touch him, he could imagine the hiss of sound and the pulse of his cock.

Maybe there was a bit more to Scotland than half-finished tattoos and colorful hair. He blinked in the low light, unable to look away from him.

Scotland had a smile on his lips, his breathing even and soft.

"Let's get you inside for tonight." He grasped the edge of the rope, tugging the knot free with a single pull. It unraveled like silk, slithering along his arms as it was freed before pooling on the ground. Scotland reached for it, expertly coiling it up.

Wait... What? Clint blinked, shaking his head to try to clear his thoughts. "Sir?"

"I won't leave you, love. Don't worry." The panic evaporated in a heartbeat, the throbbing of his cock thrusting to the forefront of his thoughts. He'd been so close, and Scotland's saliva was still cool on his shaft.

Scotland followed his gaze. "Oh. You don't get to come." His gaze was soft, despite his treacherous words. "Come on." He helped Clint to his feet, his pants tucked under his arm. "I'll take the couch. You can sleep in my bed tonight."

Chapter Eleven

Clint

Clint took another sip of his coffee, letting the bitterness wash over his tongue and settle there like it did every morning. A second later the sweetness flooded in, and he quirked his lips. He usually took it straight black and dark, tired and in too much of a rush to add anything to the steaming brew except for a shot of tap water to cool it enough to drink.

"What are you doing?" he asked, peering over his cup at Scotland, who was peeling his shirt from his body. It was chilly in the morning air, with dew still clinging to the grass that shone as the first bit of sunlight hit it. It was a good thing he'd cleaned off his blanket and pulled it over his shorts and T-shirt, otherwise, he would have been freezing.

He couldn't remember the last time he'd tried to sleep at such an early hour, staring into the darkness on Scotland's bed with his knees scrunched up at the level of his waist. It hadn't been dawn when he'd first peeked outside, giving up on the elusive dreams he craved and hated. Scotland had slept on the couch like a gentleman, his soft snores more relaxing than Clint cared to admit.

The only bad thing was that his topless streak was officially over. The air had simply been too chilly.

Scotland looked over his shoulder, his back rippling as he grabbed the closest log from the heaping pile. He'd convinced Clint to stay close to the house after he'd brewed a fresh pot of coffee, introducing him to the much larger fire pit at his own place.

The metal ring decorated with silhouettes of pine trees was a few feet across and heaped with ash and burned-out logs. There was also a pile of thick tree trunks that was haphazardly stacked a few paces away. A much larger log was sitting close by, an ax dug deep into the wood.

"Making breakfast," said Scotland, grasping the ax handle and tugging it free. His biceps strained, his shoulders going taut. He didn't seem to feel the chill of the air, his movements steady and liquid.

Clint had never realized quite how built Scotland was. He didn't look like much with a shirt on, his tattoos peeking out from every which way. Even with his sleeves rolled up, his forearms seemed thick, but nothing to get excited about. *I grossly underestimated him.*

With everything on display, it was hard not to get a little lost. His tattoos were beautiful—alive, even—as Scotland moved, stacking a log atop the thick base and taking the first swing. The ax struck the wood with a harsh thunk, the metal sinking a few inches in but not splitting it.

Does that hurt his hands? Clint could wield a whip the same as some experts, but he couldn't imagine the impact a swing like that would have on his hands. The thud and vibration would make his fingers tingle and ache.

"How did you sleep?" asked Scotland, freeing the ax with a jerk before he took another swing. On the down stroke, every muscle went tight, his pecs bulging with strength as he seemed to put every bit of effort into it.

Who chops their own wood? Clint glanced at the forest, the fog still clinging to the edges of it. Scotland had probably chopped it down himself, like some sort of beaver on steroids or something. But did he have to do it shirtless? Every ripple was distracting, and when the wood split into three pieces on the next strike, flying wide in every direction, Clint's cock twitched.

He was *not* getting hard again. He pointedly looked away at the next grunt, biting his lip as another piece of wood flew wide in his periphery. The amount of force that would take made him shudder just thinking about it. And those hands… *Those hands.*

His balls were so blue at this point that they were practically bruised. Jerking off in the shower that morning hadn't even felt like an option. But perhaps it was time to reconsider. He was never going to make it the whole day like this.

"Clint?"

Clint shook his head, dragging his gaze back. There was sweat beaded on Scotland's chest, his nipples tight and dark against his paler skin. The rose tattoo on his pec seemed to glisten, looking so real that it could have its own scent and life force.

"Clint."

"What?" He blinked, forcing his gaze back to his coffee. Coffee was safe, even if Scotland had made it perfectly for him. "I hear you, Sir. You want to make breakfast like some sort of caveman. I'm kinda pumped about it. You're a really good cook."

That didn't cover it. Scotland's skills in the kitchen so far were wasted in a tattoo parlor.

Scotland chuckled, wiping the back of his arm across his forehead. "I asked you how you slept."

Clint's face burned as he pursed his lips. *So much for not being affected.* "I didn't, Sir."

Between the strange room and the shifting shadows of evening and night, he hadn't slept a wink. He hadn't really slept since he'd been away from Unkinked. At least there he was usually so exhausted that he nearly collapsed onto his couch at the end of the night.

It was hard not to be worried about Unkinked while he was sitting here on vacation doing virtually nothing. He'd barely heard a word from Maddy, and knowing him, he was probably burning more candles or rearranging the office. He shuddered.

"Was it the pillows or the room?" asked Scotland, kneeling next to the wood block before grabbing one of the smallest pieces. With utmost precision, he lifted a smaller version of the ax, shaving tiny slices from the edge of the wood. They peeled away like a corn husk, one thin layer at a time.

"The bed," said Clint, pulling the blanket tighter. It was early, but the crickets were out in full force, the air almost vibrating with them. They never seemed to go silent here, no matter what time it was. "I don't sleep well in a big bed alone. I haven't since Ross passed."

To his credit, Scotland didn't look surprised...or even guilty. He just gathered the little shavings of wood, stacking them log cabin style in the fire pit. "Would you prefer the couch next time instead?"

Clint shrugged. "Doesn't matter. I can sleep pretty much anywhere as long as it's not a bed. Most chairs are good, and the floor will suffice in a pinch." The recovery room at the club had been his go-to on a few restless nights, the soothing peppermint whispering against his senses.

"We can work on that, too, then," said Scotland, grabbing a few of the larger logs and stacking them atop the shavings. "For now, pull your cock out and get yourself hard."

He didn't even look up. The bastard just kept on stacking neatly until the logs were a few layers deep.

Clint wasn't sure how he felt about being *worked on*. "It's too cold." He motioned to the blanket as if to prove a point. The thermometer couldn't have been much above freezing, and he could see his breath during each deep exhale.

Scotland paused, his hand still hovering over the edge of the fire pit. "I didn't catch that. Care to repeat it?"

Pursing his lips, Clint fought down his instant retort. How could he have forgotten how much Doms were assholes? He was a Dom, too, but that didn't count. He'd made peace with his asshole side.

"It's too cold, *Sir.*"

"Ah, I thought that was what I heard," said Scotland, wiping his hands on his legs. "Would you prefer the hard way or the easy way?"

It was way too early with no rest for this shit. Clint scrubbed a hand over his face, rubbing the last of the sleep from his eyes. Scotland had been trying to work him over since he'd arrived, but they were starting to get a little too close to the line for his own comfort.

"How about we talk limits," said Clint, rubbing at one eye where an eyelash tickled him. "We never did get there."

The next time he saw a couch, he was climbing right in and not moving for eight hours.

"The hard way, then," said Scotland. He nodded, his face never changing as he brushed a small pile of ash from the ring of the pit. "Go on, then. What are your limits?"

He supposed the 'no sex' limit was out, seeing as he'd recently had his ass fucked. The rest were still up for debate, though. He wasn't like Keady, who thought he could throw away his limits to spice things up. That shit was serious.

"No blood play or any bodily fluids other than cum," said Clint, reciting everything from memory. Usually, cum was on that list, but that ship had sailed. "Keep impact to a minimum because I'm not that kind of pain slut. When it comes to any devices or tools, check in first."

"Sounds good," said Scotland, wiping his hand on the grass. The blades came away streaked with black, his fingers still smudged from the deadened ash. "How are you on humiliation?"

Probably my favorite thing in the world. "Green on that front, Sir. If you want me to crawl naked down main street, I'm game."

Clint bit his tongue, his face flushing. Maybe he would have been fine with that with Ross, but Scotland? How was he supposed to know that Scotland would be there for him after that one-man parade — hopefully with bail money for when he was arrested? *Not letting that happen again.*

"Perfect. I have something in mind that will suit for your punishment." Scotland turned back to the fire pit, adjusting a few of the larger logs. "Now, I believe I asked you to get your cock out."

P-punishment? Oh shit. Besides being a switch, there was one thing that really set Clint apart from other kinksters. He craved punishment, thrived on it, even. Ross had taken him in hand so many times that a proper beating became part of their routine. The relief it brought was better than any drug that Clint had seen someone high on during his nursing days.

But if he pushed too far with someone he barely knew, he would have no idea what he was in for, which was why he had his impact limit. There was no way that Scotland could know what he craved. And there was also no way in hell that Clint was ever going to tell him. He was a brat for a reason.

"I should give you fair warning that I'm not very patient," said Scotland, pulling a lighter from his pocket and setting it on the edge of the pit. "Usually I am, but not when it comes to you. You've kept me waiting for a bit." He quirked his lips.

"Neither am I," said Clint, pulling the bottom corner of the blanket free to expose his legs. His track pants weren't nearly thick enough and gave everything away. All these threats had him hot and bothered. With one tug of fabric, he sprang free, hitting the cool air like an electric shock.

"You have a nice cock," said Scotland, staring unashamedly, the vibrant tips of his hair catching the light. "Too bad it's only for show."

Clint bit his lip, tucking his balls carefully under the band of his pants and settling the blanket back over his belly. He almost felt normal all wrapped up, with no scars on display at all. "Only part of me that the fire didn't ruin."

He tried to flash a smile, but his lips dragged down, a swallow stuck in his throat. Even the word fire felt wrong in his mouth, like something potent that could poison him.

"Clint?" called Scotland softly, moving to touch Clint's knee. His eyes were warm and open, despite the set of his jaw. "What's your color right now?"

Clearing his throat, Clint shook his head. "It's okay. I'm green. Just forget I said anything."

"No can do." Scotland pursed his lips. "There are two things I won't tolerate in a dynamic — disrespect and lies. I'll give you one chance."

"Without respect and honesty, kink can turn into abuse," said Clint, holding Scotland's gaze steady. He could almost feel the little bits of his submission slipping away, leaving only an exhausted shell behind. "I'm sorry. I can't count how many times I've preached that very thing, but I just— Well, fuck."

Tugging his pants back over his wilting cock, he let out a shaky breath, pulling the blanket tight. "You're right— I'm not green. I don't know if I can do this, Scotland. Ross was my everything. He could read my mind without even trying, and I loved him more than anything in the world. I can't just move on from that. It's too soon."

"Okay," said Scotland, his face carefully blank. "But I'm not asking you to move on, Clint."

"Yes, you are. *Fuck.*" Clint got to his feet, shoving his chair back so he didn't have to get any closer to Scotland. "I can't, okay? I *can't* with you. This whole thing — the vacation, being away from the bar, the new place and whatever you want to call what's between us — I'm not ready."

His eyes stung, and he pinched the base of his nose, fighting his hurt off as his shoulders shook. He hated crying, and he hadn't come close in so long. He took a shuddering breath, but the threatening tears refused to disappear.

"Okay." Scotland stood, holding his hands out on either side of him. "It's okay, Clint. You know you're good, right? You are strong and beautiful, and if you aren't ready, I completely respect that."

He's so beautiful. Clint tore his gaze away.

"Don't you get it? I'm *never* going to be fucking ready." Clint rocked back, covering his face with one hand as the first few tears broke loose. A headache immediately overwhelmed him, his entire face feeling like it was about to smother him. "*Never.* Ross was my one and only. Nothing you say or do is going to change that."

"That's okay," said Scotland, his words sideswiping Clint and hitting him straight in the chest.

No one had ever told him it was okay. No one had said that he didn't have to move on.

"Ross sounded like he was a wonderful person," said Scotland. "I can't imagine losing someone so dear."

"Fuck." Clint couldn't hold back any longer. Scotland caught him as he went to his knees, and Clint buried his head into his chest as the first sobs broke loose. It was like a wild animal had released itself from his lungs, his wails all but silencing the crickets around them.

"Let it out," said Scotland, hugging him close.

Clint could have stopped if he'd tried. He was terrible at crying, which was why he rarely indulged in it. A headache that lasted two days was a guarantee, and once the tears started, there was no way of stopping them until he ran dry.

How long has it been since I've had something like this? There had been tears over the years, but never someone for them to land on.

Scotland moved them back to one of the chairs as Clint's sobs slowed, holding Clint in his lap with his shoulder to Scotland's chest. It was comfort and warmth and that same strength that had pulverized a piece of wood and split it apart.

Clint's arms were sore from clutching Scotland tight for so long, his face throbbing with itchy cheeks. His lungs were airless as he curled his fingers against Scotland's chest, the only way to keep from reaching out and touching.

"Could you tell me about him?" asked Scotland, running one hand through Clint's hair soothingly. The touch vibrated over his skin, sending a rush of calm along his aching nerves. It did nothing for the pain. It did *help*, though.

"Why?" Why the hell would Scotland — with his little crush — want to know about his dead husband?

"People talk about him all the time at Unkinked," said Scotland, never ceasing his movements as he dragged his nails against Clint's scalp. "He's a bit of a mystery, to be honest. Some people said he was exclusively your sub, a few others mentioned he was a Dom. Everyone agrees he was a good guy, though."

A chuckle escaped his throat, and Clint smiled through his tears. *Yeah, that sounds about right.* "He was an asshole."

Scotland jerked beneath him, his gaze meeting Clint's. They were close — too close, their lips nearly touching. Scotland was the first to look away, staring at the stacked wood of the unlit fire. "Why would you call him an asshole?"

Clint let out a small puff of air that could have been a laugh if his heart hadn't hurt so badly. He turned in Scotland's arms so his back was to Scotland's chest, resting his head back. Memories rushed over him in an instant, with phantom limbs matching Scotland's touch.

"When I first met him, he was with another guy but looking for a third," said Clint. He could remember it clearly, as if he could close his eyes and slip back to that day when he'd set his sights on Ross. His first look at his eyes, and he'd known that Ross was a dangerous man. *Dangerous for me.*

"I heard that from Keady," said Scotland, smoothing his hands along Clint's arms before settling at his wrists. He didn't feel like the shackles Clint's imagined he would, his touch light and soft. "He said that guy got Ross kicked out of his kink community, so you kicked his ass and married Ross."

Bunch of gossips. "That's the short version, yeah." Clint wiped his face, grimacing at what came away on his sleeve. He was an absolute mess, despite the early morning shower in Scotland's home. "Keady skipped the part about me going after Ross strictly for his money, but the asshole made me fall in love with him instead."

Scotland tightened his arms, his low laugh shivering against Clint's ear. "Just money?"

"No." Clint bit his lip. "He was gorgeous." He closed his eyes and tilted his head back. His headache throbbed, but the memories burned brighter. "And rich. *So* rich. I was a step above living on the streets at that point, and I still had a year left of nursing school. I was also cute as hell and kinky. He was the perfect target for a sugar baby like me, but one scene and my ultimate plan fell apart."

"What happened?" Scotland moved his hands to Clint's hips, staying clear of the exposed strip of skin where his shirt had ridden up. The scars were bared to the light. The same thing that had put them there had stripped him of his love.

"The scene started, and he went to his knees first. That's when I figured out that I wasn't just a bratty sub." Clint shook his head. He'd been so naïve at that time of his life. "He flipped my world upside down and changed everything I knew about myself."

Everything.

"So you guys got together pretty quick," said Scotland, nodding against Clint's neck. His breath was warm and smelled of coffee and something sweet. "Love at first scene, so to speak."

"Nope," said Clint, his smile going wider as he reached back, patting Scotland on the head. "He was too good for me, and I agreed with that. So he went back to his partner, and I kept looking. I found myself a Daddy who was nearly as good looking and wasn't afraid to throw his money at me."

He let out a sigh, shifting to get comfortable. Scotland was all rugged muscle but very little squish, so he didn't make the most comfortable chair. "But it's hard to be a good boy when you're watching another man across the club. Every time Ross was there, I couldn't take my eyes off him. He'd catch me looking, and he'd give me this little glare like he was worried that I was going to stroll across the club and rip his clothes off. Turns out he was right."

The wind picked up, a few stale ashes swirling around the firepit. It was well used, with the scorched remnants of a few logs within. Warmth had started to creep across the dew-soaked ground as the sun rose, the slight wind dying down to stifling.

"He wasn't just a Dom. He was a sub, too, just like me. He had his partner and a sub he frequented with at a place the community would meet up. His partner must've seen me watching. He was a jealous thing who was so insecure it was sad. He called red right as they started a scene and claimed he was being forced and hadn't consented to anything."

It still made him angry. Safewords were *sacred.* Sometimes they were the only thing to tell you that your partner was still on board and not having second thoughts. He'd seen couples tip over the edge of uncertainty before, and it had shattered them.

"Ross was crushed," said Clint, swiping at his cheeks as a few tears slipped out. "That fire and life I loved to watch was destroyed in an instant."

Dull eyes, pressed lips and that way his face pinched when he was trying not to cry.

"I found him that night." His heart picked up, his gut pulling tight at the memory. He'd been brimming with determination so strong that nothing could have stopped him. "I was obsessed with him. Where he worked, where he lived—I knew it all. I knew his favorite restaurants that he'd take his partner to and the things he would post about online."

"Wow," said Scotland, letting out a soft breath. "Stalker alert."

"Pretty much." Clint shrugged. He'd long since come to terms with how much of an idiot he'd been when he was younger. "So, I went to his house, and I let myself in when he didn't answer. I found him standing in front of his bathroom sink looking so lost that it broke my heart."

The house had been dark, his heart beating fast as he'd looked at Ross' face, surprise etched in every feature at seeing Clint standing there.

"I asked him to punish me and beat me until I cried. I told him he was beautiful as he hurt me and how much I wanted him."

Shuddering at the memory, he licked his lips. He'd been so brave that night. He hadn't known that it was love—only an obsession that claimed every waking thought. He'd been furious at Ross, trying to rid his thoughts of the man who haunted him at all hours.

"Shit." Scotland shifted, clenching his hands on Clint's hips.

"The next day when we left the house, I told him I would take care of him. At home I belonged to him and would submit to anything he asked. But outside he was mine to cherish, protect and dominate. It was good — *heady*. What we had was perfect."

"Until the fire," said Scotland, his words like the dull blade of a knife dragging over a bruised wound before the point set deep.

"It was my fault," said Clint, shaking his head as he let out a shuddering breath. "I've never told anyone about what happened — even the insurance company and the police. They would never understand."

He could imagine their looks of horror and confusion if he'd even told them about one moment between himself and Ross. He had his kinksters and the ones who understood, but there were so many others who wouldn't.

"Cutler told me you like to play with fire," said Scotland, his voice low. He moved his hand, skimming along the edge of Clint's belly before he moved away. The scars tingled from the touch. "It's beautiful but dangerous."

"That's what everyone thinks," said Clint, squeezing his eyes shut as tears tried to escape. His heart was racing, his chest tight. He'd broken a piece of himself so he never corrected them. It wasn't worth it.

"I know what people say," said Clint. He'd heard the whispers, even from his own friends. "They think one of us was strapped to a cross getting fire flogged — or maybe having cigarettes burned into our skin. I think that's what the cops wondered once they saw what was left of the bedroom and found out about the club we'd started together."

Another sob crept from his throat, the grief crashing into his tenfold as he struggled to keep talking.

"I-I asked him for something different during aftercare. *'Light me a scented candle. I love the way they smell'.*" His legs trembled. It had played over in his mind a thousand times.

He'd never asked for that before. *Why the hell did I that time?* He should have kept to their usual routine.

"We fell asleep with the candle still burning beside the bed. A box of tissues was too close, and the flame caught…"

He'd set the tissues there, too. The feeling of cum seeping from his ass was hot as hell until it started to cool and get sticky. He always kept something close to wipe clean and had been too blissed out to ask for a cloth.

"Did you know you can't smell in your sleep?" asked Clint, his voice going high as he trembled. "The fire alarm woke us, but the bed had already caught fire. I thought it was a dream I was lost in. I stumbled through the smoke looking for him, only to realize he was still in bed. There was fire *everywhere*. I *tried*."

"You did everything you could, Clint." Scotland's grip was fierce. "It's not your fault."

Does Scotland know I've never told another soul about this? He trembled, his skin vibrating with the force of it as his nausea peaked.

"You know the worst part?" Clint sniffed, rubbing his face in an attempt to dry his tears. They were coming too quickly for it to make any difference. He wasn't sure if he'd ever be able to get them to stop. "I got what I wanted in the end…every fucking dime."

Chapter Twelve

Scotland

A few wisps of fog clung to the ditches as the morning light broke through the staggered branches of the forest. Frost had landed heavily the night before, silencing the last of the crickets and turning his raspberries to a deathly black. It was strange to see fall creep in so suddenly when he could have sworn he had just been in the midst of summer.

"I can't remember the last time I was up this early," said Clint, glancing off into the forest as Scotland hit the main road and accelerated onto the pavement. "Oh, a bunny!" He pointed at the scruffy brown creature as it bounced away, heading for the same place they'd just come from.

Clint was ruffled, his eyes wide but tired with his usual worn clothes stretched tight over his body. He'd finished the coffee Scotland had offered him in a few quick swallows and his second cup sat steaming in a spill-proof mug between them.

"I like this time of day," said Scotland, struggling to keep his eyes on the road as he picked up speed. "It's still early enough that most people are asleep, their houses dark and seemingly vacant. It's quiet."

The highway was nearly empty, which was a good thing when the man of his dreams was so focused on distracting him from the passenger seat.

He'd been fighting to keep his gaze off Clint for days. A promise was a promise, and he was bloody well keeping to it, despite how much it hurt him not to touch.

His heart had broken right along with Clint's as he'd held him, listening to dozens of stories of Ross. The way Clint had sounded, and the look on his face had made it so clear. *That* was love. Not what was between them.

I never had a chance.

But that didn't stop him from wanting and fighting the pull that haunted him. He dreaded leaving for work in the morning, looking toward the cabin and wondering if Clint had slept and if he would wake up in time to find the breakfast Scotland had left him, still warm on its tray just inside the door.

Things had become so quiet. Clint would sit on one of the chairs by the fire pit, the wood still stacked and begging to be lit. Scotland would join him, not saying a thing as they rested in comfortable silence. The walks they'd taken on the game trails through the forest had been the same, except for the few curses when the bugs managed to find their way past the bug spray and bite him.

The days were dwindling as the night turned colder, the sun disappearing for a little longer with each sunset.

"Thanks for coming with me today," said Scotland, clenching his hands on the steering wheel to keep from reaching out and placing a soothing hand on Clint's thigh. It would only lead his thoughts down a path of no good if he gave in.

"Maddy won't stop texting and asking me if I've seen your studio yet," said Clint, letting out a yawn before he squinted out of the window. "I can't figure out if that's supposed to be a euphemism or if he's serious."

Chuckling, Scotland flicked on his turn signal as they hit the edge of the city, before merging onto the main drag. The traffic thickened with every second, the first horn blaring somewhere in the distance. "Maddy is a different kind of guy. He's cute, but intense. And I don't really get his sense of humor."

"No one does," said Clint, shaking his head. "Except Derreck. That kid was new to life when I first met him at the bar. He was so innocent and naïve, with the weight of his life on his shoulders. He surprised the hell out of me, too. I didn't think much of him, to be honest, but he proved me wrong pretty quick."

That sounded just about right from what he knew about Maddy. He acted more like a teenager than a forty-something-year-old man. Scotland had been shocked to find out his age from Nav, another kinkster who frequented the community with his Dom Trick.

"This is it," he said, peering up at his building as he pulled into the reserved parking space. "I know it doesn't look like much." That was an understatement. It had used to be a bungalow before someone had converted it into a business. He'd gotten it three owners later after it had been passed along too many times by unsuccessful businessmen. Each of them had done some sort of renovation, leaving a haphazard and mismatched façade on the outside.

He hadn't thought to fix it up, focusing more on the interior than bothering with the outside.

"Huh." Clint let himself out of the car before staring at the building with a frown. "It's nicer than I imagined. I was thinking about a tattoo parlor with all the tacky signs on the windows and the bars to keep thieves out. This looks almost domesticated."

Scotland snorted. He'd never heard his work called that before. "I have a few mothers who would disagree with you."

He never touched anyone underage with a needle, but he'd had a few parents call him in a rage when they saw the new ink on their twenty-something-year-old son or daughter.

Most of the time, it wasn't what the tattoo was about or what it symbolized, but the fact that they now had an irremovable stamp of art etched into their skin.

Turning the key in the lock, he opened the door and let out an instant sigh of relief. Everything was where it was supposed to be and exactly where he'd left it. It was almost as good as coming home, with his artwork on the walls and his taste in every inch. The smell sank into him, the fresh inkiness of it soaking deep like it always did.

Clint whistled under his breath, toeing off his shoes and strolling to one of the paintings. It was something of a bestial devil, with curled horns and a devious face in shadow. The color was vibrant and clear, every brush stroke placed with utmost care and patience.

"Who did this one?" asked Clint with obvious awe, his fingers hovering over the canvas. "It's so pretty."

"I did that maybe four or five years ago," said Scotland, rubbing the back of his neck uncomfortably. "I was still at the old place, my day stacked with clients and my idiot boss always breathing down my neck. I was pissed at him for rushing clients and not giving me the time I needed to do my best work. I poured every bit of that into the painting."

"Really? You did this?" Clint's eyes went wide. "That's unbelievable." He paused, his mouth dropping wide as he looked around the room. "Did you do all these?" He motioned to the walls.

"Uh — yeah." There was a lot, and some of them were from his darkest times. There were bright ones, too, but they often lay unfinished, the passion fizzling away a little too quickly. "Art has always been my way of coping." It was more than that, really.

"Scotland." Clint turned to him, pinning him with his serious gaze. "This stuff should be in museums. I thought you were just a tattoo artist."

"*Just.*" Scotland shook his head, even as he grinned. It was amazing how people never made the connection between a tattoo and art. They were one and the same, just with a different canvas. "I don't paint much anymore. On weekends sometimes maybe, or I've got a bit of a break. I'd much rather poke someone with something shiny."

Clint broke out in a laugh, covering his mouth with the back of his hand. "The perfect job for a sadist. I never thought of it like that."

Scrunching his nose, Scotland picked up his tattoo machine. It was fully charged and small enough that it could easily fit in his hand. "It's really not like that."

He trailed his fingers over his computer keys, typing his password in with his free hand. An image he'd been working on popped up on the screen, the twisted vines and snake before him in vivid detail.

"This is sexy." He motioned to the picture, the familiar weight of the machine soothing him. "With people it's different. It doesn't turn me on to give pain to a complete stranger, especially when I'm doing my best to concentrate and not yell at them when they move."

He'd had people actually tug him away with only a dark streak on their skin before they called it quits. One guy had screamed, nearly breaking his eardrums the moment he touched his skin with the buzzing needles.

"Does it really hurt, though?" asked Clint, glancing at the machine. With the power off and no needle, it really did seem like an unassuming cylinder. Some could picture an image coming from it, steered by his hand and inspiration.

"It depends on the person and the tattoo." Scotland shrugged as he slipped into work mode. He'd been asked that question more times than he could count.

Some people expected it to be worse than childbirth, while others were surprised to feel the fleeting discomfort roll over their skin.

"I've had a few who cried through the whole thing, and I've had people fall asleep in the chair." He'd had a few people get turned on, too, but he was keeping that shit to himself. Client confidentiality and all.

"But what does it feel like? I'm curious," said Clint, looking to the chair. It was a type of material that looked like leather but was easy to keep clean and sanitary. It was close to what the club seats were made of, which Clint probably recognized.

No. I really shouldn't. "You want to try?" *Crap.*

Clint wasn't a stranger, and he wasn't just a friend, either. Relationship or not, Clint had wedged himself inside Scotland's heart a long-ass time ago, and there was no going back from that. *Still, I should be trying to resist.*

"Fuck no." Clint took a step back, his eyes going wide.

Scotland chuckled, reaching for the alcohol and petroleum jelly. "I won't ink you. I'll just stab you a little."

Clint shot him a mild glare. "Is that a pick-up line?" *I wish.*

"No." Shaking his head, Scotland pressed his lips together. "I don't go back on my word, Clint. You made it very clear you aren't interested in anything between us."

It could be that Clint was just testing him, but he didn't want to fail. Clint wasn't *ready,* and he respected that to his very soul. The moment Clint changed his mind, Scotland was going to be ready with bells on and no pants.

"Sorry." Clint rubbed the back of his head, heat flushing over his cheeks.

"Or we could just head straight to the grocery store." Scotland set the machine back on his desk for his next appointment.

"Because the grocery store is so much more exciting than watching two asses all day," said Clint, rolling his eyes. "I'll bite. But if you write 'Mother' on me somewhere, I'll sick the Russian twins on your ass."

That was a very real threat that Scotland did not want to tempt fate with. The twins were notorious mob enforcers who had been kicked out of the old club, only to be welcomed into the fold once more for reasons he tried not to be curious about. They were also terrifying motherfuckers.

"Where do you want it?" asked Scotland, his hands shaking as he reached for a few needles and set them out before preparing the other supplies. He shook out his hands. The last thing he needed was to accidentally get carried away and scar Clint.

"Where hurts the least?" asked Clint, hiking himself up onto the lounge chair that Scotland used. The seat was comfortable and soft, and Clint tested it with his hand, seemingly searching for a flaw in the material.

"Arm, I'd say. The outside of your forearm."

Clint rolled up his sleeve, the strip of flesh more tantalizing with the smell of ink and antiseptics in the room. It was funny. He'd seen Clint naked, fucked him even, but that little peek had him riled.

"I'll get some music." He turned to his computer screen, opening up one of his music apps as he waited for his nerves to calm. It wasn't even a real tattoo, just a little line that would heal into nothing. "Let's start with your forearm."

He prepped the spot the same as he would any tattoo, minus the stencil. Slipping on a new pair of gloves, he dipped a fresh needle into the jelly. He grasped Clint's wrist, turning his arm until he found a spot that wouldn't be too obvious, staring at the stretch of skin.

"Tell me if it's too much." The machine hummed softly as he turned it on, the muted vibrations of the needle calming him. It was so much better than a pencil or paintbrush. He could smell the sweat on Clint's skin and feel the nervousness radiating from him like any other virgin who sat in his chair.

But Clint was *different.*

It was relaxing, like a long drink on a warm beach with the wind in his hair and a freshness on the breeze.

It was what he knew and was best at, that artist inside him peeking out. And the moment he touched the lubricated needle to Clint's arm, routine enfolded him, his nervousness draining away.

He drew a line, grabbing a towel to wipe away the tiny drop of blood left behind. It was only a few inches long — a tiny red mark among a few freckles that would heal away to nothing. Clint had probably gotten those freckles sitting in his backyard, watching the donkeys as they grazed in the field.

Scotland had found him watching them almost every day, the sight more peaceful than he cared to admit. It was something he could stamp on his memory that was proof of Clint in his life. The freckles would take a long time to fade, and every time Clint stepped out into the sun, they would rise back to the surface of his skin.

"What do you think?" asked Scotland, turning off the machine and straightening. The machine wasn't even warm, and he was far from sated. Clint stared at the spot, his forehead scrunched in what looked like confusion.

"It didn't really hurt."

"Nope." Scotland smiled, his worry easing. "This needle is for linework, and I went pretty shallow. It's a good spot, too. Most people can take it okay." *Most* didn't get turned on by it, though.

He could see how Clint's pupils had dilated, his tongue coming out to wet his lower lip.

"Do somewhere else." Clint wiggled in his seat, his eyes decidedly bright under the spotlight. He couldn't seem to look away from the small red area that was no longer bleeding. "That was nothing."

"Let's try your wrist. Nobody likes that." He turned Clint's hand over, smoothing a finger over the delicate skin on the inside of his wrists. There were little blue lines he could see through his skin, each vein disappearing as they traveled up his arm.

He could remember getting his own wrist done and how he'd flinched every time the needle made a pass. There was very little between skin and bone in that spot, and the needle seemed to go straight through.

He prepped the spot, switching out the tip for something with a little more bite. He settled on something curved that he would normally use for shading with rows of tiny points grouped close together. "You won't have any endorphins going for you right now, so this might hurt like a bitch. Tell me to stop or say red, and I'll stop right away."

He waited for Clint's nod before he started the machine, bringing the tip to his pale flesh. Clint's gasp hit the air as soon as Scotland touched him, but he didn't pull back, sweeping along as if he were shading actual ink into Clint's skin. Letting out a breath, he passed over the spot a second time, digging in to plant the imagined ink a darker shade.

When he pulled the needle away and met Clint's gaze, regret instantly sank into him. *What am I doing?* This was supposed to be a trip to get Clint off the farm for the first time, not an excuse for some kind of scene.

Clint's lips were parted and wet, the flush on his cheeks matching the one on his neck. His eyes were half-lidded, his expression decidedly unprofessional.

"That's that," said Scotland, snatching his hand back before he did something he regretted. He was in too deep and close enough to lose himself if he wasn't careful. And Clint wasn't helping, squirming in the chair and staring at the small mark as if it were a brand.

"One more spot."

Scotland paused, just about to rip the gloves from his hand. "Clint." He let out a sigh. He couldn't do this. He couldn't betray their budding friendship. Clint was hurting terribly and Scotland had been so close to breaking him without even knowing it. *I won't risk you.*

"Please," said Clint. "It's okay. I promise. Just one more."

This is such a bad idea. He was struggling to keep his hands and lips to himself as it was.

"I've heard that the ribs are the worst spot." Clint moved his hand, lifting the edge of his shirt. "If you don't mind the scars."

Mind them? "You're beautiful," said Scotland. Hopefully, that wasn't over the line. "That's not a come-on, it's a fact. Your scars are another part of what makes you *you*. They are unique in this world and like a form of art to themselves. When I look, it's because I'm trying to see the little details — the edges — that you try to hide."

Clint paused, fiddling with the edge of his shirt for a moment before finally tugging it all the way up. He was in good shape, with only a bit of padding that probably couldn't be avoided working at a bar for so long. "Are you sure that's not a come-on?"

"Positive." Scotland swallowed, unable to tear his gaze away from the little dips between Clint's abs or the dusting of hair that disappeared beneath the waistband of his pants. "Let me find the right spot."

He prepared the lower part of Clint's ribs just above his belly. He had to lean close, the smell of Clint's body mixed with antiseptic making his mouth water. He'd done ribs before, but it had never been like this. The touch had never been electric, making his skin prickle and the hair on his arms rise up.

He bit his lip as he brought the needle to Clint's skin, digging in as if he were placing the darkest shading. Clint's gasp morphed into a moan, his stomach jumping as he clenched.

"Shhh. Stay still," said Scotland softly, bracing a hand on Clint's belly to soothe him. "Just a little bit more." He moved the needles along his side until he met the bump of the next rib. It was the same place where the edge of a scar lay, the skin pink and shiny.

He gentled his touch as he reached it, barely skimming it with the needle. Clint's moan turned into a pained cry, his stomach muscles seizing beneath Scotland's hand. *Stay still, love.* He didn't dare say it.

Something else moved that was nestled against Scotland's arm. He hadn't even known he was that close to Clint's groin until his hard cock was shifting against him at every tiny movement Clint made.

Tugging himself away, he flicked the switch off, silencing the machine before he pulled his gloves off. He paused the music on his laptop, cursing the silken notes as he silenced them.

"What did you think?" he stared at the wall, the devil grinning back at him as the flames licked at his body. There was a mirror next to him that would have a view of the chair, but he didn't dare look.

Clint cleared his throat, the leather creaking as he shifted. "Let's get groceries. You were right. That hurt like hell."

Chapter Thirteen

Clint

Eggplant, cucumber, bananas...

"Is there anything in this store that you want that's not shaped like a cock?" asked Scotland, chuckling as he glanced at everything Clint had shoved inside the cart. It wasn't nearly piled as high as it could have been, seeing as Clint had only just started to make a dent in all the food Scotland had stocked in the cabin.

Clint shot him a little smirk, heading to the end of the aisle where some fancy olive oil glistened on an overpriced shelf. He grabbed the bottle, gently setting it inside the top of the cart.

"Now we have *everything* we need for the dick veggies," said Clint. A slim zucchini on the stand caught his eye so he quickly tugged it from its spot, setting it with the rest. It was tiny next to the eggplant and cucumber. "It's okay, buddy." He patted the zucchini. "Size isn't everything."

Scotland snorted, shaking his head before he reached for two apples, setting it on top of the rest. "We might as well have some balls, too."

A man passing by shot them a scowl, grumbling something under his breath as he shuffled a little faster. So what if they were acting like a couple of teenagers? Clint hadn't had so much fun in ages. It was also a great way to distract himself from whatever else was happening with him.

In that chair, Ross had been the last thing on his mind. He'd wanted to kiss Scotland— He'd wanted *more*.

"You always meet the best people in grocery stores," said Clint, shooting the man a wink as he made eye contact. "I met Henley in one. A few dick jokes later and he had a membership at Unkinked." Clint frowned, pulling at his ear. As far as he knew, Henley was some sort of government agent—a fact that he probably wasn't supposed to know. Now that he thought about it, he hadn't seen the guy since their last off-premise munch.

"I dunno. I usually run into exes." Scotland paused at the bread section, grabbing a few loaves and gently setting them in the cart. It was probably the first practical thing in there. Clint honestly didn't know anything about cooking eggplant.

"Ouch." Clint looked over his shoulder. "I guess I'm lucky on that front."

Scotland winced, sending him an apologetic look. "I'm so sorry, Clint. I really didn't mean it that way."

"It's okay." Sending him a soft smile, Clint reached for one of the artisan loaves of bread. It was darker, with a swirl of dusted flour still clinging to the top. It also weighed about the same as three loaves of regular bread combined.

It was strange to say it was okay and not have a wave of grief make him stagger moments later. But for once, it actually was okay. He didn't wonder if Ross would have liked the bread, or if he would have urged Clint to eat it because it was a little healthier. He gave it a sniff through the plastic packaging before setting it on the shelf. *Not today.*

"Who else did I meet in a store?" mused Clint, glancing toward the freezer section. "Oh, can we get ice cream? I've got a hankering for those little ice cream sandwiches."

"Sure." Scotland turned the cart, following a few steps behind as Clint headed for the freezer section.

"Oh, I know." Clint tugged the door open, immediately shuddering at the sudden cold. "Have you met my cousin Shelvin? He's one of the designers of the new place and one hell of an architect. We'd fallen out of touch for the most part until I saw him at the store one day."

Leaning his shoulder against the door, he covered his chest with his hands. "I'm freezing. My nipples could cut glass over here."

Scotland chuckled, opening a second door and picking out a tub of ice cream presumably for himself. "I think I know why you meet people here so often. I think they probably heard that all the way at the checkout."

Clint flushed, biting his lip as he skimmed the shelf. He caught sight of the regular-sized sandwiches, but the spot on the shelf for the small ones was blank. "Sorry. I didn't mean to embarrass you. Sometimes I don't know my own volume—too long with club music, I guess."

He started as Scotland touched his arm, his grip molten in the cool air that was pouring from the freezer in thick, steaming clouds.

"Never apologize for something like that." His tone was just as serious as his gaze. "I love how comfortable you are with yourself and the lifestyle. I hope that never changes. It's beautiful—you're beautiful—when you're yourself."

Scotland was so close, the warmth of his chest right there. His lips looked softer than Clint remembered. It had only been minutes since he'd watched them, pain skirting over his ribs as his cock throbbed in the tattoo chair. His ribs still pulsed along with the spot on his wrist, like sunburn baking in bright light.

"Okay." He looked along the shelves again, shuddering as Scotland moved another step closer. He skirted his warm hands over Clint's shoulders, chasing away the chill. His nipples hardened further, more confused than he was.

"When it comes to ice cream sandwiches, size does matter," said Clint, smiling as someone approached them along the aisle. A familiar thrill washed over him, knowing that he was being heard in a public place—being naughty. "I want something I can fit in my mouth and shove straight down my throat. The big ones just trigger my gag reflex a little too much."

Scotland chuckled, running his hands down Clint's arms before settling at the level of his elbows. "You don't like them big, baby?"

Shivering at the endearment, Clint shook his head, sending a wink over his shoulder at the stranger who was looking at them with wide but very interested eyes. "I love them big, just not in my mouth."

He turned his head, freezing when Scotland was right there. *When did he get so close?* There was a small bruise on his lower lip like he'd been chewing on it all the way through the tattoo and the trip to the store. Maybe he was more nervous than he was actually letting on.

It was like trying to swim against an undertow. Even as he shifted, his arm brushing against the freezing door, Scotland loomed closer. It was Clint who closed the final distance until their lips were touching. They were softer than freshly budded leaves and so warm that Clint instantly fell into them, gasping as his senses were overwhelmed.

There was nothing better than kissing in public. You couldn't get arrested for it, and it always managed to shock and thrill someone. Grocery store aisles, restaurants, the park—it didn't matter. Anywhere there were eyes on him, longing to be him.

He turned in Scotland's arms, bringing their chests together before wrapping his arms around Scotland's neck. Threading a hand through his hair, he tugged him closer, until the kiss turned hard. He parted his lips, ready to seek out Scotland's tongue with his own.

Until everything disappeared.

Scotland pulled away, grasping his hands back as he withdrew. He was panting, his mouth parted and his lips dark and glistening. "Clint."

Clint couldn't look away. Those lips were mesmerizing. *How could I miss this?* It hadn't felt like that when Scotland had fucked him raw in the kitchen, or when he'd teased his skin with a flickering flame.

But now his body was attuned, his cock pulsing to the beat of his pounding heart.

"Clint. We can be friends, love. We don't have to be more."

What the hell was Scotland saying? Clint blinked, shaking his head as the fog started to clear. There was more than one set of eyes on him, but in moments his freedom and joy had withered.

Ross. His chest went tight as he stepped away from the freezer, letting the door bang shut. That kiss, it had almost felt like... He gripped his hand into a fist, pushing his thoughts away.

"I changed my mind," said Clint. "Let's get marshmallows. We can see who can fit the most in their mouth. Spoiler alert—I'm going to win. And we'll get whipping cream for our coffee. It's just like regular cream, only kinky."

I'm flirting. He knew it, but he couldn't stop himself. It had only been a few days since he'd broken down at the firepit but something had shifted. Something had *changed* with Scotland's arms around him.

He couldn't smile as he shuffled away from the freezers, adjusting himself to hide his reaction to the kiss. Scotland was right. Friends were better. Friends were easy. He had hundreds of them, but one more might just fill his broken heart.

Chapter Fourteen

Clint

"What are you doing?" Clint stretched out on the lounge chair that was quickly becoming his favorite piece of furniture on the property. With the midafternoon sun beating down on them, the weather was almost summerish again. The chill was sure to set in at night, though, lining the windows with threatened frost.

"We're gonna make s'mores," said Scotland. He was kneeling next to the fire pit again, a metal poker stick in one hand, and a lighter in the other. Instead of the metal flick lighter, though, this one was in the shape of some kind of fish, the flame shooting from its mouth when Scotland clicked it.

"The hell you are." Clint jerked upright, his sandals slipping from his feet as he scrambled to grab the lighter and jerk it from Scotland's grip. "We haven't had rain in over a week. All this grass could go up with a single spark." He shook his head, his hands trembling as he looked at the gaudy plastic he'd grabbed.

Why would someone make something like this? Fire wasn't a novelty. It was *dangerous.*

"I've got a bucket of water right there," said Scotland, pointing off to the pail he'd lugged across the lawn. The water was nearly at the brim, but there was no way it could cover the whole lawn.

Rolling his eyes, Clint tucked the lighter into his waistband. There were probably about three buttons on it that he'd have to push to actually light the thing, but it still settled against his skin uncomfortably. "Sometimes water just makes it worse."

A shiver flowed under his skin. And sometimes water did nothing. He could still remember flickers of the deluge coming from fire hoses aimed at what used to be his home. The flames had simply roared higher, consuming so quickly that even the steam seemed to disappear into the night.

"That's why I've got a fire extinguisher inside the door." Scotland motioned toward the house. Clint had checked the thing out himself when he'd slept in the main house for the night, making sure it wasn't expired. People always seemed to forget about that.

"I don't want to push you, Clint," said Scotland, leaning back on his heels. He was in short sleeves again, his tattoos tracing up his arms. At some point overnight he'd dyed the tips of his hair a different color. Orange suited him much better than blue or purple — not that Clint noticed or anything.

Motioning to the small pile of kindling in the fire pit, then back to the split stack a ways away, Scotland frowned. "I hate to see you afraid. Every day you sit here or at the fire pit behind the cabin and stare at the ashes for hours like you're trying to tell me something. I'm just trying to listen."

When did he get so damn stubborn? He'd been different since they'd returned from grocery shopping a few days earlier, keeping more to himself and leaving Clint to listen to the silence of the forest alone. It hurt and twisted something inside his chest.

"And I'm just trying to be practical." Clint pulled his lip between his teeth. "There is no reason to start a fire right now."

"There's no reason not to." Scotland raised one brow, pulling a second lighter from his pocket.

"Well, now you're just being an insensitive prick," growled Clint, grabbing for the lighter and tossing it back at Scotland. "I almost died in a fire, asshole. My husband did die in one."

"I know," said Scotland softly, catching the lighter with ease. "And you haven't trusted yourself since."

"That's…" *It's not true.*

A flame burst from the mouth of the lighter as Scotland clicked the button, lowering it to the paper he'd packed loosely between the kindling days before. Clint's breath cut off, his heart rate jacking as it caught, spreading across the black ink like a rising tide.

The smell hit him first, the cinders, the decay, and something that had always made his mouth water and his cock hard. His chest was in a vise at the same time he felt himself firm between his legs, springing to attention as the first piece of wood charred and caught fire.

It was *mesmerizing*. The slow dance and the way it licked at the wood the same way he remembered it flickering over his skin after Ross restrained him. The heat of it was nothing to how it was against him—*on him.*

"We went camping once," said Clint, his heart slowing as he thought about the trip that was still ingrained in his memory. The flames called him in deeper as they spread to a larger log and Scotland took a step back as the warmth grew stronger.

"There were six of us — all couples." He licked his lips. "The others went to go swim at a little lake that was close to our campsite. We were tucked out of the way in a spot that looked like someone had hacked it out of the forest with an ax alone. The nights were terrible." He rolled his shoulders. His back had ached for a week after sleeping on the ground when their air mattress decided to deflate on the first night. He'd been too cheap to go get a new one, even though Ross had had ample money.

"We were out of the house — where I was usually Dominant — but Ross grabbed me by the wrist when I wasn't expecting it, shoving me against a tree." He looked to his wrists where he could almost see the rope that had bound him in place, wrapped around the trunk completely naked. "The bark hurt the most. I hadn't expected that. It tore at my chest and scratched up my cheek." His cock had been in even worse shape when he'd tried humping as Ross had squeezed his ass before spanking him a few times.

"He had something in his hands. I didn't even know what it was until I felt the wetness on my back and caught the smell of it." His mouth flooded with saliva. It was just like smoke curling from the pit, only brighter — sharper.

"I didn't know what he was using for fuel then, but I recognized the smell deep down. We'd talked about fire play before, but I'd never thought it was something

Ross would do to me. It was so dangerous." He curled around himself, reaching for his back.

"The first letter was an 'S'. I remember thinking he was drawing a snake before he lit it. I wish I could have seen what it looked like as it burned so hot I thought I'd be scarred forever before he smothered it with a fireproof blanket." He leaned back against the chair, sweeping one hand over his groin. He was rock hard. "The second letter hurt so much more. It was an 'L' and he made it big enough that the bottom was just above my ass. When he lit it, I screamed, but not for long."

"Did he gag you?"

Clint started at Scotland's voice. He'd been so lost that he hardly remembered where he was.

He shook his head. "No. He choked me out."

Dragging his nails over the tops of his thighs, he let out a shudder. "He lit the 'U' when I woke up. I came as he smothered the 'T' and pushed me against the tree, making me hurt."

"Holy fuck." Scotland was flushed as he dragged a hand through his hair, his eyes dark in the light of the fire.

"Our friends saw me when they came back from the swim — still naked with letters burned into my skin like sunburn. I didn't think I would ever come down from that high." He chuckled, grinning.

"The drop sucked, though. Ross did everything he could, but I couldn't bring myself to smile for two weeks. It took me a month to convince him to do it again."

Leaning forward, he raised his hand toward the flames, waving his fingers as the heat singed his nerves. "That's why I don't like fire. Because I know I'll never get to have it again — not in the way I want, at least. It took that from me. I won't let it take anything else."

"I'm sorry," said Scotland, standing from his chair and heaving the bucket of water off the ground with a grunt. "I'll put it out."

No, no, no. It had barely begun, and the flames seemed so trapped within the circle, far from whipping out of control like he'd expected. *Not yet.*

"Wait." Clint bit his lip, sawing it between his teeth. "You promised me a s'more. I've been good, right?"

* * * *

Scotland

He was going to die a happy man with a hard cock, blue balls and a broken heart. *Friends. I can do this.* He'd fucked up in the tattoo parlor, and in the grocery store, too, but it wasn't going to happen again. *Hell, that sucks.*

He'd been pissy after a long day and a no-show, so when he'd spotted Clint by the fire pit again, he'd had enough. He grabbed the closest lighters at hand with every intention of starting a bonfire. *What are friends for?*

I'm done. He bit his tongue until he tasted blood. He was a bit of an asshole, so what? Belittling someone's trauma like that was one of the biggest dick moves he'd ever pulled. But he'd fucking *tried.*

He'd tried the sexy way and the conditioning way where he'd set fake flickering candles at the dinner table each night. Clint would always look at them before turning them off without comment.

He couldn't have expected Clint's reaction as soon as the flames caught. He'd been ready for fear or another breakdown. Hell, maybe that was what he'd been hoping for in his own fucked-up way.

"I think maybe you should go back to Unkinked," Scotland bit out, resting his elbows on his knees to shield his groin from view. He had to get Clint away before he spiraled any deeper into whatever was going on. Scotland had pushed people before, but he'd never been such an outright asshole.

Clint snapped his gaze up, scrunching his forehead in confusion. The s'mores were forgotten between them, the chocolate-covered cookies probably getting soft from the heat of being too close to the fire. But Scotland refused to move back when Clint was pressed as close as he could without actually getting burned, leaning forward in his chair and completely entranced.

"Why?" Clint clutched at the armrest of his lounger. From his position, Scotland could see everything from the bulge in his pants to the peaks of his nipples through his shirt. He'd been turned on since the flame had licked the first curled edge of the paper.

Dragging his gaze away, he looked to the field. The donkeys had retreated to the far side to lounge in the shelter of tall grass, and they probably wouldn't move much for the rest of the night. "I'm not sure if this was the best idea, after all." He shrugged, rubbing his hand over his face. "I thought I could help — even if it was just a bit — but I've fucked up so many times." The sex, the Dominance and now the fire... Their time together hadn't been some of his finest, even if it was worth cherishing.

"What are you talking about?" Clint scratched his chin. "I didn't think I'd last an hour out here, especially with you. No offense."

Scotland rolled his eyes. It was hard to let that slide off, especially when he couldn't quite name how much Clint had come to mean to him.

"But I can't remember the last time I was this happy and calm." Clint let out a sigh, tilting his head back and finally leaning away from the flames. "I can remember, actually, but I never thought I would get that again. You're a good friend, Scotland."

"But a shitty Dom," said Scotland, pressing his lips together. "I can't count how many times I've been dissed for being a switch, but maybe they were right all along. I can't be both—not really. I can't submit as much as a natural submissive, and it's the same with Dominance. I'll always have that little spark inside telling me to do the exact opposite."

Clint nodded, his gaze locked on the fire. Scotland wasn't sure when he'd looked back, but he couldn't seem to keep his eyes away for long. At least he was farther back in his seat now and not teetered on the edge like he was ready to dive in at any moment.

"Tell me about it," said Clint. "When I discovered kink, I'd thought I'd finally found somewhere I truly fit in, but that didn't last long. I didn't think any Dom would ever want a boy who sometimes wanted to be the boss. It seemed no sub wanted a Dom who chose to kneel on occasion. You're not a shitty Dom, Scotland."

"I didn't do right by you." As soon as he said it, he knew it was true. Clint's entire stay had been a clusterfuck of pushing boundaries that should have been left alone. "I never should have fucked you, knowing that you weren't in it for the long run. I never should have started this fucking fire."

He knew he wasn't talking about the flames—and maybe Clint did, too. There was something burning between them, and he wasn't sure if he'd be able to put it out. "I never should have kissed you."

Clint cleared his throat before reaching into the package of cookies and chomping down on a chocolatey edge. "For the record, I'm glad you did."

What? Clint had resisted him nearly every step of the way. Where the hell was this coming from? Scotland stared at him and the slight swell of his lower lip. All it would take was a single move, and he could feel them again. Somehow, he knew Clint wouldn't stop him this time.

"I thought of something," said Clint, running his hand through his hair. "I'm surprised I didn't think of it earlier." He turned until Scotland could see the flush on his cheeks. "You know I scened with Cutler, right?"

Those rumors had spread through Unkinked like a contagion, courtesy of Maddy and Keady. He nodded, swallowing the jealousy that instantly threatened.

"Cutler is a friend." Clint's throat bobbed as he swallowed.

He hadn't thought they looked that friendly the last time he'd seen them speaking. Rumor had it that Keady had almost been kicked out of the club, and Cutler had had *words.*

"Okay." Scotland reached for a cookie of his own as Clint slid the package his way. The marshmallows were open but most of them hadn't been touched, their sweetness filling the air.

"So…" Clint raised one brow before licking his lips and catching a stray bit of chocolate. "*We're* friends."

"Yeah," Scotland said slowly. "We just talked about this. We're friends but nothing more… Oh." He widened his eyes, giving Clint another look. *How the hell am I going to do this?*

On one hand, he wanted to yell out 'yes' and kiss Clint right there, but the pang in his chest stopped him.

"I don't want you to get hurt, Clint. I'm talking about an emotional hurt." He cut off whatever Clint was going to say with a wave of his hand. "I need a personal connection with my partner, and I think they need that, as well. It's too easy to get wrapped up in kink and forget about what's more important."

"This *is* personal," said Clint. "You've been following me around for months, and hell, I'm practically living with you right now. I know you aren't going to walk out on me after a scene or a fuck. I trust you."

When he'd started the fire, he'd been hoping to offer reassurance, not drown in the deep end. His heart could only take so many hits before it gave up for good.

But maybe Clint was right. It wouldn't be perfect, but if they were friends, at least he could be there for Clint in whatever way he needed. Hell, some friends were even closer than married couples.

"But I thought you weren't ready," said Scotland, the final tether of hesitation holding strong. "Ross —"

"Would want me to have this," said Clint, tilting his head to the sky. Sun washed over his face, his freckles standing out with vibrance. "He loved me, even if he was an asshole. He always knew what was best for me. Something's telling me that *this* is best."

Maybe he believed in heaven, Scotland wasn't sure, but it didn't matter. Love like that didn't just fade away, and it wasn't something that was ever forgotten or replaced. He'd never had a chance. *But I can't walk away.*

"Let me think about it," said Scotland, letting out a huff before grabbing another cookie. "We're going out tomorrow night—you and me. I'll have an answer for you by then."

Clint grinned, every engraved worry line relaxing. Fuck, he was beautiful. *I have to say yes.* He clenched his hands into fists, willing his Dominant side to stay strong. He wasn't telling Clint. *I'll see how long it takes him to figure it out tomorrow night.*

Chapter Fifteen

Clint

"I've been here before," said Clint, eyeing the apartment building. It was his kind of place, with a lived-in worn look and a menagerie of busted cars in the parking lot.

Places like it were always more real than the shiny newbuilds, and the people could hide nothing from their neighbors, who were only a few inches of insulation away. A fight would be known by everyone in a few hours, and you always could tell who fucked the best.

"I used to live a block from here," said Clint, pointing down the street that was still so familiar. "I used to eat at that restaurant all the time before I learned how to cook more than spaghetti and soup."

It looked exactly the same, down to the rusted-out sign that was missing a few letters and the 'help wanted' posted in the front window. His heart ached. It had been years since he'd even come close to visiting the neighborhood. Between the club, and well, the club, everything had seemed to blur together.

Scotland was smiling at him, his eyes dark. He'd been quiet all day and had hardly said a thing in the car. Somewhere in those lips was Clint's answer to the question that had been burning through him the whole time. Anticipation was curled right next to nervousness, but there was no regret.

"Tonight, you call me 'Sir'."

Goosebumps prickled over his skin, which was suddenly too tight over his frame. His mouth was dry, words lost as his heart pounded. *Yes.* He let his eyes fall shut, leaving any worry behind.

Ross flickered over his mind, but only as a memory of his sweet smile. The ache was still the same, but there was something new next to it. It had been a long time since he'd had hope.

"Yes, Sir."

Scotland reached out, tracing his thumb over Clint's bottom lip. Dipping the tip inside, he paused until Clint parted his teeth, shuddering as Scotland stroked his tongue.

"You have your safewords, and I trust you to use them," said Scotland, pinching Clint's tongue between two fingers and tugging softly. "Any limits for tonight?"

Clint shook his head as much as he could with his tongue trapped. Drool was pooling in his mouth, and he let it fall, dribbling down his chin. Some of the limits he'd given Scotland the last time they'd talked about this probably didn't exist anymore.

I trust you.

"I only have one rule for tonight," said Scotland, moving his fingers deeper until he tested Clint's gag reflex. His jaw ached as he licked Scotland's fingers, letting his saliva fall. "Anything I ask you to do, you do it without question while we are here. You can brat all you want when we get back to the car. Until then, I need your complete submission. I think you need it just as much as I do."

Clint hated when Scotland was so fucking right. Ross had always accused him of using his bratty behavior to be defensive. The asshole had always been able to read him.

"Let's go," said Scotland, releasing Clint and stepping out of the car. Before Clint could wipe his chin and follow him, Scotland was opening the passenger door wide and holding out his hand. "Let me help you."

Clint flushed, lowering his gaze automatically as he stepped outside. He'd never been able to meet someone's eyes when he was in a submissive state, much preferring the view of the floor.

He didn't release Clint's hand as they walked to the door past a crowd of teenagers who gave them nods as they approached. It was almost a blockade of sorts, but Clint wasn't nervous.

"You guys friends of Derreck and Ice?"

Clint blinked, giving the group and the apartment a second look.

"Yeah," said Scotland, his hand twitching against Clint's. "I'm not sure who Ice is, but Derreck — yes."

This is Derreck's place? Clint had never visited, even though Derreck had been at the bar and his old apartment too many times to count. Glancing over his shoulder, he spotted Derreck's beast of a car in the lot. He was surprised he hadn't noticed it before. It was the only one in the lot that had four of the same tires.

"That guy of his," said one of the teenagers, scuffing his shoe against the cracked pavement, "he's a fucking legend, but the first time I saw him I thought he was an ice cream cone. The name stuck."

"Maddy?" asked Clint, scratching at his cheek. That was classic. Maddy was the most naïve and masochistic man he'd ever met. 'Ice' fit him perfectly.

"Yeah." The kid nodded. "Anyone who can fuck in a graveyard is a legend."

Clint snorted, leaning against Scotland as he chuckled. Scotland pulled him closer, wrapping his arm around Clint's shoulders. He fell into the embrace, letting out a sigh. "Why did you guess we're his friends?"

"You guys all have that same kind of look," said one of the other teenagers, grabbing his phone from his pocket as it dinged. "Like you know your way around too many things to risk a fight."

Scotland snorted, flexing his arm. Clint couldn't tear his eyes away as the muscles of his arm rippled before his eyes, his tattoos stretching and bulging.

The teenager eyed the display, not seeming nearly as impressed as Clint was. "You guys don't give a shit about where you get laid."

Clint nodded. "That's so true." He glanced up at Scotland, his cheek dragging over the scruff of his chin from how close they were. "We should get badges for the club or something. Like a 'never have I ever fucked on a rooftop or a movie set'. You'd get a badge for every place. We could do prizes! Oh, Maddy would love that."

Scotland chuckled, nosing along Clint's jawline, despite their audience. "I love it when you're like this. You're so fucking good."

The first teenager narrowed his eyes, tilting his head to the side. "That's another thing, too. You're always saying 'good boy' and 'Sir' and other weird shit like that. Dead giveaway."

Clint's smile flitted away in an instant, his teeth clacking together as he clenched his jaw. Scotland had gone tense, and Clint rolled his shoulders, shrugging him off. "You're a kid, so I'm gonna let that last comment slide."

"I'm nineteen, man." The teenager seemed to puff out his chest a bit as he glanced at his friends.

He's just a kid. Take it easy on him. "Then you should know to have some respect, especially if you know we're Derreck's friends. We don't use words lightly in kink…or titles. I call my Dom 'Sir' because he deserves it, and I trust him completely."

The teenager flickered his gaze to the door, his eyes going a bit wider. "Sorry, man. I really meant no offense. I was just talking shit."

"Oh." Clint grinned, advancing a step. "Perfect then. I was all prepped for a little knife play there, but I guess I'll keep it in my pocket for now." He winked, grinning when the teenager took a sudden step back.

Scotland looped his arm through Clint's, pulling him off balance before leaning over to whisper into his ear. "Give the kid a break. He looks like he's gonna piss himself."

Without looking back, Scotland led them to the door and pulled it wide. As soon as they let the door close behind him, Clint let out a laugh. "When I worked as a nurse, I got to understand punks pretty well. They were just testing us—probably making sure we're worthy of being Derreck's friends or something."

He bounced up on his toes, landing a kiss on Scotland's cheek. He couldn't explain it, but he was more excited than he'd been in a long time, bubbly energy rushing through his limbs. "Why are we visiting

Derreck and Maddy, Sir? It's not that I don't want to see them, but we weren't exactly on the best of terms before my vacation."

"No questions," said Scotland, putting his hand on Clint's lower back and propelling him toward the door. "I have a surprise for you."

Anything that Clint could have said was cut off as Scotland knocked and the inside door swung open a moment later. He blinked, his breath catching in his throat and his cheeks burning as he caught sight of who was standing there.

"Hey, I'm Scotland. Nice to meet you."

"Rowes." Rowes took Scotland's hand, shaking once before he turned his gaze on Clint. Clint gaped his mouth like a fish, his brain stuttering to a complete halt. *The* Rowes Keppel — the star of his favorite show on earth and the only show he watched religiously. Lately, he'd even downloaded it onto Maddy's phone so he could watch it while chilling in a chair at the club.

Over his shoulder was Isthmus Linton, the supposed star of the show and Rowes' partner. Clint had always assumed something was going on between them, but he hadn't known for sure until they'd show up at Unkinked one day.

"Nice to see you again, Clint." Rowes dropped his hand as Clint continued to gape, a smile on his lips. "Derreck asked me to grab the door while he pulled dinner out of the oven. Come on in."

Rowes turned away from the door, his presence still looming, along with the smell of expensive cologne.

He didn't belong in a run-down apartment building, even if Clint loved the place already. He probably had four penthouses and a summer home somewhere exotic with palm trees and freaking coconuts growing in the yard.

What the hell? How? He lifted his hand, staring at it. Rowes Keppel and Isthmus Linton were two of the hottest actors on television, their show gaining even more popularity after a recent stir in the media. They'd been to the club a few times, but they lived out of town. Clint had never expected to see them again.

"You are such a fanboy," said Scotland, kissing Clint's neck as his brain blipped. "The last time I saw you this awestruck was when you saw my cock."

"Yes, Sir." Because wasn't that the fucking truth. The two actors looked even better off-screen than they did on, and Scotland's cock had been a sight to behold.

"Take a seat next to Rowes, and I'll grab us some food." Scotland grabbed the door as it started to ease shut in Clint's face, holding it open and letting Clint through.

Sit…next to Rowes? Clint toed his shoes off without looking down, flinching as Maddy and Derreck's cat started howling at him for pets. Maddy told him all the time how much he loved the little furball, but also how terrible its yowl was. It suited its name, which was Demon.

Rowes was seated in front of the couch, his head leaned back against Izzy's knee. There was a collar around Rowes' throat, matching the one on his wrist that Clint had heard so much about on celebrity news. He'd known exactly what it was as soon as he'd seen it.

He took a deep breath before he crossed the small space between the door and the couch. Rowes gave him a small smile and a wave before he trailed his gaze back to the television.

It's okay. It's okay. They're only superstars — ones you've been crushing on since season one.

"You guys get your stuff sorted okay?" asked Clint, immediately slapping a hand over his mouth and letting out a small groan. "Sorry. Not my business. You are just both so beautiful. Beautiful *and* kinky...like heaven."

"*I'm* beautiful and kinky," said Scotland, saving Clint from digging himself any deeper as Izzy started to chuckle. Rowes was covering his mouth, his eyes sparkling. "Sit down, love."

"Yes, Sir." He dropped to the ground, shuffling until his back was against the couch. Instead of ending up to one side of Scotland's legs, he landed between them. He grabbed each ankle, shuffling them closer until he was effectively caged. He let out a soft sigh. *So much better.*

Izzy and Rowes seemed much calmer than the time he'd last seen them when they'd been close to their breaking point. With the stress from the show and exploring their kinky side, they'd looked ready to snap.

"Truth be told, I thought you were a Dom, Clint. My apologies," said Izzy, letting out a sigh as he weaved his fingers into Rowes' hair.

"Everybody does."

Clint looked up at Maddy's voice. Hell, he was a sight for sore eyes. He'd spent more time with Maddy than anyone else, and he'd never admit how much he missed him while he'd been away.

Maddy looked good, and not at all like the club had been too much to manage for him. There was a smile on his lips, and he looked calm and well-rested. There were times when Clint worried about him. *Maybe I don't need to worry.*

"But I know Clint's secret," said Maddy, shooting them a wink. He had the most adorable blue polka dot oven mitts on, which happened to be Clint's favorite pattern, and the tray he was balancing between his hands smelled divine.

"Brat," said Clint, surging to his feet to adjust the wooden cutting board on the table before them so it would be easier for Maddy to set the food on. "How have you been? How's the place holding up? You started a brat night, didn't you? I knew you would. All you subbies getting together to plan something…"

Clint grinned, adjusting the tray with his fingertips until it was in line with the edges of the table. "Can I help with anything? Do you have plates? Or, did anyone need a drink?" He turned to Scotland, who was looking at him with one raised brow.

"Clint?" asked Maddy, pulling him in for a brief hug. "Go sit down. You're still on vacation."

"But—" He looked to the kitchen where he was sure he'd just heard the sound of a breaking plate. "You hate serving food. Let me help?" He bounced on his toes a little, his hands itching to grab the oven mitts right off Maddy's hands. If they hadn't opened a bar together, Clint had planned to convince Ross to let them start a restaurant. They would have hired a chef so Clint wouldn't have had to do the cooking part, but he would happily deliver every plate himself.

"What he's trying to say," said Derreck, peeking his head through the door of the kitchen, "is that his ass is getting punished, so he has to do this himself." Derreck was surprisingly done up for the occasion, wearing the first button-down that Clint had ever seen him in. He was usually more of a jeans and T-shirt kind of guy, with varying degrees of dirt on him from his job as a gravedigger.

"Oh." Clint took the two steps back to the couch before dropping to the ground between Scotland's knees. He landed closer to Rowes than he had before, his skin prickling from the proximity. *Is it rude if I stare at him?*

Clint cupped his hand over his mouth, aiming his voice away from Maddy, who was making his way back to the kitchen.

"What did he do?" he asked Rowes, ignoring the way Scotland bumped him with his leg. "I mean, he's great at pushing Derreck's buttons, but I don't think I've actually seen him in trouble before."

Rowes shrugged, smiling as Izzy reached for a plate and loaded up on a few potato skins. He took a small bite as Izzy held one to his lips, licking the bacon bit that clung to his lip. "Something about candles? I didn't hear the whole story."

They are so sweet. Clint's heart melted as he watched Izzy feed Rowes another bite before reaching for his drink and carefully bringing the cup to his lips. Thinking about them as actors had his heart pounding, but as a cute and kinky couple, he could let himself relax.

"Oh, God." He rubbed a hand over his face when Rowes' words caught up with him. "Maddy must have started a freaking candle club at Unkinked. I knew I shouldn't have left the kid in charge."

Scotland touched his cheek, dragging Clint's attention to him. There was something soft in his eyes that probably shouldn't have been there with a friend. Clint couldn't bring himself to care. He was loose and free, a laugh in his throat, despite the threat of candles near his life's work.

"When Derreck found out Maddy didn't ask you about the wax play scene, he had a few choice words," said Scotland, moving his hand to Clint's hair before digging into the strands. "Word on the street is that his punishment is going to last the entire time you're on vacation."

"And you say *I'm* the gossip," said Clint, closing his eyes and letting out a hum as Scotland scratched his nails over his scalp. His hair was softer than usual since he'd started using Scotland's shampoo, and he'd fallen in love with the deep scent of it. All it was missing was the hint of donkey, and it would match Scotland perfectly.

Chuckling, he leaned his head back, tilting to the side to follow Scotland's hand as he moved.

"You like that?" asked Scotland, his voice lower than normal.

"Yeah, Sir." Clint cracked one eye open, bending so he could catch sight of Scotland. It was good that he wasn't the only one enjoying it.

"You want me to feed you, love?"

It did look nice the way Izzy brought the food to Rowes' lips, letting him take little bites and even wiping his cheek with a napkin when a small piece went astray. He nodded, not trusting his voice. Isolation must've turned him sappy.

"Here." Scotland held out a piece of potato skin, the grease probably stinging his fingertips. Clint opened wide, accepting it onto his tongue with a moan as flavor burst in his mouth. Maddy was a damn good cook.

"What are we watching?" Clint looked to the television when Derreck silently entered and started setting something up on the screen. His heart was beating way too fast as Scotland offered him another bite, his fingers stroking Clint's tongue like he had in the car. Any more and he was going to be sporting a hard-on next to his idols.

"The season premiere of a certain show that's not out yet," said Maddy, strolling back into the room with yet another plate. "Rowes and Izzy seemed to think they owed you a favor, so they got their hands on it for you."

Clint's jaw dropped toward the floor, a piece of potato spilling out and rolling onto the ground. *Gunlover* was only his favorite show of all time, but the season finale had been the last, despite so many unanswered questions. He'd heard about Rowes' and Izzy's new roles and had been waiting to get his hands on more than just a few sneak peeks.

"It feels kind of self-centered to be watching this," said Rowes, playing with a loose thread on his pants.

"You just don't want to see the wall I fucked you against on set." Izzy's voice was a deep grumble that took Clint's brain almost completely offline.

Fucked on set? "Oh! I have to do one like that for my new 'never have I ever' game. It was totally one of my ideas. I may have suspected something like that happened a few times during the last show. You guys are *intense.* I saw a leaked video of a kiss— Amazing." He let out a wistful sigh.

"A lot like this?" asked Scotland, grasping Clint's chin and tilting his head back. Their lips met a second later, and Scotland immediately opened his mouth, his tongue skirting between Clint's lips.

Fuck. Clint groaned, carefully moving to his knees and turning before his neck could strain any farther. Burying his hands in Scotland's hair, he tugged him closer, deepening the kiss. His heart pounded, the music for the beginning credits starting up behind him, but he didn't care.

Tilting his head, he tried to deepen the kiss, dragging Scotland harder against him. He didn't want Scotland to get any ideas and pull away.

"It's starting," said Maddy, his voice coming from somewhere to Clint's side. "You're gonna miss it."

Clint drew back, licking his lips as he pressed his forehead to Scotland's. They were both panting, his lips throbbing from the force of the kiss. "That's what the pause button is for."

He dragged Scotland back to him, who put up zero resistance, slipping his tongue into Clint's mouth and stripping Clint's Dominance from him in a heartbeat. Scotland's grip on his hair turned fierce as he dragged Clint onto the couch to follow him as he leaned back.

Clint scrambled, landing on Scotland's lap and immediately grinding down to bring their groins together. The touch was like a shock of both heat and electricity, his balls aching and full already. Considering he hadn't emptied them after so much prolonged edging, he wasn't surprised.

Scotland jerked Clint's head back, clicking his tongue. "I don't want your idols to see how much of a slut you are, Clint. And Maddy made all this wonderful food."

Clint blinked his eyes open, looking slowly to the side. Every eye was on them, the show paused with a shot of Rowes screaming, his mouth open in horror.

"I don't mind," said Maddy, leaning his chin on one hand. "I've only been with two guys, so it would be interesting to see how other couples do it." He winced as Derreck flicked his ear from his position seated next to Maddy. "What?"

First off, how was Maddy not a virgin when he met Derreck? Secondly... "I'm your boss."

He spotted Rowes' flushed cheeks before he quickly looked away and leaned his cheek against Izzy's knees.

"Sorry," said Rowes, muffling his voice behind his hand. "I didn't mean to stare." Izzy didn't seem to have any qualms.

"Sorry." Clint scratched the back of his head, hissing as he shifted in Scotland's lap. That almighty treasure of a cock was right against his, teasing him, even as he tried to stay still. "I'll watch—I swear. I just got distracted."

As soon as he tried to turn, Scotland grabbed his hip, stilling his movements. "Where's the fun in that?" The grin on his lips was malicious. "You guys are all fans, but I've never heard of this show. Give me something else to watch."

What? Clint looked to his pocket where his phone lay. There was nothing on there unless Scotland wanted to play shitty games on a flip phone.

"Take your shirt off, Clint," said Scotland, releasing Clint's hip before patting it. "I need to check that spot I tattooed yesterday anyway."

Clint swallowed, choking when he wasn't able to get it all the way down. *My shirt?* Sure, more than a dozen people had seen him without a shirt on at Unkinked, Maddy and Derreck included. But Rowes and Izzy were another story. They were both so goddamn perfect that he would look like a disaster next to them.

His gut throbbed, but not in the familiar way from sweet humiliation. Biting his lip, he gave Scotland a wary look. "Yellow?"

Scotland froze with his hand midway through petting Clint's ass. "Is it the shirt?"

Clint nodded, glancing at Izzy through his lashes.

"I'm willing to compromise. How about you lose the pants instead?" asked Scotland, resuming his strokes.

Now *that* had him throbbing in an instant. There was nothing wrong with his cock, and the scars along his hip would mostly be covered by the hem of his shirt. "Green."

"Good boy," said Scotland, giving him a quick kiss. "Thank you for letting me know you were uncomfortable. Now turn around and take those pants off."

Maddy hit play on the television as Clint awkwardly spun around, almost kneeing Scotland in the balls when he moved too quickly. The opening credits bloomed before his eyes, his excitement building for more than one reason as he slid his pants from his hips.

When he settled, his naked ass brushed against Scotland's clothed cock, his chest burning into Clint's back. Scotland immediately snuck a hand around his waist, brushing his fingertips against Clint's cock.

It was fucking torture.

Every time he was dragged into a scene on the television, Scotland would stroke him slowly. Clint would stop mid-comment, glancing to either side, but no one was looking their way. It was only when his breathing started to come in fast that Maddy or Derreck would glance over.

Maddy's gaze lingered, burning over Clint's flesh, but Derreck didn't pause before looking back to the screen. Izzy and Rowes either didn't notice or didn't care, their eyes locked on the screen as they called out a few critical comments.

"We had to wait three days to finish this scene," said Rowes, reaching for Izzy's leg and squeezing. "A storm rolled in the first night and completely trashed the set. Our agent Lorena nearly had a meltdown."

Then Scotland would stop, stroking his thigh or the scratchy bit of hair above his prize, and Clint would throb and struggle not to squirm.

Maddy looked at him for a long time, flicking his gaze everywhere. Maybe he couldn't quite believe that

Clint was in this position, blatantly grinding his ass against Scotland when it became too much.

Clint couldn't believe it either.

"We need to head out to catch our flight," said Izzy, about a half-hour into the show. "It was good meeting you again, Clint." They didn't shake hands, but Rowes turned pink when he caught sight of Scotland's hand resting around Clint's cock, his fingers tight but not moving.

Clint sent them an awkward wave.

"Sorry about having my dick out the whole time. It was great to see you guys again. Good luck with the new show, and seriously, come by the club any time you want to get your kink on."

Rowes flushed bright red, missing Izzy's soft smile as he looked at him. The two were so in love it was nearly disgusting.

"We're still new to kink," said Rowes, clasping his hands together. "Well, kind of. It was cool to see a different kind of dynamic. And hot…really hot."

Clint could agree with the 'hot' part. He'd been hard for so long that he was sweating, his shirt sticking to his back and probably to Scotland's chest as well.

"They were really nice people," said Maddy as he started to clear the table, stacking the trays on top of each other. "I have no idea how Derreck got them to come, though. He wouldn't tell me the details, but something about them being in town."

Derreck shifted in his armchair. He'd been typically silent the entire evening, his gaze locked mostly on the screen and Maddy. He steepled his fingers, letting out a grunt. "They owed me a favor."

"Um." Maddy bit his lip, his cheeks flushing as he nearly dropped the trays. "Like a work favor or a kink favor?"

That was a good question. A work favor for Derreck would have to mean either digging a grave or burying a body. *Holy shit.*

"Does it matter?" asked Derreck, reaching for the disc that Izzy had signed for Clint before they left and flipping it over to eye the shiny bits underneath. "We're even now."

Clint had nothing but respect for Derreck, but he was freaking terrifying sometimes. He was probably even scarier than the twins, who were actual gang enforcers. Maddy seemed completely enamored, however, with stars in his eyes and the trays steady as he shook his head and turned to the kitchen.

"It was a kink favor," said Derreck lowly as soon as Maddy disappeared as he gave Clint a rare smile. "I just like freaking Maddy out."

Just Maddy? "Hell, my heart is pounding, and I'm not the one sleeping with you." He moved his hand to Scotland's thigh, squeezing the muscle as it flexed beneath his hand.

"Oh, are you guys sleeping over?" asked Maddy, his eyes sparkling as he returned with a tray that looked like Jell-O topped with whipped cream. "I've never had a sleepover before. Derreck, can they stay? *Please.*"

Derreck rubbed his temples, letting out a sigh. "Since you asked so nicely. It's after ten, anyway. Probably best to stay off the road at this time of night in the country unless you want to hit a deer."

Clint let himself sink a little farther, grinning as he squirmed in Scotland's lap. "Can we? Can we?" he asked Scotland, cranking his neck to the side to place a kiss on his throat. "I've been good." He wiggled his ass, Scotland's cock throbbing against him.

"We don't have a spare room," said Derreck, standing from his chair. "Plenty of blankets and pillows, though. One of you can take the couch. I guess Clint can have the floor."

Aw, less fun.

"Sounds good," said Scotland, before Clint could protest. *Bastard.*

Maddy's spoon jiggled as he laughed, the whipped cream nearly landing on the carpet before he managed to catch it with his mouth.

A frown tugged at Clint's lips. No matter what anyone had to say, the only reason he was here was Maddy. Without him, so many people in his life would have ended up in a different spot. He'd probably be amidst his own mental breakdown, the weight of the club and the never-ending paperwork too much to think about any sort of future.

"Hey, Maddy?" said Clint, laying a hand on Scotland's wrist to pause his movements. "I'm sorry."

Maddy dropped his spoon, a bit of Jell-O going flying. Derreck eyed the spot of green on the carpet with a look of exasperation. Demon chose that moment to sneak out from under one of the chairs, going up to the glob and sniffing it.

"It's okay," said Maddy, setting the bowl down before loosely wrapping his arms around his middle.

Shaking his head, Clint leaned over, placing one hand on Maddy's elbow. "I've made a lot of mistakes in my life, but you aren't one of them. You're the best thing that's ever happened to Unkinked."

Maddy sniffed, his eyes going shiny as he swallowed and looked away. "Thank you. For the record, I'm sorry, too. I should have asked about the wax stuff."

Clint shrugged. They'd both made mistakes. He hoped they still had enough friendship left that they could truly move on.

"That's nothing," said Scotland as he moved his hand to Clint's hip. "I started a campfire yesterday. You want to talk about fuck-ups? I get the gold *and* silver medals for that stunt."

Chapter Sixteen

Scotland

Worst idea ever. He shuffled his hip against the ground, attempting to find some carpet that was softer than concrete. It was probably a bit better than hardwood or something similar, but the plush had obviously worn out a long time ago. He wasn't going to let Clint sleep on the floor, though.

As soon as Clint had settled on the couch in a T-shirt, he'd promptly passed out. Sleep had obviously been escaping him for longer than he'd let on, because he'd barely even moved. And he snored, which was absolutely adorable.

Scotland sat up, shuffling until his back was against the couch. Turning his head, he watched Clint in the low light, memorizing the soft outline of his sleeping face. Every so often a car would pull into the lot outside, the beams flickering over the window and casting a temporary beacon.

He hadn't heard anything from Maddy and Derreck's bedroom since they'd retreated to it, but the door was open a crack. Sound would easily be able to slip both ways.

"You asleep?" he asked softly, running his thumb over Clint's lips. Clint scrunched his forehead in his sleep, letting out a little whimper. He was almost painfully beautiful, his face relaxed and his worries nowhere to be found.

He trailed his fingers along Clint's chin where his scruff had returned in full force since he'd shaved yesterday. It gave him a rugged appearance, that wasn't nearly as desperate and unkept as it had been before. His neck was soft until the top of his chest, where his hair began. Scotland weaved his fingers into what he could reach through the neck hole of Clint's T-shirt, tickling over Clint's warm flesh beneath.

Scotland watched as Clint's cock twitched in his sleep, his lips parting with a soft noise that wasn't quite a moan. Awake, he was responsive, but in sleep, his guard was completely gone.

They had talked about this exact thing before — the memory burning through Scotland as he moved his hand so he could dip under Clint's shirt. His abdomen was firm but relaxed, his pecs the perfect size to fit in Scotland's palm. It didn't take much to drag his boxers down past his hips.

Clint had told him about his time with Ross one of the evenings they'd sat around the empty firepit, and the days he would get fucked awake. He'd said those were some of his best mornings — already sore and open before he'd had his first coffee.

"What're you doing?" asked Clint, his voice thick with sleep. Scotland let out a sigh filled with relief, teasing over Clint's nipple. He wasn't going to push any limits with Clint when he was asleep, especially if they hadn't negotiated the kink.

"Thinking about fucking you," said Scotland honestly. Clint's cock twitched against his arm, a bit of moisture dragging over his skin. "How would you feel about taking your shirt off for me now?"

Clint rolled slightly, pressing his cock hard into Scotland's arm and thrusting his hips. "You aren't fucking me in here. Derreck would bury me alive if I got cum on his couch. I'm pretty sure he already dug the grave earlier."

Scotland grinned, pulling away to tug his own track pants down. He was already throbbing from watching Clint—hell, he'd been hard since Clint had first sat in his lap that night. Clint hadn't opened his eyes yet, his lashes dark against his cheeks. "Who said anything about *you* coming?"

"Fuck." Clint let out a loud breath before shuffling to pull his shirt over his head. "Are you ever going to let me come?"

"Quiet," said Scotland, lifting himself onto the couch and hovering over Clint. "You're louder than you think. I wouldn't want Maddy to wake up to see his boss getting fucked on the couch."

"Who said I'd *let* you fuck me?" Clint poked him in the middle of the chest.

Scotland froze for a moment, going over every conversation they'd had. Even if he was just playing kinky friend at the moment, Clint hadn't mentioned sex being a limit. A smile stretched over his lips as he realized what Clint was implying.

Oh, so that's how you want to play it? If Clint wanted to push some boundaries, then Scotland was all for it.

Consensual non-consent happened to be one of his biggest turn-ons — and Clint's, it seemed.

"You can't stop me," said Scotland, gripping Clint's hip and squeezing hard. "We both know that I'm the stronger one, and you're the slut." He gave Clint one final soft caress across his belly before he sank into the scene.

It wasn't difficult to let the hardness settle over him, his muscles already tight and hot from thinking about Clint naked beneath him. He didn't have to pretend when it came to the longing and lust, nor the desire to see Clint squirm and whimper.

I want it all.

When Clint tried to sit up, Scotland slapped a hand over his mouth as gently as he could, pressing him back into the couch. With his other hand, he grabbed Clint by the balls, squeezing them tight. Clint let out a muffled whine, trying to close his legs.

"Are you going to be good?" Scotland asked, bringing his lips close to Clint's ear. He cast a glance at the open bedroom door, but there was no sound except soft snores.

Clint nodded, his eyes wide as he sucked heavy breaths through his nose. He seemed just as lost to the scene as Scotland was.

Releasing Clint with both hands, Scotland grabbed for his hips a second time, attempting to flip Clint again. He only got halfway before Clint seemed to come awake, kicking out and wiggling at the same time.

The blow was light, but it still stung where Clint managed to nail him with one knee. He touched the spot on his thigh, gritting his teeth through the muscle spasm.

Scotland hadn't been lying. He was stronger than Clint, even if the margin wasn't all that wide.

Before Clint could react, Scotland reefed him around, pressing his face into the armrest of the couch. As Clint scrambled to get his face out of the soft leather, Scotland grabbed his hips, tugging him to his knees and moving close until his cock slid between Clint's cheeks.

"So easy," he reached a hand back, touching Clint's entrance with a single finger. "All I need is a little slick, and you'll take me right inside." He spit on his fingers, rubbing over Clint's entrance before lining up his cock.

"Fuck no." Clint arched before throwing his weight back and effectively breaking Scotland's hold. The couch creaked from the sudden move, the leather groaning as they struggled.

Scotland had his reflexes to thank for how quickly he was able to recover, slapping a hand over Clint's mouth and pinching his nose at the same time. "Quiet. They'll be able to hear you if you pull that stunt again."

As he released Clint's nose, letting him drag in a few deep breaths, he spit on his other hand again, slicking up his cock. With Clint still distracted, he lined his cock up, pushing inside with relentless pressure.

Clint froze as soon as he was breached, clamping around Scotland like a fucking vise as he let out a loud whimper. Scotland pressed his hand harder against Clint's mouth, muffling his cries.

"You can call for help, but they won't stop me. Maybe Derreck will even want to join. I've heard rumors about his cock, and I've always wondered how true they are."

He lifted his hand from Clint's mouth as he eased forward, giving him the opportunity to speak up if he needed to. They had non-vocal backups just in case, but he'd rather play it safe during an intense scene.

"Fuck." Clint trembled as Scotland was finally inside, his groin pressed hard against Clint's ass. "It hurts. It hurts. Fuck, so good."

I love masochists. They were literally the best—Clint especially.

Scotland wrapped his arm around Clint's neck, dragging him upward so he could seat himself a little deeper. Clint was hot around him and so fucking tight that he knew he wasn't going to last long. He couldn't give in yet, or he would never hear the end of it.

"You can't seem to stay quiet. Let me help you." Scotland took one quick glance toward Maddy and Derreck's bedroom before he surged his hips forward, tensing his arm at the same time to cut Clint's air off.

Clint didn't grab for him or try to pry his arm from his throat. Instead, he reached for Scotland's hips, tugging him closer—deeper.

Rocking as much as he could without making the couch creak, Scotland curled his body around Clint's, trying to find that spot that would blow Clint's mind. From the way he jerked in his arms, he knew exactly when he found it.

He pulled back, slamming deep as hard as he could. The slap of skin rang out in the darkness, loud enough to startle him. But Clint's response was worth it as he jerked, a cry vibrating against Scotland's arm before it was cut off.

He loosened his grip, and Clint drew in a shuddering breath, turning his face as much as he could toward Scotland. His eyes were closed, his lips parted. Headlights flashed at the window, lighting up the tears on Clint's cheeks.

"I'm going to come," said Clint, his voice absolutely wrecked. His whole body was shaking, his lower lip trembling.

So fucking good. Scotland changed his grip so he was holding Clint by the hair, drawing his body away so his cock slid into cool air. Grabbing the nearest discarded piece of clothing, he wiped his cock off, hesitating as he throbbed fiercely.

There really was no reason that he couldn't come himself.

"Come here." Scotland leaned against the back of the couch, guiding Clint's head between his legs. When his lips brushed against his cock, he let out a harsh hiss. "Safeword now if you need to." He could totally understand someone safewording in this kind of situation, especially Clint, who seemed to have a touch of germaphobia.

He groaned when Clint stayed silent. Tugging Clint onto his cock and pushing his head down until his cock bumped against the back of Clint's throat, he let out a soft sigh.

There was nothing like getting good head, and even if he was out of practice, Clint was *good.*

He held him there, even as he let out a gag that wasn't exactly quiet. The bedroom was still silent, Maddy and Derreck hopefully still sleeping on the other side of the wall. The noise was part of the thrill — the risk of getting caught thrumming through him.

He knew Clint loved it as much as he did.

"I thought I saw the doorknob turn," said Scotland, forcing Clint to take him deeper, even as he tried to tug away. "Can you imagine Maddy's face if he walked in here to see your ass gaping as you choked on my cock? He would know exactly how hard you like it — his high and mighty boss who never lets anyone step out of line, getting fucked raw with no lube."

Clint whimpered, taking Scotland into his throat until his nose pressed against Scotland's groin. He was so tight, the suction like none other even as drool pooled on Scotland's cock.

"Trick told me what you said to him—how dangerous it was to fuck someone without lube. Not to mention breath play… I wish he could see you now and see how fucking good you take it."

Scotland eased Clint back, making sure he caught his breath before he took him again. There were so many things that people said in the club that could make a newbie uncomfortable. Scotland liked soaking it all up, usually keeping it to himself.

"What about Maxim and Nikita?" asked Scotland, reaching to flick on a lamp light so he could watch the tears roll down Clint's cheeks. He flinched in the sudden light, but it was perfect. Clint was absolutely wrecked, his eyes red along with the tip of his nose with his lips stretched wide around Scotland's cock.

He didn't look like he was quite there as he relaxed, allowing Scotland to take what he wanted. *Let go, love.*

"I heard you gave them a lecture on gun safety." Scotland bit the inside of his cheek as Clint sucked him hard. "I wonder if they would have listened if they saw how good of a cocksucker you are. They probably would have just been imagining something between your pretty lips."

Clint slapped the couch, fresh tears falling. Scotland jerked him free, leaning in to kiss his forehead. "You need a break?"

"Don't talk about them like that," said Clint, his voice thick with tears and the achy remnants of Scotland's cock.

"Is that a safeword?" asked Scotland, stroking Clint's cheek.

Clint looked away, lowering his gaze to the ground before he shook his head.

Some truths were harder to hear than others. Clint was loving it if his cock was anything to go by. The head was nearly purple, pre-cum dripping down the shaft.

"You okay to continue?" Scotland tested the waters a second time, a bit of uncertainty seeping in. He'd fucked up before, and he didn't want to do it again. At Clint's nod, he kissed his forehead before putting Clint's mouth back where it belonged.

"I heard Henley used to hit on you," he groaned as Clint choked once before settling. "It sounds like he was a badass, and he was drooling for you. He must've known how good you are with your mouth. Isthmus and Rowes certainly know how pretty your cock is now. You couldn't wait to show it off to them."

He must've struck a chord, because Clint put his hands on Scotland's knees, digging his nails in. It wasn't a safeword, but maybe it was supposed to be a warning.

When do I ever listen to warnings? If Scotland hadn't fucked up so many times, he wouldn't be here living out one of his greatest fantasies.

"You helped every single one of them," said Scotland, his leg jerking as he grew closer. "I knew it as soon as I saw you. 'There's a guy who helps people and likes to get fucked.' You kept acting shy, like you didn't know what a cock was, never thinking of yourself."

He thrust deep one last time, holding Clint tight so he couldn't escape. "They love you—every single one of us. Maddy and Derreck, Trick and Nav, Copley and the twins—none of them would be together if not for you. You're the best man I know."

He came as Clint let out a choked-off sob, tears streaming down his cheeks as he locked his watery gaze with Scotland's. His grip was painful on Scotland's knees, but his fight was gone. Clint went limp, swallowing every bit of cum as Scotland watched subspace take him like a rising storm.

"So fucking good."

He wasn't letting Clint sleep alone on the couch tonight or any other night. Clint was his.

Chapter Seventeen

Clint

Clint shifted his grip on the ax, raising it up to near eye level as he zeroed in on the thick wooden log. It weighed more than he expected, despite Scotland calling it soft wood. And the ax was hefty, on top of that. Apparently, the wood hadn't dried out yet, which made it heavier, whatever the hell that meant.

"Not like that," said Scotland, looping behind him to adjust his hand placement and stance. "You look like you're trying to bash someone's skull in with a baseball bat. You'll end up hacking into your leg with that approach."

Clint shifted his feet wider, flexing his hands until his hold was steady again. He'd been a shaky mess for days, especially when Scotland got as close as he was now. The warmth of his skin made Clint want to close his eyes and lose himself to the mad calmness that he'd floated on for hours at Maddy's. He'd still been in a daze the next morning when Scotland had said their early morning goodbyes and had driven them back to the farm. Maddy had given him a knowing look and a smile.

Sun filtered through the trees to the small stretch of lawn where Clint had piled the few logs he'd wanted to chop that morning. He'd ignored most of Scotland's advice so far, letting his battiness reign. It was the only thing keeping him from slipping.

"Let it fly, boss." Scotland took a step back, and Clint had to correct himself so he didn't topple over. He just needed something to occupy his mind, and tossing a heavy and sharp object around had seemed to fit the bill.

He hadn't been ready for lessons on how to chop wood when he'd first jerked the ax out of the stump, but Scotland was like that. Now he was hovering close by, his coffee abandoned but still steaming in the cool air.

Taking aim, Clint swung the ax down, letting its own weight carry it through the move. It struck the log with a sharp thud before bouncing off to the side, nearly making him stumble from the unexpected reaction. His hands immediately ached, the vibrations making his fingers go numb.

"What the hell?" The top of the log was completely flat, other than a narrow dent from the tip of the blade, barely noticeable between the rings of the log. A blister was probably already working its way under his skin, leaving him more marked than the wood.

"Close," said Scotland, reaching around and placing his hand on Clint's chest. He pulled until Clint stood straighter, his shoulders farther back than they would normally be. "Just at the last second you tilted a bit, so the ax skimmed off. Stand as straight as you can and bring it right down in the middle.

"This has to be some kind of trick wood," said Clint, skimming his finger over the edge of the blade. He hissed, drawing his finger back as it cut into his skin.

Scotland chuckled, bracing his hand on Clint's belly as he moved closer. Dipping his hand under the edge of Clint's shirt, he laid his palm flat out, his finger stretching over the skin there.

Clint shuddered, closing his eyes as his legs started to tremble. It felt so good to be touched again with soft hands and so little expectation. Part of him wanted to shrink away, knowing that Scotland was touching the scars that marred him, while the other part screamed at him to be proud of them. It was hard to be proud of something that had flooded him with guilt for years.

He was still guilty. Every time he closed his eyes, he saw Ross' face and the way he used to twitch his eyebrows when he didn't approve. But it was getting easier to shake that off and remember the smiles and the soft moments when there had only been happiness.

He was happy *now* with Scotland's hands and his touch.

"It's not a trick," said Scotland, his breath whispering over Clint's ear. There was something hard pressing against Clint's ass that did not feel like a belt buckle or a jackknife. "Try again, and tighten your core on the down swing. You can't just let it fall. You have to put some effort into it."

"Effort?" Both of his wrists were killing him, and he was pretty sure he'd fucked up a muscle in his shoulder. "Stand back. I don't want you to get splintered." Clint shrugged Scotland off, grinning as he forced him away with one finger to his chest. "I'm going to hit this wood so hard that it can't help but split in half. I've got a great up-and-down game, but I'm a bit out of practice."

"Just don't—"

"If you say chop your leg off, we are going to have problems." Clint sucked in a breath, squinting at the log that was leaning just a bit to the left. Tucking his tongue into his cheek, he hauled the ax over his head, bringing it down with every bit of force he could muster.

With a crack, the ax sank into the log, stuttering to a halt just past the blade as it caught on something within the wood. The handle quivered in Clint's hands, his body off balance as he went from sixty to zero in an instant.

"Fuck." Clint stumbled to the side, sinking against Scotland as his shoulder throbbed. Even his toes ached from the swing, but the wood was still in one piece. "That's just not fair." He glared at the block, gritting his teeth. He hadn't even sheared off a splinter. "Not trick wood, my ass."

Scotland chuckled, a sound that was both soothing and infuriating. His wandering hands were slightly less exasperating, especially when he tucked one in Clint's back pocket, cupping his ass through his jeans.

He'd officially run out of track pants to wear, so he'd jammed his ass into proper jeans that morning. It had nothing to do with trying to impress Scotland, even if it had worked.

"Let me try, baby." Scotland kissed his neck, palming Clint's pec and scraping a nail over his nipple. "I told you it's hard." He rocked his hips.

The wood wasn't the only thing that was hard. From the feel of it, Scotland had a bit more than Clint's own semi. With the sun beating down on them, and the fresh breeze, it was almost as indecent as when Clint had been naked in Scotland's kitchen.

"Let's make it a bet," said Clint, grinning as he passed the ax over. There was no way he was losing. There had to be rebar embedded into the log or something. "You split it in one go, and I'll grant you one wish — genie-style."

"And if I can't?" asked Scotland, not looking phased as he adjusted his grip on the handle before edging his feet apart.

"Then you grant me one wish — BDSM style." Clint winked. He had a lot of wishes stored up from over the years. That's what happened when he got to watch but not touch for so many scenes.

"Should I be worried?" Scotland raised one brow, flexing his hands on the grip. The ax looked small in his hands, especially when he tensed. The log looked like it didn't stand much of a chance, either.

There's no way he's winning. Clint rolled his shoulders, trying to relieve the strain. His hands were still numb and tingly, the palms a darker pink than usual.

"So many options." He tapped his chin before strolling to the nearest tree. It was some kind of maple, with low sweeping branches that were just out of reach. "I haven't practiced my Shibari skills in a while, but this here looks like the perfect set up."

Scotland's eyes went dark as he dragged his gaze over the trunk and branches.

"Or we could do a little role play," said Clint, leaning against the bark. "Oh, please help me, Mr. Lumberjack, only you don't come to *help*." A shudder worked its way up his spine.

"I could go for a little CNC anytime," said Scotland.

Yeah, because consensual non-consent is the best. But that felt like a little bit too much of a win for Scotland. *I've gotta think darker.* "Or I get to tattoo my name on your side, right where it will hurt the most."

Clint swallowed thickly at his own idea. That shit was permanent, but fuck if that didn't make him hard. "I'm not talking the fake tattoos you did on me...or henna. Something permanent and big, right over your ribs where it will sting like hell."

Scotland let out a breath, looking a tad unsure for the first time. "I knew you were a sadist, but shit."

Maybe that is taking it a bit too far. "Okay, fair enough." Clint scratched the back of his head. He probably shouldn't be branding someone unless he was prepared for a full-time relationship with them. "A public scene of my choice — very public."

Scotland quirked his lips, hefting the ax over his head. "Deal." He brought it down, his arms bulging as he met the edge of the wood. Instead of stalling, it kept going, slicing through the pale surface as if it were mere tissue paper. From the force of the blow, the wood splintered, flying in different directions with one nearly striking Clint in the foot.

Clint glared at the piece of wood, the size of it much too small to be half. Scotland grinned as he gathered the pieces, holding up three nearly identical bits. "Look — a bonus." He waved the third piece in his hand. "Does that mean I get two wishes, genie?"

Grumbling under his breath, Clint grabbed the piece that had flown the closest to his leg. *This isn't possible.* He'd watched enough videos of lumberjack men to know that it was, but it still pissed him off.

He nodded, begrudgingly handing it over to Scotland when he loomed close enough. Instead of grabbing it, Scotland bypassed his outstretched hand, pinning Clint to the tree. The rough bark scraped against his back, probably cutting into his shirt and his skin.

Scotland leaned in, tracing his lips over Clint's ear. His breath was shallow, his cock burning through the front of his pants as it met Clint's. "Thanks for all the ideas, Genie. I'll make sure to surprise you."

Chapter Eighteen

Clint

Why did I give him all those ideas?

They'd been driving for nearly thirty minutes, the countryside well behind them until they were smack-dab in the middle of the city with office and antique buildings alike staring at them from all sides.

"This brings back some memories," said Clint, gazing longingly at a passing street. "I can't count how many times I've been down this street." He pointed at the corner of an old crumbling building. Inside, was one of the best-kept secrets in the city. "I stopped at that bakery almost every morning when I slept at home. They have the best pretzels known to man. Dip that in their specialty whipped cream cheese and yum."

He licked his lips, his mouth watering at the memory of the taste.

"We can stop and get some," said Scotland, already turning on his signal to pull over to the side of the road.

Clint shook his head. "On the way home. I'm not sure if I can eat right now." It was a fancy way of saying he was nervous as all hell. He was back in kinky action, but the ball was solidly in Scotland's court.

Scotland shifted his grip on the wheel, checking his blind spot before merging back into traffic. "You know you don't have to be worried. You still have your safewords and all the power here."

Clint scoffed. "*Please.* Me? Worried? There isn't a kink out there that I haven't tried."

How many times had he said that lately? Sure, he had a tally that he'd subconsciously kept, but most of that had been with one man. Scotland was nothing like Ross.

"You can't love them all," said Scotland, sending him a soft smile. "And if you did, I'd be worried."

"I didn't say I loved them all." There were a few he decidedly hated…like needle play, which just brought back memories of his nursing days with grown men screaming at him when it took more than two seconds to find a vein for a blood draw. *No thank you.*

"I'm nervous, I guess…excited. I haven't been excited like this for a long time." Clint looked out of the window in time to catch sight of an adult store on a street corner. The place didn't look like much, but it was another gem. And it probably would have gone out of business without Unkinked's support. He still made sure to order his weekly supplies from them.

"So, what are we doing?" asked Clint, bouncing his leg up and down as Scotland turned down another street. "Streaking? Oh, a little romp in the park? Or maybe some action in a movie theater?"

Streaking was probably in his top ten, but he had to do it somewhere safe and controlled like the club where he wasn't going to accidentally stumble upon someone underage.

"Nope."

He slumped his shoulders before scratching at the inside of his wrist. "Are you going to tell me?"

Secrets were fun, but the way Scotland did them always seemed to give him a heart attack. He was never going to forget how unprepared he had been to see Izzy and Rowes like that.

"We're going to a gym. I have a membership at one of the bigger places in town here. They've got a boxing ring that I thought you might want to try out." Scotland sent him a smirk. "You can't believe that I got these arms just from chopping wood."

Scotland flexed, and Clint had to fight to keep from drooling. That may have been exactly what he'd thought. He'd spent far too much time picturing Scotland chopping wood with no shirt on, his tattoos rippling with each strike. He'd even considered starting a fire on his own just to see Scotland rush over and split some extra logs.

"Is it kinky boxing?" That was a great idea. *Maddy would love it.* Even better would be boxing while covered in lube and armed with a few toys. The first one to get stuffed would lose. "Hold that thought. I have to send Maddy a text."

He dug out his phone, powering it up. He ignored the few notifications before sending the idea off to Maddy and powering it down again.

* * * *

The place was fancy as all hell, with more machines than Clint could easily count and mirrors on every wall.

It was packed with people in way better shape than him and a few others he could see himself bonding with. Anyone who wanted to better themselves with exercise was someone worth talking to.

He glanced at his belly, which wasn't as flat as it had once been. He still made sure to keep in shape, but there were only so many hours in a day. Not having the bar anymore had helped. Even a single beer per night could pack on the calories, which he certainly didn't burn while bent over paperwork.

"This place makes my dumbbells and yoga mat look very softcore." He watched a few videos online every once in a while, following along to keep himself limber. And on quiet days at the club, he set an hour or two aside for lifting. It had been a lot easier lately with Maddy looking after things.

"This is nothing," said Scotland, raising one brow. We're headed to the basement. Once we're down there, you call me 'Sir'."

Clint swallowed, his throat clicking as a bolt of heat went straight through him. How did Scotland always seem to know what he wanted three steps ahead of Clint himself? Public scenes were his absolute favorite. There was something so dirty about being himself in public, with others none the wiser. There was also a thin line that couldn't be crossed.

Scotland will know that, right?

Clint tucked himself one pace behind Scotland, falling into his submission with a sigh. It was getting easier to go there, with his mind quiet and his thoughts focused on Scotland. There was no need to worry about himself or how he looked. Scotland would let him know if there was an issue.

He still couldn't believe he actually trusted the guy. Scotland had pestered him for so long, and Clint had kept that wall built high with the sturdiest bricks available. *Bricks erode, too.*

After stepping through the doors of an unexpected elevator, Clint leaned against the wall, eyeing up the array of buttons. Scotland swiped a card through a slot before pressing the button marked only as 'B'.

"How big is this place?" It appeared to be maybe three floors from the outside, but there were a hell of a lot more than three buttons.

"I've met a lot of different people on my table," said Scotland, skimming his hand over one of his tattoos. Had he done the art himself? Or had someone else carved the marks into his skin? Clint's hands twitched as he tried to rid himself of the image of someone else's hands piercing Scotland's flesh.

"Jealous?" said Scotland, quirking his lips. "My needle gave a woman an orgasm once. I was doing a small piece on her inner thigh and *bam.*"

Clint narrowed his eyes before crossing his arms. "Definitely not jealous, Sir. I love watching women, but I don't want to make one come. I think we're in the same boat on that front. Besides, if you would have tattooed *my* thigh, I would have come, too. All the cock rings in the world wouldn't have stopped me."

Of that, he was absolutely certain.

The after-effects of the invisible tattoo he'd received had been slightly less pleasant. He'd itched up a storm for a few days, and there was a small red area left behind that was dry and scabby. If he hadn't been looking for it, he wouldn't have noticed it.

Scotland's hands were on him in a moment, one wrapped around his throat as he pressed Clint into the wall, and the other at his chest. The elevator dinged as it slid to a halt, the doors sliding wide to reveal a dark room. Clint couldn't budge an inch with Scotland pinning him, the weight of his body like a drug.

"I would put a needle on you again in a heartbeat," said Scotland, dragging his lips over Clint's ear. "But first I would light a candle, and hold it close enough that you could feel the heat of it, dripping wax on your skin until you would be blushed bright red. I'd have so much fun scraping the wax from your skin, bringing the flame closer and closer until all you could do was feel the burn. After you started whimpering, I would put a needle on that same spot. You'd scream for me."

His throat clicked as Clint swallowed, his cock instantly hard in the track pants that Scotland had insisted he wear. The doors creaked, sliding shut and locking them tight in a small room with only their breaths.

"Please, Sir." Clint wasn't sure how much longer he could take it. It had been days of edging, and even more before that when Scotland had taunted him, following him around the club until he'd haunted Clint's dreams.

Scotland shrugged, pulling away all at once and pressing the button to open the doors again. He held his hand over the gap so they didn't slide shut, looking over his shoulder, as if he were confused that Clint hadn't moved. He didn't seem to notice the flush on Clint's cheeks or the way his cock was attempting to poke its way right through his pants.

"You coming?" asked Scotland, his voice way too loud in the small space.

Clint gritted his teeth, doing his best to tuck his cock so he didn't get it caught in something at the gym. "I fucking hope so, Sir."

Chapter Nineteen

Scotland

How could a forty-something-year-old man be so incredibly cute? Clint's blush hadn't faded since they'd stepped off the elevator, his eyes wide and his thoughts hopefully calm.

From the upstairs, no one expected what was in the basement. Hell, Scotland hadn't expected it that first time, either. It was a high-end establishment with a bit of a front. *No judgment here.*

The smell of sweat was thick, despite the air circulation, the sound of fists hitting padding and flesh like an unstoppable rhythm. There were few actual fighters who trained in the two rings or on the bags, but there were many others who had no business being in a legitimate establishment.

"Maxim," said Scotland, reclining his head at the enforcer who almost had more tattoos than he did. Scotland had done a few of them himself, including the manacles that wrapped around Maxim's identical twin brother's wrists. That had been well before he'd been part of Unkinked's community.

Maxim inclined his head before nodding at Clint. Clint returned the gesture, not looking nearly as nervous as he should have. Maxim was a wild card who had only seemed to calm once he'd found his sub, Copley. He was still a dangerous sonovabitch.

"Haven't seen you in here in a while," said Maxim, grabbing his towel that he'd left on the bench before slinging it over the back of his neck. He was shirtless and dripping with sweat, his chest heaving.

"I've had a guest."

"Hey, Maxim," said Clint, circling around Scotland before touching the bag that was still swaying a bit from Maxim's hits. "Good seeing you again. Are you taking care of Nikita for me?"

Maxim scoffed, wiping his face with the towel and tossing it to the side. "Copley takes care of him for me. Domestic bliss, baby." His grin was enough to put Scotland on edge. He wasn't exactly sure how a sweet guy like Copley managed to handle both of them.

"It's good to see another kinky fucker here, though," said Clint, pushing the punching bag. It wobbled with a clank of chains as Clint grunted, throwing his shoulder into it. "This thing is way heavier than I thought."

Scotland covered his mouth with the back of his hand as Maxim raised one brow at Clint's display.

"This isn't some kinky gym," said Maxim, stalling the punching bag with one hand.

"He's right." Scotland reached out, dragging a finger down Clint's spine. He was already sweating, his shirt clinging to his back. "Besides Maxim and me, I'm pretty sure everyone on this level is straight and vanilla."

"Then why did you bring me here?" asked Clint, panting as he tried to land a hit on the bag. When he failed to move it much, he put his shoulder to it again, seeming to attempt to pull it from Maxim's grip. His voice was playful, as he let out a soft little growl, but Maxim looked anything but amused.

Waiting three beats, Scotland turned away, before settling with his back against the nearest wall. Shit wasn't mirrored on this floor. Nobody wanted to see their own face bloody after a round in the practice ring.

"Sorry. *Sir*." Clint looked over his shoulder, biting his lower lip.

Maxim's eyebrows shot up, his mouth wide as he lost his grip on the bag. He dropped his gaze to Clint, furrowing his forehead a moment later. "Never took you for a sub."

Clint cleared his throat, dropping his hands to his sides as he took a shuffled step back. There was a tension in his jaw that hadn't been there a moment before, his biceps flexing for no apparent reason.

"We're switches," said Scotland, speaking up before Clint could say a word. He could sympathize with how Clint felt. He hadn't expected judgment from a fellow kinkster.

If anything, Maxim looked even more confused. "What the hell is a switch?"

It was Scotland's turn to be surprised. Maxim gave him the impression that he'd been around the block a time or two, but he looked genuinely confused.

"Someone who is both a Dom and sub," said Clint, a professional mask slipping over his face. "If a person enjoys both roles or needs them, then they can often switch back and forth. Sometimes it depends on their partner or just the situation."

Depends on their partner? Scotland swallowed, looking at the laces on his running shoes. He'd been in the Dominant role the entire time with Clint, and he'd hardly noticed. But submission was something he needed, too. Hopefully, that was something Clint realized. He couldn't be in the lead all the time.

"Oh," said Maxim, scratching at his chin. "Niki needs to explain some of this shit to me. Doesn't matter, though. Nothing kinky in this gym — you got it? I vouched for Scotland 'cause he's a cool guy. I don't want to have to rescind his membership."

Maxim cracked his knuckles, looking far too intimidating.

A nervous chill raced through Scotland's body. "No problem. But it's not my fault if he gets turned on by a little pounding." Scotland shrugged, the lie rolling off his tongue like molasses. A little fib never hurt anyone, and he was pretty sure Maxim was just talking out of his ass. He'd spent a good twenty minutes on the phone already with Maxim to set up this scene, so he wasn't worried.

"Fair enough," said Maxim. "Copley can come just from a little spanking, so I get it. Are you here to work out, then? I can help you get your hands wrapped."

"Thanks, man, but I've got it."

Scotland led Clint to the far end of the basement, passing about a dozen guys he knew. He paused at each one, starting up a conversation until Clint was shifting from foot to foot, flicking his gaze around the room. With every one, he introduced Clint as a friend, and Clint narrowed his eyes.

After grabbing some wrapping material, he sat Clint on one of the benches, grasping his hand as he started to bandage his knuckles.

"Friends," said Clint, spitting out the word like it tasted foul. "This is why I stick with kinky shit. I feel like I'm back in the closet." He jerked his hand as Scotland made another round.

"You're sexy when you pout," said Scotland, finishing off one of Clint's hands and starting on the second. "You can't go everywhere in life strutting your kink and expecting to be accepted."

"Yes, you can." Clint drew his hand back, placing it on Scotland's chest to stop him. "There isn't anywhere in the world where you shouldn't be able to be yourself, and nobody is so much better than you that they can't accept you for exactly who you are. I gave up hiding a long-ass time ago, and I have no plans to go down that road again."

Scotland swallowed before glancing away. Maybe he'd been wrong to bring Clint here. But maybe Clint was right. He hadn't realized it, but there were places where he hid himself.

"Not everybody has Unkinked all the time, Clint. This is the real world."

"You know what?" Clint pushed himself off the bench, crossing his arms over his chest. "Fuck you." He turned toward the rest of the gym, raising his voice. "Hey, assholes, guess what? I'm gay as hell, and I like BDSM. I'm not talking a little wax play, but full-on fuck me against the wall and choke me out, 'cause that's what makes me come the hardest. This asshole here" — he jabbed a finger in Scotland's direction — "is too afraid to get it on outside the house. Hell, he hasn't been able to make me come in weeks."

The sound of fists never ceased, but a few people glanced over to Maxim before they returned to their workout. Most of them probably had earbuds in, except for the two in the closest ring who had definitely heard and cared about Clint just as much as they did about getting an inevitable concussion.

"What did I say about making trouble?" called Maxim, stretching out a leg muscle as he glanced their way. "No fucking in the gym. Looking's free."

"I'm not making trouble." Clint dropped his gaze before kicking at the edge of a mat. "I'm just doing a warmup. You know — letting all the frustration out."

"Or, you think you can get your way by putting on a big pout," said Scotland. "I don't have a problem with being kinky, Clint, but these are my friends, and they didn't consent to a scene in the middle of the mats."

Clint bit his lip at that, his face flushing. "I may have gotten a bit carried away, Sir." He didn't look that apologetic. "But you can't stop me from making dick jokes."

"Go ahead." Scotland shrugged, trying to squash the unease that remained. He was out and proud and didn't give a crap what people thought of him. But there was a time and a place to be a brat, and this was not it.

I'll just have to make that clear.

"Now let me finish wrapping your hands so we can get to that pounding we talked about."

* * * *

He may have underestimated Clint a bit.

Maybe more than a little.

Scotland's arm was currently pinned behind his back with Clint sitting on his ass and wiggling around like he was trying to hold on to a wild stallion. Scotland's shoulder protested with each movement, but he was not tapping out.

"That's fucking cheating," Scotland ground out, trying and failing to get his arm free. Something in his back popped, making him go numb for a split second. Clint only writhed more, grinding his cock into Scotland's ass. It probably seemed dirty as all hell to any onlookers, of which they had a few.

"Were you not ready, Sir? I'm sorry." Clint cackled, shifting his grip on Scotland's arm. He was strong as hell, with a grip that seemed unbreakable. "But now that you're a little stuck and I'm a bit hard, let me tell another joke."

It was the joke that had caught him off guard in the first place. Scotland had laughed, letting his fists sag for just a moment, and Clint had been on him with surprising agility and strength.

Sweat dripped into his eyes, momentarily blinding him as his chest was pushed harder into the padded floor of the ring. Scotland groaned as his shoulder ached from the angle. *I'm not tapping out.*

"What's the difference between a cock and a hundred bucks?" asked Clint, dragging his hips and grinding his semi into Scotland's ass. He let out a laugh, the sound bouncing off the walls as someone let out a whoop.

Is that Maxim? Ah, what the hell. "I dunno." Scotland gritted his teeth, scraping the nails of his free hand against the mat.

"Someone is always down to blow a hundred bucks." Clint cackled, even as Scotland bucked, finally sending Clint tumbling to the side. He was on his feet as fast as he could, dragging his arm across his forehead to wipe some of the sweat out of his eyes. By the time he recovered, Clint was sitting on his ass, his lips split in a wide grin as he leaned against the ropes.

"I've got a better one," said Clint, holding out his glove and fist bumping the closest onlooker. It was Felix, which just wasn't fair. He'd always been the sweetheart at the gym, helping everyone else work out, even if it meant neglecting his own routine. His eyes were glowing with mirth.

Things were definitely going differently than he'd imagined.

"A cock is a lot like life...hard all the time for no reason at all," said Clint.

Fuck, he looked good when he smiled, with his cheeks flushed from exertion. It was hard not to think about pinning him and jerking his loose track pants off right in the middle of the ring.

Keep in control. He took a slow breath, but it didn't stop his own chuckle that rose in his throat.

Maxim threw his head back in a laugh, leaning against the ropes. "I changed my mind about you, Clint. You can bring all your kinky friends down here anytime. Maybe you can convince Niki to get his ass here more often. He's packed on a few pounds with Copley's cooking."

That sounded nice—not only the kinksters in the gym, but also the part about gaining a few pounds from cooking. In his case, Scotland had been overindulging since Clint had arrived. That's what happened when he tried to seduce someone through their stomach.

"One more round," said Clint, taking Scotland's offered hand and getting back on his feet. "No headshots. Concussions can cause severe and lasting neuro damage."

Yeah. That was the third time Clint had said that. "I'm not gonna punch you, Clint. I'm just letting you win to gain your confidence and get you ready for what comes next."

"Oh." Clint wiggled his eyebrows. "I like the sound of that."

Too bad it was mostly a lie. Clint had definitely won the last round fair and square.

"Show me what you got," said Scotland, raising his fists to just below eye level. Clint did the same, hunching his shoulders in an automatic move that made him look like a natural-born fighter.

Moving first, Scotland feinted left, only to swing his right arm out, landing a blow on Clint's forearm. The wrap and gloves took most of the hit, but Clint would probably have a bruise later. *I'll kiss it better.*

Clint hissed, taking a step away only to dive right back in, his shoulder low as he collided with Scotland's gut. The move sent Scotland right into the ropes as the air was driven from his lungs. Scotland stumbled, reaching for the rope to right himself as Clint withdrew.

"You can fight," said Scotland, still not quite sure he could believe it. The Clint that he'd been wanting all this time spent his days giving people advice and mixing drinks, not taking down people in the ring. *What the hell?* He couldn't even chop wood, for Christ's sake.

"I can *brawl*," said Clint, shrugging before he raised his hands in an imitation of Scotland's pose after he peeled himself off the ropes. "Why do you think there is hardly ever anyone stirring up shit at the club?"

"Yeah, but..." He distinctly remembered seeing Clint wield a baseball bat once, but he hadn't thought much of it. There were props all over the club, but he couldn't imagine Clint hitting anyone if the opportunity arose.

Then again, he seemed to have no issue hitting Scotland.

Clint smashed into him again at high speed, his arms open in a tackle as Scotland tried to recover. *Maybe we should have worn mouthguards?* Scotland's head struck the mats as Clint's weight hit him, the remaining air in his lungs whooshing out.

Don't give up. He twisted, taking Clint by surprise and catching his arm in a grip strong enough to throw him off. He doubted the move would work a second time from the way Clint sent him a feral grin as soon as he stopped rolling.

"You gonna stop playing around?" asked Clint, wiping a bit of spit from his lips. "Or is that really all you've got."

"Don't say I didn't warn you, little subby," said Scotland, hauling himself back onto his feet. Mustering up every bit of courage, Scotland stalked ahead, raising up his arm as if to strike as soon as he closed the distance between them. Clint landed a punch of his own—a light tap on Scotland's shoulder that barely zinged off his muscle.

Clint must've meant to hit hard, though. His eyes went wide as he stumbled, his weight off balance as he shuffled his feet. If Scotland hadn't been training at the gym for a while he wouldn't have noticed the opening it created for the brief flash of a second.

Scotland swept out his legs, catching both of Clint's ankles and sending him tumbling. He hit ass first, letting out a soft gasp as he fell back, sprawling across the mats with his arms thrown wide.

It had never been so good to pounce. Scotland pinned Clint's wrists above his head hauling them straight and high so Clint could barely struggle. When Clint tried to move, he straddled his hips, settling his full weight on Clint. Scotland felt his own arms bulge as he leaned in, refusing to let Clint move or escape.

The corner of Clint's shirt rode up as he squirmed, their groins coming precariously close. The trail of blond hair on his belly was dark with sweat, his skin slippery with it. Scotland could almost taste it on his tongue, and on his breath, every sense filled to the brim with Clint.

"Got you," said Scotland, unable to stop himself from leaning in and licking a stripe along Clint's neck. He was salt and sweetness and every other good thing that Scotland knew. When he closed his eyes he could smell the hit of his own laundry detergent and soap. *Home.*

"It was a lucky shot," said Clint, his struggles going weak as he let out a soft moan. "Let me up, and I'll show you."

Scotland shook his head, taking a deep breath. "I don't think so. I like you like this—so vulnerable and soft."

"You two need a minute?"

Scotland drew back at Maxim's voice, flushing as he realized that he had been seconds away from making out with Clint like teenagers in the middle of the gym. Most of their audience had already taken off, although Garry was looking pretty darn invested in the outcome.

"We'll hit the showers," said Scotland, releasing Clint and offering him a hand as he rose to his feet. "I think there were a few guys done for the day, so we'll keep it clean."

Clint's face was just as flushed as his own felt, his lower lip between his teeth as he stared at the ceiling, with his chest rising and falling fast. Scotland was going to fucking *ruin* him.

"Go ahead, baby. I'll just have to ask Maxim about the schedule, then I'll join you." Scotland leaned down to drag his thumb over Clint's lips, giving him the only kiss he could at the moment.

"Okay, Sir." Clint staggered a bit as he rose to his feet, his gaze bleary and lost when he stumbled through a door clearly labeled 'showers'.

"Can you keep everyone out of there for the next hour or so?" asked Scotland, giving Maxim a pointed look. "I'll owe you a favor."

Maxim cracked a smile, throwing an arm around him as Scotland ducked out of the ring. "An hour? You're spoiling him." He glanced at the closed door. "I've been thinking of a tattoo for Copley. You do that for us, and I'll keep everyone out of there for the rest of the day."

Scotland grinned, doing nothing to hide his semi. It was pointless. Besides, it happened all the time during workouts. Once the blood was flowing, the rest was a write-off.

"But what's the schedule you're talking about? I don't know shit about that," said Maxim, withdrawing his arm and wiping it with a towel. *Okay, so, I'm a little sweaty.*

"Nothing, man," said Scotland. "I just didn't want Clint to know the coast is clear. He's gonna think someone is going to walk in on us at any time. Nothing like a bit of risk to spice things up. And hey, Maxim, one more thing…"

Chapter Twenty

Clint

Oh God. Clint shuddered, leaning his back against the nearest locker and sliding slowly to the ground. He'd never been so turned on in his life. Sore muscles and aching knees just added to the warmth in his gut and the thrumming through his veins. *So good.*

He couldn't wait to get Scotland back to the farm and push him against the nearest surface. He didn't care if he was the one getting fucked or if it was his turn to rail Scotland's ass, but he was coming. There was no cock ring in the world that was going to stop him.

Dragging himself to his feet, he stumbled across the locker area around the corner where he presumed the showers would be. There were three of them, made up of nothing more than a tiled strip with drains carved into the floor and three spouts protruding from above.

With no walls or even curtains, it was like a dream. Even if he had to keep his hands to himself, he was certainly letting his gaze stray. Scotland had an amazing physique, but it would only be better soaking wet and with a bit of soap spiraling down his leg to the drain below.

Fuck, keeping it clean. Clint reached for himself, pressing the heel of his hand to his groin to try to ease the ache. Anticipation would only make it better. Plus, he could plan a surprise for Scotland and pounce on him as soon as they got to the lane at the farm. Clint could easily maneuver over the center console, straddle Scotland's cock right there and let the bounce of the first pothole grind their cocks together.

He shucked off his track pants and T-shirt, tossing them on a bench outside the tiled area before toeing his shoes off and stepping into the shower. The first jet of water that hit him was freezing cold, pushing a gasp through his lips. It was probably for the best. Anything warm on him right now might just make him come.

His teeth chattered as the stream warmed to something much more reasonable, the water stripping the sweat from his skin as steam started to rise. He ducked his head under the water, turning toward the wall as he caught the sound of the shower room door opening and closing.

It wasn't that he had any modesty to speak of — quite the opposite, really — but the worst of his scars were on his front. His back was still marked extensively, the skin shiny and tight, even beneath the warmth, but people were much less likely to ask him about them if he was looking away.

Facing them, he could see the pity in their eyes — the sadness. *"That must have hurt so much."* Or, his personal favorite, *"You poor thing."*

That was one thing about kinksters. They all had scars — some more visible than others. It was rare to see someone without a mark from a past scene or even a bit of red skin on their ass or bruises on their knees from kneeling. Some, like Shelvin and Elliot, had their scars buried well beneath their skin, but they were still there. Clint could see them in the way Elliot would flinch from the sound of a belt or the way Shelvin had fainted from lack of food.

He flinched when he felt warm hands on his shoulders, pulling him from his thoughts.

"If your name isn't Scotland, be prepared to have your ass kicked," said Clint, shivering as those hands went from his shoulders to his wrists, pinning him in the same way he'd been in the ring. A cock pushed against his ass at the same time he was shoved into the tiled wall, his cheek pressing against the limescale-covered squares.

Closing his eyes against the water spray, he sucked a breath through his mouth, choking on a bit of water that managed to seep through his lips. The hands never let up, not even as the person ground against him, their cock coming dangerously close to penetrating him.

"Water doesn't make good lube," Clint choked out, turning his face into the tile so he could breathe better. Lips against his neck were his only answer, then teeth dragging over his skin. The grip on his wrists tightened, two hands becoming one and holding him with utmost strength.

"I thought you said we had to keep things from getting dirty," said Clint, flinching as that cock breached him the barest amount. It fucking stung, dragging against him in a way that he absolutely loved and hated at the same time. He was persistent, too, returning with even pressure as he tried to squirm away.

"Scotland?"

Teeth snagged his ear, dragging the same spot that he'd pieced years ago. He rarely wore piercings anymore, but the skin was still extra sensitive, the bit of scar tissue, making him shiver.

"Not even going to ask me my color?" asked Clint, tugging at his wrists. The grip was too steady and completely unbreakable. He hadn't realized Scotland was that strong.

Unless. His heart pounded as he twisted, the ruthless cock coming way too close to penetrating him again. Scotland had planned to talk to Maxim about something. Maybe it wasn't him at all, but someone else who had slipped in, hoping for a quickie after the show. There had been a lot of guys bigger than Clint with rippling muscles, and Clint had made it very clear he was looking for cock.

"Lube or I safeword," said Clint, hissing as his hips were forced into the tile, water momentarily slamming into his face as it pounded down on them. He spluttered, struggling to turn his face away and choking as some made it into his nose.

With a squeak of a nob, the water disappeared, a single drip echoing in the room. His breath was loud in his ears, water sliding down his chin to his throat.

He blinked his eyes open, squinting against the water that instantly stung. The sound of Scotland spitting had him instantly on guard. And it was Scotland. Without the water he could catch the scent of his body wash and that clinging bit of donkey that never faded.

"Close enough," said Clint, relaxing against the wall and spreading his legs. "So much for keeping out of trouble." His cock throbbed, scraping against the wall in an aching dance. It was more friction than he'd had in a while and he bucked into it, seeking the way the rough wall scratched against his sensitive skin.

"Baby, you're so fucking dirty that I never stood a chance," said Scotland, his voice rumbling next to his ear.

Fuck, he sounded good. It was strange to think that it hadn't been that long since Clint refused to even think of Scotland as anything more than a pest. Attractive hadn't even been on his radar. *God, I want to come.*

But someone walking in on them was a distinct possibility. In theory, it was fun, but Scotland seemed to like this gym. He didn't want to get him kicked out. That, and Maxim had made it pretty clear on the no fucking part. This was the gangster's territory, not Clint's.

"Did you lock the door?" asked Clint, tugging against the grip on his wrists. Scotland was digging bruises into his wrists, and he trembled at the possibilities. One look, and everyone would know exactly how rough he'd been fucked. Their minds would race, picturing every scenario, but none of them would get it right. The real thing was just for him.

He could already picture himself staring at the bruises and poking them once he crashed in his cottage for the night, Scotland only a few steps or a text away. Or maybe Scotland would take him back to the house and let Clint toss and turn in the bed as he stood guard on the couch outside.

"I'll be quick," said Scotland. "I'm close already. Tossing you around is like fucking foreplay."

"Yeah, but." Clint tried to look over his shoulder, but his neck couldn't twist that far in his position, especially when Scotland scraped his teeth over him. "Maxim…"

"Will probably kick my ass, yeah. But not before I get some ass myself. Relax, baby, or this is gonna hurt."

He didn't get more warning than that before Scotland slicked up his cock with another layer of spit, slowly pressing inside. Clint cried out, slamming his mouth shut when his voice echoed off the walls. They could definitely hear him in the gym, if they hadn't heard him on another floor already. Nothing carried farther than the sound of something explicit.

"Fuck." Clint scrambled against the tile, trying to find purchase. "They probably heard that. If you pull out now, we could play it off that I slipped in the shower."

Scotland chuckled, not stopping until his groin was settled against Clint's ass and sticking together from the dampness between them. "I'm sure you heard that all the time when you were a nurse. How many people slipped in the shower and managed to accidentally get a shampoo bottle jammed up their ass?"

Squirming, Clint tried to angle away so Scotland's cock would slip free. He only managed halfway before Scotland caught him by the hips, easing home again with a sharp thrust. It pushed more than one of his buttons, filling him to the brim.

"But no one is going to mistake that gape, even if you tell them that. You're so beautiful all fucked open. I love it."

Fuck. Clint bit his lip to stifle his moans, but when Scotland picked up the pace, there was no mistaking the sound of skin slapping skin, the dampness from the shower making it so much worse.

A tap at the door made his heart nearly stop. It was a quiet rap, nothing more than a quick blow of knuckles, but he heard it clearly. Scotland seemed none the wiser, even as it came a second time.

Reaching back, he grabbed Scotland by the hip to try to still him, digging his fingertips in when he didn't immediately stop. Scotland let out a groan against Clint's ear, picking up his pace.

Someone was knocking on the goddam locker-room door. *Do I care anymore?* What little pain there had been had faded to pure pleasure, Scotland's cock like a wet dream as it carved a spot inside him.

He would never forget that cock. Every ridge, every vein, was engraved on his memory. And the way Scotland throbbed when he was all the way in, made his own cock leak and pulse. He was so fucking close.

"Did you lock the door?" asked Clint, gasping out a breath when Scotland changed the angle and slipped that much deeper. Clint dug his nails in, forcing Scotland to stop. It was the best when he paused all the way inside, filling him up in a way only a cock could. Toys were never the same. Even the most realistic one out there could never replicate it.

"No," said Scotland. "I don't think the door has a lock."

He felt Scotland freeze as the knock came again, so much louder this time. "Scotland, you in there?"

Fuck. It was Maxim. He was probably pissed, and that was one person in the world who Clint had no desire to piss off. He didn't need to be on the Bratva's bad side for any reason, even if Niki had helped him out of a bind or two in the past.

"Yeah, come on in," Scotland shouted back.

Clint jerked, a flash of cold and hot shock running through him. Was Scotland insane? He was eight inches deep at the moment with no room to spare.

The grip on his wrists tightened as it tried to wiggle away—anything he could do to salvage the situation. The door clicked open a second later and he froze, the sound of footsteps getting closer.

"What should we tell him?" asked Scotland, grinding his hips until he dragged against Clint's prostate. His eyes watered, a whimper on his lips that he tried and failed to bite back. His heart pounded as he flexed his fingers, but he was caught.

How am I supposed to survive this?

"You better think of an excuse really quick," said Scotland, dragging his teeth over Clint's ear. His nerve endings prickled, everything on high alert. It sounded as if Maxim would be rounding the corner in just a moment. Any second and he would see them.

An excuse...an excuse. Clint's mind went blank as those footsteps shuddered to a halt. Scotland kept going, though, moving his hips in a steady motion.

"What's going on in here?" asked Maxim, the darkness in his voice leaving no room for rebuke.

Oh God, I'm going to die. Maxim was going to toss them in an alley behind the gym and leave them to rot in a dumpster. Maddy would take over the club and put candles in every room before the first flies found Clint's body.

"I slipped in the shower and fell," Clint blurted out, closing his eyes as he flushed with humiliation. Maybe it was even better that he was facing the wall. *Really? That's all I could think of?* "Scotland was helping me up, but then he slipped, too."

Maxim snorted as Scotland trembled against him, stilling his hips for a moment. It took Clint a moment to realize that Scotland was laughing. *Bastard.*

"Scotland, I wanted to talk to you about that schedule," said Maxim. "Is now a good time?" He moved until he was just at the edge of the tile and within Clint's range of view. His arms were crossed, his lips set in a line. He looked fucking terrifying, his muscles still bulging from his workout.

"Yeah, sure," said Scotland, sneaking a free hand around Clint until he met his nipple. He pulled Clint against him to give himself room, immediately clamping his fingers down and twisting. His fingers were slippery and cool, the heat at Clint's back a stark contrast. "You know me. I'm just getting my cardio in."

Are you fucking kidding me? When Scotland pulled out an inch, only to slide back inside, Clint realized that he wasn't kidding at all. It was worse than anything to have his cock throbbing but neglected, one of his members standing next to him chatting with his Dom about some kind of game night get together that didn't even sound real. Scotland didn't seem like the type to watch hockey.

"That would work," said Scotland, picking up the pace as he released Clint's hands, pressing against the back of his head instead. With his other hand, he grabbed Clint's hip, pulling him into the next thrust. "Just a second."

A few staccato beats later, Scotland let out a groan, settling all the way inside as his cock pulsed. Clint panted, his eyes closed and his breath buzzing against his ears. A drain dripped in the distance, echoing as Maxim let out an annoyed-sounding sigh.

"Thursday?" asked Scotland, his voice frustratingly steady. "I'll bring my homemade salsa."

"You don't have to bring anything," said Maxim, rubbing his hands together as Clint panted against the wall.

His legs were weak, his will to keep standing only holding on because of Scotland's hands on him. His cock was so hard it hurt, but the way Scotland was starting to pull away, it looked like he wasn't going to get to come...again.

Maxim's goodbye was lost as Scotland kissed the back of his neck, sucking the damp skin into his mouth. He must've been more sweaty than damp right now, shuddering from the fight of hot and cold along his skin. Scotland dragged his teeth over the same spot, adding the edge of agony to it.

"Please." Clint whimpered, sliding his palms over the surface of the wall. He was hovering in the best place, subspace descending like that warm blanket that he missed so much. "*Please.*"

He hadn't thought he would ever beg again. He hadn't expected to find anyone who was worthy of it.

"Do you know how fucking good you are?" asked Scotland, moving his hands along Clint's skin. His sides, pecs, ass—he didn't miss a single spot, even sliding between his cheeks and playing with the slickness there that belonged to him.

"Yes," said Clint, tears prickling against his eyelids. He let them fall, too far gone to hold back. He never wanted to hold back again. The truth of it hit him straight in the chest.

Scotland was perfect and sweet, giving him everything he needed even when Clint had denied him over and over. "I'm good. Please."

"That's my boy," said Scotland, moving one hand to Clint's cock.

The reaction was almost instantaneous. One sweep from base to tip and Clint curled his toes, aching against the tile. The second jerk of Scotland's hand had a moan pushing through his lips as heat burst at the base of his cock, flowing from his balls all the way to the tip. By the third he was shooting against the wall, his breath gone as his heart pounded.

"My sweet boy. Let it all out. Your cum, your tears — I want it all."

Chapter Twenty-One

Scotland

Scotland rolled over, pressing his body against Clint's as Clint murmured into his phone. It was dark out, and far past the time they should have both been sleeping. The crickets were chirping outside the cracked window as they had been most of the late summer, starting to get softer as cooler air swept in.

But in the club not too far away, the night hadn't ended, people probably packing the walls until bursting and getting their kink on in every which way. Maddy had called ten minutes ago as Scotland held Clint in his arms, drawing circles on his naked arms as they dozed.

The sound of the cell phone had jolted them both awake. It was the first time Scotland had heard anything more than text notifications from it. It was one of the rare nights that Clint had kept it on, usually turning it off as soon as he skimmed over his texts.

"I'll be right there, Maddy," said Clint, shifting until he could sit up. Scotland let out a groan, wrapping his arms around Clint's waist and refusing to let him go any farther.

It had been three weeks since he'd dragged Clint into his bed with every intention of not letting him go. Twenty-one days since he'd fucked Clint in the gym showers with their breaths echoing against the walls. After they'd come home together, Scotland hadn't been that rough again, making love to Clint on every surface in and outside of the house.

The front porch had been a great spot, with Clint laid out beneath him and the sun shimmering low in the sky. Halfway through a walk in the bush hadn't been quite as nice, the bugs leaving bites on both of their asses with how long Scotland had teased Clint.

But reality was a bitch.

Scotland would wake up in the middle of the night sometimes to find Clint staring back at him, his eyes red but sleepless. Other nights Scotland woke to whimpering, and he would pull Clint close. Clint would flinch when he woke, grabbing the nearest shirt and dragging it on, putting his hand against his scars as he trembled.

The only time he truly seemed to rest was when Scotland fucked him sweet and slow, letting him come, then fucking him through it. Clint would get a few hours of rest then before he pulled away to pace the bedroom, only coming back to rest under the sheets when Scotland pretended to be asleep.

"Wake up, baby," said Clint, tapping his cold fingers against Scotland's arm. "I know it's late, but you've got to let me go."

Scotland jolted, rubbing his face into Clint's back. He hadn't realized he'd started to drift back to sleep again while clinging to Cling like a giant monkey.

"No." Scotland tightened his grip, pulling Clint back to the bed so he could shove his face into Clint's belly. It was his favorite part. Every time he looked at Clint, he would find something he hadn't noticed before — something that begged him to never forget.

His scent had changed during his time in Scotland's bed, some of the cleaners from the club finally fading until there was fresh air and home with the sweat of someone who was a quick study at learning to chop wood.

He couldn't imagine the warmth of Clint's skin gone, nor the end of their morning coffees together. His fridge was bursting at the moment with so much more to cook for Clint — enough that he would never go hungry.

"I'm not letting go," said Scotland, shaking his head and breathing deep through his nose. Letting out a hum, he kissed Clint's belly, his lips lingering on the swirled skin. "If you go, you won't come back."

It was the thought that had been plaguing him since the first day when he'd spotted Clint on the porch of the little cottage and his heart had refused to listen to reasoning. It was temporary — Clint in his arms, his partner in kink and in his home. His heart hadn't listened.

It was almost painful to look at Clint most days and watch that beautiful smile that had gone from forced to genuine in a matter of days. When he'd successfully chopped wood for the first time, that grin had lit up his world.

"I...I'll be back," said Clint as he touched Scotland's arm.

Scotland blinked in the darkness, all hints of sleep gone in an instant. In the few times he'd caught Clint lying, it had never been over something so real. Clint had lied about being okay so many times he'd lost count, but something like this... It could break him.

"Maddy called with an issue at the club, that's all," said Clint, running his fingers through Scotland's hair even as he slipped away and stood from the bed. "Derreck will be here to pick me up in a few minutes."

"Then I'll go with you," said Scotland, releasing Clint and grabbing the edge of the blankets to throw them back.

"Okay."

Scotland froze, every muscle losing power. *I didn't expect that.* "Oh."

"You can come with, and we'll crash at the club after. Maddy said something about cops, so it might not be short."

Cops. Scotland shot up, scrambling from the bed and grabbing the nearest pair of pants. "Shit. What happened?" Now he just felt like an asshole. "We can take my truck and get there faster."

"Derreck will be here soon," said Clint, flicking on the lamp before rubbing sleep from his eyes. "I'm not sure of all the details, but someone called the cops, and they are at the club right now. It didn't sound like they were trying to arrest anyone, but if someone like Maxim shows up, that'll change. I just need to get there."

Scotland grabbed a hoodie, throwing it on just in time to hear two honks right outside the bedroom window. He winced a moment later when he caught the sound of two braying calls as the donkeys sounded the alarm in the darkness. The remaining crickets fell silent, the night going still.

"Ah, hell." Scotland grabbed the wall as he nearly tripped trying to get a sock on. Adrenaline pulsed through him, sleep the last thing on his mind. It wasn't that he *disliked* cops, but they had a way of misunderstanding kink. *Unless handcuffs are involved.*

"Here." Clint grabbed the sock from his outstretched hand, cradling Scotland's foot and slipping it on. He was on his knees, his gaze focused and his tongue between his teeth as he caressed Scotland's bare ankle before reaching for his other foot and slipping the second sock on.

"Thanks, love." Scotland leaned his head back, letting it thud against the wall. Thrusting his hand into Clint's hair, he let out a sigh. *Is this going to end?* Clint was so fucking *good* for him. He'd never be able to go back to the way things had been.

The horn blared again, followed by another bray, shattering his peace with a burst of sound. There were a few moments in his life that he wished would last longer, and his time with Clint was among those.

When Clint tried to stand, Scotland tightened his grip on his hair, keeping him on his knees. His chest was tight, breath barely making it into his lungs as his eyes stung. He let out a shaky breath, but his voice still trembled when he spoke. "Is this going to end? I need to know before we leave this room."

"Scotland—" Clint started. *That tone.* Scotland had heard it before from subs, Doms and boyfriends alike just before they parted ways. The tentative softness was always a lie—the pickax ready to jab him straight in the heart.

"I had the time of my life, Clint." He couldn't stop the tear from rolling over his eyelid, tracing down his cheek. "These weeks with you have been some of the best in my life. You're the best man I know."

The horn blared again. *Does Derreck have to be so fucking persistent?* One more moment, that was all Scotland was asking for. One more fairytale second to be with someone he'd never expected to fall in love with.

Looking back, he'd never had a chance. Clint was everything, but Scotland was just a tattoo artist with some land and a couple of donkeys. He had friends, but no one who would understand. They all thought they knew who Clint was—someone unreachable, even for him.

"Can we talk about this another time?" asked Clint, trailing his fingers over Scotland's wrist, his voice calm and soft.

Scotland released his hold, dropping his hand to his side. It was now or never. Once Clint stepped through that door, he would be gone like a leaf on the wind. There was nothing to hold him here. No threats of vacation, or forced time away from the club. He would go back to his friends—his life—and Scotland would return to whatever he had been doing before.

"Sure." Scotland wiped the stray tear away, offering his hand to help Clint to his feet. "We'll have lots of time." It was a fucking lie.

* * * *

Three cruisers? Scotland almost couldn't believe his eyes as they pulled up the gravel drive. The area had expanded since the club first opened, leaving room for twenty or so cars. The cruisers blocked off any chance of exit, trapping anyone who may have wished to leave. Since it was pushing one o'clock in the morning, that would have been most of the patrons.

One officer was at the front door, the door itself wide with a few people gathered around. Another was standing at his car, his arms crossed as he glared into the light as they approached. Derreck flashed his lights before shutting the vehicle off in a move that could have been considered accidental if Scotland hadn't known him better.

Derreck was usually a quiet guy, but their entire drive had been silent, the air thick with so much tension that Scotland had felt like cowering in the back seat. Clint hadn't said a word, staring out of the window and perking up as they had finally reached the right road.

Clint was out of the car before the engine had shut off, Derreck not far behind. Scotland ran a hand through his hair, shaking off his nerves. He'd had his fair share of run-ins with cops, but he had a lot of respect for them. Despite some of the hits they took in the media, he was still calling the cops if someone ever broke into his house.

Cops and kink didn't go so well, though.

"Can I help you, Officer?"

Scotland caught Clint's question as he ducked out of the car. The closest officer — the one leaning against his cruiser—shifted his stance, widening his feet as he dropped his hands to his sides. He was built with a few tattoos on his arms. It wasn't Scotland's work.

"Are you the owner?" asked the officer, his eyes sliding over Clint and landing on Scotland.

Scotland gripped his fists tight, stepping just behind Clint. Hopefully, it would offer him some moral support. Clint snuck his hand back, tangling his fingers with Scotland's before giving him a soft squeeze. The act was enough to extinguish every bit of unease.

"Yes, I am," said Clint, glancing at the door where another officer was approaching. "Did you have a warrant or did you just feel like trespassing tonight?"

Oh shit. Scotland blinked. Clint could be a fiery son of a bitch, but he hadn't seen him quite so sassy before.

"We had a complaint that there was someone underage on the premises. When we arrived on scene, we heard a scream, which is more than enough probable cause to enter."

Clint let out a sigh before running his hand through his hair. "Well at least someone was having a good time." He glanced at Scotland, a flash of a smirk on his lips before he turned serious. "Since I assume you've searched the whole place by now, did you find anything other than consenting adults having a good time?"

"Uh…" The officer's flushed face was obvious, even in the dark.

"Every person that comes through the doors has a membership," said Clint, his grip going tight again. Scotland dragged his thumb over the back of Clint's knuckles, trying to soothe him. "To get a membership, you have to show ID, have a criminal background check and sign about three dozen waivers. If someone managed to slip past all those checks, then the Dungeon Master will escort them off the premises before they make it past the first hall."

The second officer arrived mid-rant, the furrow in his forehead more pronounced because of his lack of hair. His sleeves were rolled up, a familiar dragon tattoo carved into his arm.

"We've made three arrests." The second officer flexed his arm, and Scotland had a sudden realization. The tattoo was familiar because he had done it himself, from the epic scales to the dark tail that had literally made the man cry.

"Hey, Duncan," said Scotland, speaking up for the first time. The second officer's eyes went wide as he looked at Scotland, obviously recognizing him.

People said a lot of shit when they were in his chair, the needle buzzing between them and gentle music playing in the background. The adrenaline messed with people's heads, making them spill their secrets as Scotland gently tortured them. Duncan had been chattier than most.

"Who the hell did you arrest?" asked Clint, apparently oblivious to Duncan's shock. "There are no weapons permitted on site, and anyone breaking the rules is shown the door."

"There were two offenses of open liquor," said the first officer, ticking off two fingers.

"This is a private establishment, asshole, and I have a license," said Clint, his arm bulging as he clamped his hand down tight.

Ow, ow, ow. Scotland winced, trying to keep a straight face as his hand was squeezed.

"There was also someone practicing medicine without a license, but we let that one slide..." The officer seemed to wilt at Clint's intense glare.

"Are you fucking with me? I'm a nurse, and there are three doctors who are members. If someone was doing some stitches, it was probably one of them. Also, most of the members are certified in first aid. I taught and certified them myself."

Scotland shifted, trying to adjust himself. Clint was *good* and smart, hitting his competence kink head on. He also seemed completely fearless, despite the tremble of his grip.

"That doesn't account for the drugs," said Duncan, finally seeming to get over his shock. "There was more than one person with marijuana, although we are only charging one."

"So you're charging people for legal drugs now?" asked Clint, bristling. "I have some Advil in my bag. Did you want to arrest me, too?"

Scotland cleared his throat, catching Duncan's eye. "Seems a bit better than what we would find in your center console, Duncan."

Clint cast him a strange look as Duncan took a step back, stuttering out a single word before he continued to retreat. Scotland kept his glare mild. He didn't have to do anything more. He remembered every little word about Duncan's admissions over his addiction. He hated to use something like that against a guy, but come on.

"The blatant display of honestly despicable behavior in there is sickening," said the first officer. That had Clint grumbling under his breath. "I'm surprised you haven't been shut down before. Even if the concerned caller was a hoax, I'm glad they called. There were a lot of dangerous situations in there that we luckily got diffused before anyone could get hurt."

Clint tugged his hand free, cracking his knuckles in front of him. "So that's how you want to play." His grin was nearly deranged, his eyes narrow and feral.

Holy fuck. If he had known about this side of Clint, he wouldn't have faced him in the boxing ring without a hell of a lot more focus. Sure, he'd seen Cint take care of a few assholes in the club before, but the Dungeon Masters had always been at his back.

"You give me the word, and I'll have so many lawyers crawling up your ass that you won't be able to help but come. Everything that happens in these walls is not only fantastic but completely legal. The last asshole that tried to take on people like us failed in spectacular fashion. So, I'm going to give you one last chance. Apologize to everyone who you've inconvenienced, and get the hell off my property."

"Clint!"

Clint's head shot up and Scotland's gaze followed a moment later as someone appeared at the open door of the club. People parted to let him through, his uniform looking different than the other officer's. He seemed vaguely familiar, like someone Scotland may have seen a time or two passing through, but his features were common enough that he would have been easily forgotten.

"Tensall," said Clint, holding out his hand as the other approached and shaking his hand once. "It's good to see someone intelligent here."

Tensall rubbed the back of his head, a strained smile on his lips. "Sorry for the disruption tonight, Clint, and for coming out here so quickly. I'd hate to interrupt your vacation for long, so I'll keep this short."

The blue and red lights flashed against his face, casting a shadow over his features. It was impossible to tell if he was thirty or fifty, but his hair looked dark. His eyes were dark, too, but strained in a way that suggested he had seen more than his fair share of things in life.

"We aren't pressing any charges here tonight, and everyone has been released. It sounds like the one who called it in was a Phil something—an ex-member? I'll take care of him."

Scotland watched Derreck crack his knuckles beside him, narrowing his eyes.

Tensall glanced from Clint to Scotland. "I'm glad I caught the call on the radio before things got out of hand. I wanted to check in myself to see if a certain person made an appearance and that was what all the kerfuffle was about."

There was something Scotland was obviously missing.

"I haven't seen Henley in a couple of months. I'll let him know you are looking for him when he pops by next," said Clint, a hint of a smile on his lips. "I still can't believe he won't return your calls. Are you sure you have the right number?"

"No need to say anything to him," said Tensall, shaking his head. "I'll catch up with Henley another time. I'm hoping to make it a surprise the next time I see him. That guy loves surprises."

"That he does," said Clint, a real smile touching his lips. "I'll keep it as our little secret."

"Come on, guys," said Tensall, looking to the other officers. "There is nothing to see here. Let's get this show on the road."

Duncan grumbled, jerking his car door open and slamming it shut once he was inside, gravel kicking up as he hit the gas. It left small ruts behind, but it was a relief to see him gone. Tensall stared after him, his arms crossed and forehead furrowed.

"Who the hell is that guy?" whispered Scotland as the remaining cops readied to leave, the stragglers coming out of the building and returning to their cruisers. A few members started over to Clint, one nearly naked in the cool air.

"A member named Henley used to work with him in some kind of special forces outfit," said Clint, shrugging as he turned to Scotland. "Henley moved away a little while ago and shortly after, Tensall stopped by. He started working with the local police a little bit ago, and he's hoping to connect with Henley when he's back in town. Something about an old case they were working on."

'Cause that sounds completely plausible…

Scotland wrapped his arms around Clint's shoulders as the others approached, pulling Clint back into his chest. He was exhausted, hungry and wanted Clint back in his bed where he belonged.

A few people gave them strange looks, and Scotland tried not to wilt. It didn't help when Clint went tense in his arms when he squeezed tighter.

Was it already time? One step back to Unkinked and what they had was over?

Clint pulled away, and it was like a stake through his heart. Scotland tried to play it off, wiping the nonexistent dirt from his pants and staring after the last of the flashing lights as they trailed out of the lane.

He glanced down at his legs when he felt something tickle at his ankle. He realized for the first time he'd accidentally grabbed Clint's pants instead of his own, the waist cinched tight and uncomfortable.

He couldn't stop looking at Clint and the way Scotland's pants sagged from his hips, the hem dragging on the ground and catching under the sandals he'd thrown on. They were Scotland's, too.

"Time for damage control," said Clint, stepping toward the club.

Chapter Twenty-Two

Clint

What a fucking mess. He respected police officers for everything they did, but when they showed up on *his* turf and threatened him and anyone else in the lifestyle, he got riled. Thank goodness for Tensall or he probably would have spent the night in jail. Only amateurs thought metal cuffs with no padding were a good way to get kinky.

"You sure you're okay, Maddy?" asked Clint, patting Maddy on the shoulder again. Maddy was seated, clutching his sweater tight and pulling it down his hands over and over in a tick that he always did when he was nervous.

"You didn't do anything wrong. To be honest, I'm shocked this place is still standing and not on fire…"

Derreck gave him a glare, and Clint chuckled awkwardly.

"I'm joking. There is no one else I would trust to take care of Unkinked. I mean that. It's probably even cleaner than when I left."

"And I signed on three new members while you were away." Maddy sniffed, wiping his nose with a tissue. "There was a fourth I turned away. I'm guessing he's the one who made that call. He was a real asshole. About a dozen red flags with him."

Obviously Derreck hasn't mentioned Phil. Phil was an asshole who had almost put an end to Maddy in every sense of the word. Clint had thought he'd taken care of him by making a few phone calls and some threats. Last he'd heard, Phil had been rolling around in a gutter somewhere, but apparently he'd managed to haul his way out.

He wasn't sure if he'd have to worry about it. Derreck had had a strange look in his eye ever since he'd heard the name.

Clint nodded at Maddy, his hand bumping into Derreck's as he tried to rub a small circle on Maddy's back. Wincing, he lowered his hands to his sides. *I know when I'm not wanted.* Derreck had practically cocooned Maddy in the last few minutes, and Clint wasn't exactly a hugger.

"Well, I'm back now," said Clint, glancing around the open play area. They'd shut down for the night, sending everyone home with assurances and some hefty apologies. "Did you want to take the next few days off? I'm more than happy to cover for you. I'm vacationed out, frankly."

Now that's a fucking lie. When he closed his eyes, he could almost feel the gentle heat of the sun and the crackling of the small fire Scotland had built for him. The air was tinted with sweat from Scotland chopping wood, and the buzzing of a few distant flies that were probably driving the donkeys crazy. Better them than him.

His favorite part had been watching the donkeys play, and listening to their call that exceeded their small frames with abundance.

"I'm taking Maddy home," said Derreck, grasping Maddy's hand and helping him from the couch. "He'll be back when he's back."

Maddy rolled his eyes. "Derreck, seriously…"

"Do you want a beating or not?" asked Derreck, raising one brow.

Maddy nodded so quickly that it probably made him dizzy. "I'll see you in a few days, Clint."

Clint collapsed against the same couch as soon as they left the room, rubbing his hand over his face. Man, it was good to be back, but at the same time…it wasn't. His gut was tight in the way it hadn't been for so long, his to-do list longer than he cared to think about.

How much equipment needed to get wiped down? There was a flogger on the ground a few feet away, not to mention the mess of ropes that would need to be coiled and returned to their rightful owners.

Weeks of rest and he was exhausted, every limb sinking into the couch until he wanted nothing more than to sleep. It would be best if that sleep wasn't alone. At least with Scotland, he managed to catch more than a few short winks threaded with scattered nightmares.

He hadn't seen him since he'd gone into super-save-the-day mode when the cops had taken off. In fact, it was completely possible Scotland had hitched a ride home with another couple.

It was probably for the best. Clint's night had just begun. It didn't make the ache go away, though.

It took him almost two hours to get everything cleaned and put away, antiseptic clinging to his skin, despite how many times he washed his hands. Maddy had obviously been looking after things in his absence, but kinksters were like toddlers. You could spend hours putting all their toys away, and they have them all back out and played with in ten minutes.

By the time he approached the door to his section of the house, his feet were nearly dragging on the floor, his eyelids drooping. He'd had too much of the good life lately, and despite catching up on years of lost sleep, he was still exhausted.

He half-expected it to be locked, but the knob turned under his hand. It was a good thing too. He'd left two bags of milk and a crap ton of veggies in the fridge that he told Maddy to feast on. It would have been awful to come back to that rotted mess.

And luckily, he trusted a few of his members enough to crash on his bed if they needed to. He hoped no one had christened the damn thing, not that it mattered much. He'd be heading for the couch. The last thing he needed was a reminder that he was sleeping alone tonight.

I hope he made it home okay. He bit his lip as he thought of Scotland. He'd been so damned busy, he hadn't even said goodbye. If he hadn't been so worried about Unkinked, the guilt would probably drag him the rest of the way to sleep. *I'll make it up to him. I have to.*

Clint blinked as he rounded the corner into his bedroom, intent on finding the softest pair of pajamas so he could get out of Scotland's pants. They kept catching on his heel, trying to drag down his ass every time he bent over.

There was a pair of feet in his bed. He blinked again, hesitating as he reached for the lamp. Whoever it was probably didn't mean him any harm, but he didn't want to wake them up with a lamplight to the face. That would make the gentlest soul grumpy.

They were lying on top of the covers, their face buried in the pillow. There was something so familiar about them that he realized who it was, even in the darkness.

Sleep was the last thing on his mind as he reached for Scotland's ankle. His legs were naked, his ass covered only by a thin pair of black boxers that cupped the curves perfectly. He didn't stir as Clint trailed his fingers up the back of his leg, fine hairs tickling his fingertips until he reached that smooth spot on the back of his knee.

It was vulnerable and sweet, and in seconds, Clint's chest was full to bursting. While he'd been worrying about Unkinked, Scotland had figured out exactly where he belonged. *Why am I still trying to fight it?*

Ross should have been the one in his bed, snuggled up behind him and spooning him as he snored into Clint's ear. It felt so fucking good to give himself up to Scotland, but what about taking control? With Ross it had been so easy that they'd hardly even needed to speak about it. His switch had been like a visible knob that Ross could turn on and off at will. *Sub or Dom.*

Can I be Scotland's Dom?

There was so much power in being a sub — taking pain, restraint or anything the Dom gave him and being strong enough to take it and pull pleasure from it like a drug. It was the sub's say, but the pressure was on the Dom. Everything had to be perfect, and they had to keep their sub happy, healthy and horny.

"Scotland?" Clint asked softly, dipping under the lower cuff of Scotland's boxers until his fingertip met the curve of his ass. He was soft there, too, with only the finest hairs. Clint delved deeper until his finger traced the edge of the warmth between Scotland's cheeks. *So tight.*

"Scotland?" he asked a little louder, unable to tear his hand away. He was treading a fine line of consent that he'd rather not tumble down.

"You're good, love," said Scotland, his voice filled with sleep. He shifted on the bed, adjusting his hips as he pressed his hole harder against Clint's finger.

Fuck. "You're such a good little slut," said Clint, pulling his hand back to spit on his fingers before he moved right back to the same spot. "Sitting up here waiting for Daddy to get home to take your little ass." He sucked air in through his teeth. It had been so long since he'd felt like a Daddy Dom, but it was just as good as the first time. "Let Daddy in."

"*Please.*" Scotland's whisper was breathy as he pushed against Clint's finger, letting the tip inside. Silky heat engulfed Clint, the slide easy from his saliva.

"Such a greedy boy. Did you want more?" Withdrawing, Clint tugged Scotland's boxers free, dragging Scotland to his knees. His face was still buried in the pillow, leaving him open and…vulnerable— something Clint had never expected from Scotland.

It was hard to picture a guy who could split wood with one hit and stab someone with a hundred needles as vulnerable. It was heady as hell, too. How many people had seen Scotland like this? Probably only a select few that Clint had no intention of thinking about. As far as he was concerned, this moment was just theirs.

"I didn't know if you were coming back," Scotland mumbled into the pillow, taking a deep breath as Clint breached him again.

His heart was thudding in his chest, his mouth dry in a way that resonated deep within him. The words slipped out of his mouth without stopping, but he didn't realize how true they were until they were reverberating in his ears. "You can't get rid of me now."

Scotland tensed beneath his hand, snapping his spine rigid as he turned his head. He blinked his sleepy eyes at Clint. "Do you mean that?"

"Not unless you're calling red," said Clint, nibbling Scotland's ass cheek as he hovered closer. "That's the only way to stop me. As far as I'm concerned, this is exactly how you belong — ass up, with two fingers in your needy hole." He slid a second finger to the knuckle, relishing the slight drag as the saliva dried. He spit once, watching the bubbles slide down Scotland's crack until they met his buried fingers.

"I thought — "

Clint cut Scotland off as he twisted his fingers, nailing his prostate dead-on. "It's not time for you to think right now. Put your subby hat on, and let me make you come." Clint pressed harder, easing up when Scotland let out a whimper. His cock was red and hard, dangling toward the bed.

"I know what you thought," said Clint, easing away and scrambling for his lube. He still kept some at the bedside table, just in case. He did run a kink establishment, after all. Turning the bedside lamp on, he got back to work.

Scotland's breath hitched as Clint slicked his hole up, sliding three fingers deep and scissoring them wide. The pink of Scotland's rim glistened in the lamplight. Scotland's face was flushed, those beautiful eyes closed and forehead furrowed in obvious pleasure.

"You thought that as soon as I came back to the club, you could escape and find another man. Well, let me tell you something." He bit Scotland's ass cheek, sucking a mark into his skin as Scotland groaned, low and long. "I'm not sure how we are going to make it work, but we will. Someone like you, I can't let slip through my fingers. Right, slutty boy?"

"Uh-huh." Scotland whimpered as Clint pulled out, slicking up his cock and jamming the blunt head against Scotland's hole. It was so soft and open that he could probably slide right inside if he wanted.

"Fuck yourself on my cock. Show me how much you want to be my sub."

It was less than a second before Scotland raised himself on his hands and knees and shoved himself back, taking Clint's cock to the inevitable base in one long move. It was tight and perfect, bringing him to the edge in a heartbeat. *When was the last time I felt this good?*

He couldn't remember.

Scotland was *perfect* for him—the perfect sub, the perfect Dom and the one he wanted to risk everything for.

"Make me come," said Clint, struggling to hold still as Scotland did just that. *Yeah, I'm not letting this go. Not for anything in the world.*

Epilogue

Scotland

"You sure you're ready for this?" asked Clint, stroking Scotland's back for what felt like the hundredth time. His palm was hot and sweaty, sliding against Scotland's own perspiration. It felt smoother than it usually did after a round of waxing the day before. Clint hadn't wanted any body hair to interfere.

"I'm not worried," said Scotland, trying to portray every bit of calm when his heart was pounding. He shifted on the table, the padding sticking to his naked skin. He'd taken everything off from his clothes to his boxers until he was completely exposed.

Not that there was anyone to see him but Clint. After months of planning and working on the kinks of their relationship together, Clint had finally brought up the scene that both of them had been longing for.

One of the shower heads in the wet room dripped, echoing along with his breath. They'd decided it was the safest route. Not only had Clint grabbed close to a dozen fire extinguishers, but he'd moved the table until it was directly beneath one of the shower heads. Those, along with the fire blanket, and everything was as safe as it possibly could be.

The waft of alcohol hit his nose a moment before he heard the flick of a lighter and the gentle roar of an ignited flame. The heat hit him an instant later, flaring against his ass before Clint's hand skimmed over his skin.

It didn't sting, or even hurt, but was more like a whisper of warmth as if he'd stuck his sunburned arm into the daylight. Clint soothed him with his hand, his palm so much warmer than it had been.

"That was just a little taste," said Clint, his voice thick and low. Scotland turned his head, trying to catch Clint's expression. It was almost as blissed out as his own, the fire dancing on the tip of the wand-like tool he had in his hand.

As he watched, Clint rubbed the fire quickly over his palm, bringing his hand to Scotland's skin as blue fire clung to it.

The heat was sizzling this time and surely would have singed his hair if he hadn't already waxed. The smell of alcohol clung to the air, tickling his nose as Clint did the same thing again in a fresh spot that hadn't been ignited by the flames.

He squirmed, trying to get used to a feeling that he wasn't quite sure of. It wasn't a tickle, but it wasn't exactly a burn, either. He shuffled up on his elbows, trying to spot where Clint had last touched him. It was tinged pink like a sunburn and tingled harshly.

"Keep still," said Clint, dropping the tool into a bucket of water so the fire hissed out of existence.

Placing a hand on Scotland's shoulder, he eased him back down to the table to lie flat. "You ready for more?"

Scotland nodded, swallowing as Clint grabbed the next wand before igniting the soaked end. The fire was on Scotland in seconds. Clint scraped the wand along his skin, the fire lingering for less than a second before Clint moved his hand to the same spot, extinguishing it with a touch.

He couldn't help but squirm again, nudging his cock into the table and relishing in the ache. Clint's hands were steady on his skin, never flinching or faltering, despite the fire that was literally at his fingertips.

"You look so fucking good," said Clint, extinguishing the second fire wand before reaching for a third. "How are you feeling?"

Scotland let out a low groan. He'd been anticipating this scene for weeks, but his imagination hadn't held up to the real thing. He'd expected burning, and maybe something unpleasant, but this was more like a tease. It wasn't enough — merely a threat that could've been so much more.

"I like it." Scotland let out a shuddering breath. That was such a fucking understatement. "I'm really hard."

Clint chuckled, probably smiling wide as he lit the third wand, flicking it against Scotland's skin. He felt the fresh alcohol splash in a few places, the flame testing the edge of his tolerance as his nerves were tortured. Clint extinguished it all with his touch before dragging his nails over the same spot, scratching into Scotland's oversensitive skin.

"Here's my little surprise."

He caught the clink of ice against glass a moment before a shock danced over his skin. It was like touching something metal in the middle of winter, the cold sinking straight into him in one wild second.

He'd never quite played with temperature like this before. He'd once set a knitting needle in the freezer and had drawn it over someone's skin once it was cooled. They had been blindfolded, and they'd swore to him that they had felt a blade slice into them.

But this was something else entirely.

"Oh, God." Scotland shivered as the cold dragged from one shoulder to his other, before striking the same spot where the flame had been mere moments before. It was so much colder than a simple ice cube should have been, the melting liquid dripping over his skin to the table below.

"Look at that," Clint mused, touching Scotland's cheek until he turned, blinking at his Dom and lover. Clint held the ice cube where he could see it, rolling it between his fingertips. "You're melting it so quick. You're so fucking hot."

Clint's eyes were dark—darker than Scotland had ever seen them. He was lost in the scene just as much as Scotland was, but from his steady hands and the way he carefully rolled the ice over him made every bit of Scotland's worry relax.

He didn't have to worry—not really. Clint was the local king of kink, and Scotland had discovered very honestly that he deserved every bit of that title. When Clint was in his Dom space, they did scenes that Scotland never could have imagined on his own. And Clint seemed to know his limits down to the exact breath.

Scotland pushed his ass out, trying to reposition his cock so it wouldn't hurt quite so bad. The water was tricking his senses, making the echo of fire burn hotter than it had before. The fire hadn't been on his skin nearly long enough to cause any real damage, but it certainly didn't feel that way.

"There's my needy boy — my little pain whore." Clint slapped his ass with his empty hand before sliding what was left of the ice cube between his cheeks, pressing it inside. "Here you go, baby — something to fill that hungry hole of yours."

"*Fuck.*" Scotland gripped the table, arching his back as the cold went from unbearable to perfect in an instant.

Clint wiped a cloth against his skin, cleaning the rest of the water that hadn't dried or fallen to the table below him. He was so meticulous, with steady hands that could pin him or make him come in an instant.

When the fire touched him again, Scotland almost screamed. It fucking hurt, even if it was only a trick of his nerves. With how quickly Clint put it out, it had no chance to truly burn him.

His throat was hoarse as he gasped, his breath catching in his throat as Clint wiped the flames against him with his palm. *So hot.* He trembled, caught between the battling sensations of his body.

"Here, honey, this will keep you cool." Clint pressed another ice cube inside him, then another, going until they clacked together, shifting over his prostate and chilling him from the inside. It was so cold — too cold, as the fire was washing over his ass, Clint's hands like a molten inferno that soothed and beat him perfectly.

"I *can't.*" Scotland shook, pressing his forehead into the table as he arched his back. "Please, I'm going to come." His cock was throbbing and leaking on the table, probably making a terrible mess that Clint would have to clean later. He'd never been so caught, so fucked out in a scene that didn't involve a gangbang.

"You can come. Here." Clint reached between Scotland's legs, touching his cock. Scotland cried out, half-expecting to feel fire on his most sensitive skin, but it was just Clint, his callused hand rough with the perfect amount of pressure. "You're so hard. You like it, don't you? You like it when I light you up like this? Did you need more ice, baby?"

"Fuck no." Scotland bit his lip, whimpering as Clint tightened his grip. "The next thing in my ass better be your cock."

Clint chuckled, flicking the lighter and bringing bliss and agony back to Scotland's flesh.

He wasn't sure how long it went on. Each time he thought he'd finally caught up to the sensations, Clint would press another ice cube inside him or bring another flaming wand to his skin. *How many does he have?* They had to have gone through more than a dozen, the burn like a low simmer that never ceased.

Clint's breathing was as heavy as his own, the distant dripping of water long since lost to the pure overwhelming awareness that had wrapped itself around his world. He wasn't sure if he'd come or not, but he was floating somewhere far, far away, where fire and ice were absolute bliss.

"You okay, baby?"

Clint's voice was steadiness through the fog, but Scotland had no desire to answer. He never wanted to leave this moment. Even if he wasn't sure if he were on the table anymore or not. He had a distant thought of Clint walking him back to their bed, but it had to have been a dream. The sheets against his skin and Clint's kisses on his body didn't feel real.

Clint sliding his cock home was the first thing that broke through the fog. Scotland cried out, grabbing for Clint's ass, bringing him closer and forcing him all the way inside. The ice had long since melted, but he hoped he was still cold, torturing Clint's cock in the same way he'd been teased.

"Fuck, baby." Clint's lips were on his, the cool sheets of their bed soothing the warmth of his back. It was so fucking good—so sweet, and soft. He'd never thought he would ever see this softness from Clint.

"Use me, Daddy. Come inside me," Scotland begged, digging his nails into Clint's ass until he hissed, slamming his cock as deep as he could go.

Even if he hadn't come before, Scotland felt himself shoot the moment Clint did. He could feel him, his cum a contrast to the coolness of the ice. It was molten, filling him deep until he was sure he would never descend from his high. His own body clamped down during his release, begging Clint to go faster, longer— as long as he could.

"Fuck," Clint whispered against his neck. "You okay, Scotland?"

He couldn't feel most of his limbs, his back was on fire and he was pretty sure he was leaking cum-laced ice water all over their sheets. "I don't think I've ever been so green."

Clint chuckled, kissing the top of his head before curling around him. He liked to snuggle, something that Scotland absolutely loved.

"You okay? With the fire, I mean?" asked Scotland, a tendril of worry creeping in. They'd been working on Clint's anxiety about fire for months, but that was a whole different ballgame to the scene.

"I was scared at first," said Clint, rubbing his face into Scotland's chest. "When I lit the first one, I thought I was going to have a heart attack—until I touched you with it. I remembered what it was like to have control over something that is completely uncontrollable—both you and the fire. I feel fucking invincible right now."

"Me, too," said Scotland, brushing his lips over Clint's head and humming at the smell of his own shampoo. "Did you set the alarm? I have to be back to feed the boys in the morning."

Clint grunted before nodding. "I figured I could go with you. Maddy offered to look after things for a few days when I told him about our scene. I could help with chores and stuff."

Scotland hummed under his breath. "That sounds fucking perfect, love."

**Want to see more from this author?
Here's a taster for you to enjoy!**

The Little Things in Love
M.C. Roth

Coming September 2024

Excerpt

Elgin

Something was wrong with Wallace. There was a paleness to his cheeks as he flitted his eyes across the busy restaurant, tracking random people as they passed by the small cove that obscured their table. He was usually so focused, so spirited, but ever since Elgin had come home for dinner, only for them to immediately turn around to head out to the restaurant, things had been *off.*

"Is it a sex thing?"

Wallace spluttered, grabbing for his glass of wine and smothering his laugh against the rim. It was clearly too late. His eyes were already sparkling, color flushing into his cheeks again. His soft cheeks and the smattering of freckles were some of the first things that had made Elgin realize he was in love.

That hadn't changed…not for years.

"Are we getting dessert and leaving early?" asked Wallace, waggling his eyebrows. The server chose that moment to walk by, a grin touching her lips as she swiftly changed direction.

"No way." Elgin shook his head, running his finger along his lower lip. *I must've been imagining things.* Nothing had changed. They still had the same jokes and laughter. Maybe it was time for him to give Wallace a break. The man was a CEO and worked for a living.

Wallace leaned in, pushing his half-eaten soup to the side so he could lean his elbows on the table. "Then do tell. What is the sex thing—and when are we having it?"

Anyone who looked at Wallace probably had no idea about the mouth on him—or that dirty mind that was locked behind blond hair and blue eyes that were so expressive he could see the world in them. He was the type of guy who stopped to help someone pick up their groceries if they dropped them or would fund a kid's university tuition because the teacher had called him up.

Elgin was the only one who really *knew* him.

"Did you see the bathroom at this place? There's a couch in there, along with crested hand towels. Not many places have that type of thing anymore." It helped that they would drop a thousand dollars between the two of them over dinner. The hostess would probably stand guard at the bathroom door if he tipped well enough. *Which I always do.*

"A bathroom?" Wallace quirked his lips. "Kinky."

The door to the restaurant must've shifted open, as a bit of cool air swept into their bubble. They always had the same spot in the private area just inside the place. It was far away from the kitchen, so it was quiet, and it was the best place to people watch. Most didn't notice the small inlet tucked to the side that had a view of most of the main dining room.

Two men shuffled by their little hiding spot, the second one catching Elgin's eye. "He's going to propose. I bet you five— No…twenty dollars." He narrowed his eyes. "The excessive cologne, tie and the way he's overdressed makes me think wonder if it's a surprise. And the way he keeps reaching for his pocket tells me that's where he must have the ring."

Wallace let out a soft sigh, running his hands over the tablecloth. "I love weddings." His smile brightened. "Oh, look. We'll have a front row seat."

The couple was seated just outside their bubble of privacy, the scrape of their chairs audible against the floor. They would be able to hear every single word from their spot.

The hostess reached over, lighting the small candle at the table before sweeping away and leaving a trace of her perfume. With the low lights and soft ambiance, the candle was almost the brightest thing in the room. Elgin narrowed his eyes, straining to catch every detail.

The one who was reaching into his pocket every few seconds was tall, with visible sweat gathered at the edge of his dark hair that was styled to fall just above his ears. His gaze wandered the restaurant as he shifted, pulling his chair up tight to the table before he rested back again. He fiddled with his napkin, running the material through his fingers over and over.

"He's so nervous, poor guy," said Elgin, staring shamelessly. Glancing at Wallace, he was momentarily caught. "What? This is exciting."

Wallace's cheeks were flushed, his lower lip red as he released it from between his teeth. The sweater he wore was perhaps a size too big, but it dragged Elgin's thoughts to how light Wallace would be when he tossed him on the bed later.

"It's okay," said Wallace, his eyes dark. "You're just really invested in another man right now."

As if. Wallace was his everything, and he meant that in every sense of the word. His husband was sweet, like a cinnamon heart that had the hidden bit of spiciness he was never expecting. But that wasn't the half of it.

"You just don't want to bet against me," said Elgin.

The second of the pair had no nervousness to speak of and didn't seem to notice his partner's state — or much of anything, really. He was buried in his phone, the glow of the white screen flashing against his glasses with the video's reflection glaring on the pane.

"This is a nice place. Do you like it, Ralph?" The nervous one asked, running his hand through his hair. He must've had gel in it or something because he scrunched up his face, wiping his palm on his pants a moment later.

"Meh." Ralph shrugged, running his finger over his phone screen. "I told you I didn't care, Annan. Sophie was here last week, and she didn't like her vegetables much. She said they weren't even cooked."

Elgin turned his head away from the scene, taking a sip of his water. *Poor guy.*

"I might take that bet, after all," said Wallace, smiling at the server as she brought their main course. Elgin's steak appeared seared to perfection and topped with a crusting of cheese and two thin spears of purple asparagus. Wallace's portion was tiny in comparison.

"Fifty bucks says Annan will back out. Another fifty if Ralph leaves before the main course arrives," said Wallace as soon as they were alone again.

Elgin glanced at the couple out of the corner of his eye. "It doesn't seem like as much fun without a wedding at the end." He wiped his cheek dry of a pretend tear. "I could have been the best man."

Wallace bit his lips as if he were struggling to keep the smile off his face. "You're right. Everyone should propose the way you did—no chance of rejection that way."

That's not fair. Elgin shook his head, grabbing his fork and knife and cutting into his steak. The blue cheese coated his tongue as it melted in his mouth, a groan catching in his throat. Ralph didn't know great food if he was worried about a few al dente vegetables.

"I gave you a heads up when I proposed," said Elgin, eyeing up Wallace's food. "Is that all you're going to eat?"

"Gotta save room for dessert." Wallace licked his lips, dragging his gaze over Elgin's form.

How fast can I finish this steak? Elgin wondered.

"But sending me a message on social media is not a heads up," said Wallace, laughing as he shook his head. "I'll never forget when Lenny called to congratulate me when he saw a picture of the ring on your feed and told me that you had updated your profile to 'engaged'."

"Hey." Elgin pointed his fork at Wallace. "You're telling it all wrong. I got down on one knee just a few days later when you got back from your business trip. The post was my heads up."

Wallace sent him a light glare. "You are as romantic as a jar of peanut butter—sweet, satisfying and unexpectedly dangerous."

"Please put that on my tombstone." Elgin framed his hands. "Here lies Elgin, sweet and unexpectedly dangerous."

Wallace's smile dropped as he swirled his spoon in his bowl of soup. He'd barely touched it, a few vegetables floating around the top of the thick cream base. There was bread on the side that was sprinkled with herbs and a dusting of cheese that smelled divine.

"Are you sure you're feeling okay?" Elgin lowered his voice. "We can get the rest to go, and I can light the candles and get the massage oil out. You look tired."

Wallace rubbed his forehead before shaking his head. "No. I'm fine — really. It's just been a long week. Rachel at the office thought it would be a great idea to bring in a crock pot of chili for the potluck this week, and everyone got food poisoning. Two general managers and the COO were all out of commission. The vegetarians were safe, at least."

"Thank God," said Elgin, shoving another forkful of steak into his mouth.

"Besides, I can't miss this." Wallace looked to the side, his not-so-subtle gaze focused on the couple. Ralph still hadn't looked up from his phone, and Annan was pulling at his tie, his hair ruffled and shiny where sweat dotted his temples.

"I feel bad for the guy," whispered Elgin, leaning his head on his hand. He'd never admit it, but he'd been too terrified to propose to Wallace in person, taking the easy way out and telling the world first to give Wallace a chance to make a break for it while he could.

It had been worth it to see his husband laugh when Elgin had picked him up in the airport, holding a 'future Mr. Bekker?' sign in his hand. And every time they revisited the story, Wallace's eyes lit up. *Worth it.*

The nervous one named Annan shifted in his chair, and Elgin perked up, turning sideways so he had an even better view. With one hand in his pocket, Annan stood, rounding the table and dropping to one knee. He winced as he landed, grabbing for his tie as if it had choked him.

"Aww." Wallace reached across the table, tangling his fingers with Elgin's.

Ralph raised one eyebrow without looking up from his screen, his posture stiffening in his chair. "What are you doing? Unless you fell, get back in the chair. You're making a fool of yourself, Annan."

Ouch. Elgin winced, trying to look away, but he couldn't. Annan seemed like a nice guy, in a rugged sort of way, with blue eyes and a five o'clock shadow that was genuinely attractive. His throat bobbed as he swallowed, pulling a small case out of his pocket.

"Ralph," Annan started, clearing his throat when his voice caught. His voice was deep and smooth but had a nervous waver to it.

You can do it, buddy. Elgin gripped Wallace's hand tighter. All joking aside, he was fully invested, just about ready to grab Ralph's phone from his small hands and toss it across the restaurant.

The server paused her approach, turning around and heading back to the kitchen. She, at least, had qualms about eavesdropping on what should have been a beautiful moment. *Not me.*

"Ralph —"

"Seriously, Annan, get off the floor." Ralph slammed his phone on the table, the sound of the hit putting Elgin on edge. "I'm leaving." He reached for his coat that he'd hung on the back of his chair, despite several hooks being available.

"Can I ask you a question? Then we can go home, Ralph. I promise." Annan seemed to falter, clutching the box tight in his hands. His knuckles were white, the little velvet package looking close to buckling.

"No." Ralph pushed his chair back. "I can't believe this." He shook his head, his eyes going wide.

"Oh no," said Wallace, squeezing his hand tighter. "Elgin, I can't watch. Tell me when it's over."

Elgin couldn't look away, every muscle in his body going progressively tighter. He knew how fucking hard it was to be in Annan's position. *At least give the guy a chance.*

"Will you marry me?" Annan blurted out, his fingers slipping on the box as he tried to pry it open. After a moment of fumbling, he managed to reveal a thin black band nestled on a pillow of white. The jewel in the center was small and barely noticeable in the low light, but it was beautiful, nonetheless.

Ralph snorted, covering his mouth with his hand as he laughed. The high-pitched sound drew every eye in the restaurant, another server peeking around the corner as the room went quiet. Forks and knives hovered above plates, as people held their collective breath.

"No," said Ralph, slipping his coat over his shoulders. "Why the hell would I want to marry *you?*" He spat the last word, an icy venom dripping from his lips. The way he crinkled his nose gave him a semblance to a pig who had just rolled in its own waste.

Elgin narrowed his eyes.

"Why not?" Annan muttered, dipping his gaze to the box to stare at the ring. His hands were trembling and his gaze unsteady as he stared at it. It was tiny in his large hands, and Elgin could almost smell the sweat that seemed to pour from him.

"Don't get me started." Ralph shoved his phone into his pocket. "You're boring as hell, you don't have any friends and you're not even that attractive—not to mention, all you care about is your stupid animals, who smell terrible, by the way. I can't stand getting into bed with you, even after you've had a shower, because you reek, just like they do." A cruel smile spread across Ralph's lips. "To be honest, I'm just here for the food."

Wallace gasped, ducking his head while Elgin clenched his jaw.

The box fell from Annan's hand, and he dropped his arm to his side, slowly standing. His head was ducked, his eyes glassy as he looked at the floor, his forehead scrunched. "I have friends."

"No, you don't, because there isn't a single person in this world who can stand you."

Elgin rose to his feet, releasing Wallace's hand before he even knew what he was doing. Crossing the short distance, he strolled to the couple's table, relishing in the way Ralph's gaze snapped to him, his eyes going wide.

"Annan, is that you?" asked Elgin, grinning as he stopped a pace away from the table. "Oh wow, it is! I haven't seen you in years." He didn't spare Ralph a glance as he held his arms out, pulling Annan into a bear hug.

A woodsy, earthy scent tickled his nose, along with something else he didn't recognize as he embraced Annan. Their heights were near level, but Elgin was broader, his frame dwarfing Annan a bit as he drew close to his ear, whispering quietly.

"Just play along."

Elgin drew back, catching Annan's eye and releasing his grip. Annan blinked, his forehead still drawn in confusion. "Hell, it's so good to see you. It's been, what? Six years? You look great."

He did look even better up close. His hair had some natural curl to it that was trying to break free from the product, little wisps going astray. That, and he was built under his suit that didn't fit all that well.

"Elgin, remember? Elgin Bekker." He spied Ralph's eyes widen in recognition. It felt good to throw his name around a little for a good cause. Wallace was probably hiding his head in shame, though. "We met at the retreat. Those was some of the best three weeks of my life."

He patted Annan's back, turning to Ralph for the first time. Letting his smile drop, he stood a touch straighter. Wallace always claimed that Elgin had the patented 'resting bastard face', and the best part was, it was as natural as breathing.

"It looks like your friend is leaving. Care to join us for dinner?" asked Elgin, dismissing Ralph with a glance and putting his back to him. Annan was holding onto himself, his eyes still shiny but dry. "It will be my treat."

"Sure." Annan drew out the word as if he wasn't exactly sure what he was saying. He glanced to the floor, spying the box that had snapped shut and rolled under the table.

Elgin ducked down, grasping the small velvet box and pressing it into Annan's hand. "Wouldn't want to lose this."

"I can stay. I don't have anywhere to be."

Elgin turned at the sound of Ralph's voice, giving him the same unimpressed look. Ralph's gaze was flitting from Elgin's watch to the cuff links on his jacket, then down to the very expensive shoes he'd worn to the restaurant. He would have much preferred sandals, but he'd dressed up for Wallace.

"I'm afraid I don't know who you are," said Elgin, grabbing Annan's chair and hefting it off the ground. "Here, Annan, follow me. I've told my husband so much about you. He didn't believe me when I said I saw you in the same restaurant where we were grabbing dinner."

With his back to Ralph, Elgin held out his arm, looping it through Annan's. The poor guy still looked as if he were in shock, staring at the box in his hand. Helping him across the space was an easy task, and he tucked the chair at the end of his own table, clearing away the breadbasket and the tiny plates so Annan would have room.

"Wallace, this is Annan." Elgin grinned at his husband before peering back over his shoulder. Ralph was staring at them, his jaw hanging slack and something like determination in his gaze.

Elgin narrowed his eyes at the man, jerking his head toward the exit. *Get the fuck out.* Ralph stumbled back, nearly tripping over his chair in his rush to get away. It was the same way a new intern would scurry away if they didn't realize that ninety percent of Elgin's body was made of dry humor and sarcasm, and that he had only fired two people in his entire career.

Wallace groaned, holding his hand out to Annan as he shook his head. "Elgin, you are in so much trouble."

About the Author

M.C. Roth lives in Canada and loves every season, even the dreaded Canadian winter. She graduated with honours from the Associate Diploma Program in Veterinary Technology at the University of Guelph before choosing a different career path.

Between caring for her young son, spending time with her husband, and feeding treats to her menagerie of animals, she still spends every spare second devoted to her passion for writing.

She loves growing peppers that are hot enough to make grown men cry, but she doesn't like spicy food herself. Her favourite thing, other than writing of course, is to find a quiet place in the wilderness and listen to the birds while dreaming about the gorgeous men in her head.

M.C. Roth loves to hear from readers. You can find her contact information, website details and author profile page at https://www.firstforromance.com/

PUBLISHING

Sign up for our newsletter and find out about all our romance book releases, eBook sales and promotions, sneak peeks and FREE romance books!

www.ingramcontent.com/pod-product-compliance
Lightning Source LLC
Chambersburg PA
CBHW020823260626
47169CB00003B/804